Red
River Stallion

Also by Troon Harrison

The Horse Road

Red River Stallion

Troon Harrison

BLOOMSBURY
LONDON NEW DELHI NEW YORK SYDNEY

Bloomsbury Publishing, London, New Delhi, New York and Sydney

First published in Great Britain in January 2013 by
Bloomsbury Publishing Plc
50 Bedford Square, London, WC1B 3DP

A CIP catalogue record for this book is available from the British Library

ISBN 978 1 4088 1936 4

Typeset by Hewer Text UK Ltd, Edinburgh
Printed and bound in Great Britain by CPI Group (UK) Ltd,
Croydon CR0 4YY

1 3 5 7 9 10 8 6 4 2

www.bloomsbury.com

For my husband, Trevor.
Every morning I awake with thankfulness
into a world made rich and joyful by your love.

Chapter 1

I was alone in the canoe when the great creature swam out of the fog.

I heard the gusts of its heavy breathing before I could see the creature itself. Chills of fear slithered up my neck. Around the canoe's fragile hull of birch-bark, the muddy Hayes River swirled down to meet the salty waters of Hudson Bay. The current was running fast; although the tide was slack, the river was filled with eddies and long ropes of water like the muscles in a hunter's arms.

I had been warned, for most of my fourteen winters, about the dangers of the river. Only last year a man from the trading fort had drowned here, stranded on a sandbar as the tide rushed in. What had possessed me to come out alone in a canoe taken from the beach?

It was the arrival of the supply ship that had caused my foolishness. It had sailed over the horizon that morning from England, a tiny island far away across a wide ocean. Only once a year it arrived in the months of July or August, and dropped anchor at a place they called Five Fathom Hole, on the edge of the great bay. Then the men of the fort went out in light boats and schooners to bring ashore the precious supplies that the Hudson's Bay Company sent to its employees. There would be Dutch cheese, and British beef to cook with, and fresh supplies of oatmeal for porridge and of flour for bannock. Women would have fresh lengths of calico cloth to sew with, and strings of bright glass beads. Letters would arrive from loved kin, and newspapers filled with pictures and stories about things that happened in that other place, the place that the white men called home.

For the two weeks that the supply ship lay offshore, the fort at York Factory would be filled with bustle and laughter despite the hard work of unloading the cargo and carrying it up the wooden landing stage to the warehouses. There would be wild games of football, the winning team celebrating with extra rations of rum, the laughter and shouting turning into fist fights. Men would play their fiddles while my mother's people came into the fort from their lodges, and danced their Swampy Cree dances, the Rabbit dance, the Kissing dance. And maybe some girl with coppery skin would catch the eye of a trader, newly off the ship, and she would marry him. The way that my mother had, twice.

My father, a man named Simon Mackenzie, had left when I was still a baby swaddled on a cradle-board, peeing into moss. He had gone with a canoe brigade, paddling west along hundreds of miles of water to a fort in a place called the Red River valley. Before departing he had promised my mother that he would return and that they would always be together but, instead, he had abandoned us. His broken promise had lain in my mother's eyes, hard and still, like stones lying under shallow water at the margin of a lake. She had waited many years for him to return, clinging stubbornly to his promise while she lived amongst the Homeguard Cree, the bands that lived near the fur-trading fort. She refused even to marry a young chief though he sent bolts of fine cloth to her tent door, and piles of trade blankets. Finally, though, she did remarry; my second father, Ronald McTavish, was the fort's baker, his heavy arms and cheeks always pale with flour and even his sandy hair dusty-looking. With this second husband, my mother had Charlotte Bright Eyes, her second daughter and the person dearest to my heart.

When Charlotte was five winters old, my mother died of a white man's illness called the measles, her soul gone along the wolf road that shone overhead on clear nights, a ribbon of stars. For one more year, Charlotte and I lived inside the fort's tall palisade of logs with the only father we knew, but when the supply ship came again, Ronald McTavish called us to the bakery to tell us that he was leaving on the westerly wind.

'Ah, lassies, I'm sorry to go without you,' he told us, his voice as soft and heavy as his bread rolls. Charlotte was seated on his wide lap but I stood stiffly in the doorway of the bakery, numb with disbelief.

'But you know how I hate the cold winters,' he continued, 'and how the gout aches in my joints. Oh, girls, I long for green fields. Now that your mother has passed on, I haven't the heart for this wild land any more. You will be fine; your mother's people will take you in and care for you.'

He had been right; my mother's people did take us to live in their lodges of poles and deerskin, to sleep on boughs of spruce around smoking fires. But all had not been fine, for in the final moons of winter many of our kin died of starvation, including my grandfather. My grandmother had died many years before; I scarcely remembered her. And so, when the supply ship had dropped anchor this morning, I had climbed into a canoe and paddled along the shoreline, hoping for a glimpse of her three tall masts and of the other boats scuttling across the water like beetles to meet her. I had hoped to slip away from my melancholy, my deep sadness. At the fort, they called my sadness the Blue Devil. I had hoped to paddle away from it, like a moose being hunted and doubling back, shaking off its hunter and vanishing into its own solitary life again. I had hoped to forget about all the spirits.

The fog had fallen upon me like a blanket after I had already paddled a good distance east along the shore from the fort. Now, instead of being able to glimpse the ship being unloaded, I was in danger of being swept out to sea and drowned. After the fog had fallen, a great dead spruce had sailed out of the yellow murk. It must have been standing on the riverbank, and the water had eaten away the clay beneath it until one day it toppled over with a wild splash, and was sucked away. Though I had strained over my birchwood paddle with the strength of both arms and my whole back, the current swept the canoe sideways, and the roots of the tree, reaching out for me like dark arms, had pierced the birchbark sides of the canoe above the waterline. The canoe was held fast in a tangle of roots, and the tree, the canoe and I were being swept out to sea.

Faintly, I could hear the cries of the water birds along the mudflats or flying overhead: the brown geese, the white geese, the beautiful pale swans, the eider ducks. Water gurgled against the tree roots, pulling away chunks of bark from the trunk.

Once, the ghostly shape of a fishing stage flew towards me out of the mist. Here, some Cree man had built a willow weir beneath the water, and a platform five feet above the water, so that he might catch porpoise as they leaped and splashed upriver, eighteen miles inland to the great waterfalls. For a moment, I thought that my spruce tree would lodge up against the legs of the stage, and that I could cling to it and climb out. I leaned from the canoe, stretching my arms towards the stage's looming posts. I was a leg's length away from the closest post, then an arm's length, then closer . . . my muscles quivered with the strain of my stretching. I would be saved when the fog lifted, when fishermen saw me on the stage. All would be well!

Then a whirling eddy of dark green water caught my tree, and it revolved away from the stage, its whole waterlogged length spinning in the current. I sank back into the canoe, my heart hammering.

A little while later a tiny bird decoy, fashioned from bent willow, bobbed past me and was swallowed by the fog. Some hunter had made it to lure the ducks down close to his hiding spot on the mudflats, so that he could shoot them. I shouted, hoping a hunter might hear me, but the fog ate my voice whole.

I will die out here, I thought. *Then who will look after Charlotte Bright Eyes, my little half-sister with her face shaped like a heart? Who will finish making her coat, cut from a trading blanket with stripes of green, red and yellow? Who will sew the beads on to her leggings, and smoke the moose hide to make her a fine new robe?*

Out here, in the fog, the *misipisiwak* or underwater panthers might come for me, sensing how alone I was and how defenceless. They would rise out of the depths of the underwater world, the world

6

where powerful spirits dwelled, with their horns and their bodies like lynx, and would devour me.

I broke into a cold sweat, although tiny chips of ice bobbed against my canoe with a gentle scraping sound.

This is happening because I failed in my vision quest, I thought. No spirit wanted to be my *pawakan*, my spirit guide. Now I was going to die alone in the salty mist, trapped in the roots of the black spruce, without a spirit guardian to save me with its power. All I had was a song, the song I'd been given in my vision dream, which neither I, nor the elder healing woman Betty Goose Wing, could understand. Was the song directed to an animal, or to a wind spirit? And which wind was I calling to? Sawanis, spirit of the south wind, would be a gentle force to call upon but if I sang to Kiwitin, the malevolent being of the north, then harm would surely befall me. All dangerous animals came from the north – the wolverine, the snake, the underwater panther – as well as the terrible Witiko monster with its heart of ice, which gnawed its own lips with its sharp, blue teeth, and which stalked people and ate them. The words of my song might bring me power or might be treacherous, might be a trick played upon me in my dream.

Nonetheless, these words were all that I had brought back to the lodges after my vision quest's three days of fasting, and so I began to sing them now in my canoe, in the fog. My voice was thin with terror. I drummed the palms of my hands on the canoe's thwart as I sang the words over and over, imploring my missing *pawakan* to come to my aid and save me. *'Far Runner, Wind Runner, Water Runner, come to me, carry me onwards.'*

I paused for breath, gulping air, tasting on my tongue the wet mist, the salt, the muddy banks, the ice, the rotting roots of the tree that held me fast. Then I heard it, the breathing of the great creature. Was it a water panther? I peered into the mist, my heart plugged in my throat like the wooden stopper in the neck of a powder horn.

The creature's long head parted the fog.

It was larger than the head of a caribou, as large as the head of a moose but more tapered, and with bones that were lighter and more slender. Both caribou and moose were animals that I knew well, and this creature was neither one of them, and neither did it have any antlers or horns. Around its head was fastened something like a harness, made of strips of hide, and a rope trailed from this harness and sank down into the water. The creature's fur was red like the fur of a summer fox, and it had pricked ears, longer than the ears of a sled dog but shorter than the ears of a rabbit. Between its ears hung down long red hair, and its nostrils were wide and fluttering with its heavy breath. Its back was beneath the water but I glimpsed its length, and saw how the long red hair of its neck and tail floated on the surface of the water. Around it, the current swirled in circles so that I knew it had great legs, churning the depths as it swam towards me. Its large rounded eyes rolled white as it glimpsed the shadowy tangle of the spruce tree and my pierced canoe. Air snorted from its nostrils. Was it a *manitou*, a great spirit, summoned by my song? I clutched the canoe's cedar gunwales and stared at the creature as it came closer, closer.

Twice a year, the spirit chiefs of the caribou commanded the herds to journey: northwards in summer along the edges of the long days, then southwards in winter, fleeing the darkness. On their journeys, the deer swam across lakes and rivers; they could find the far shore even in darkness, even in fog. They could smell the land; its scents of moss and muskeg swamp, black mud and pale clay, spruce needles, water lilies and cranberries, the green leaves of poplar. Perhaps this red creature too could draw smells deep into its lungs; perhaps it was not lost, as I was, in this world of fog and water, but was swimming strongly towards the invisible shore.

There had been fog in the dreams of my vision quest too. The previous fall, in the moon when ducks begin to moult, Betty Goose Wing – who was an aunt of my mother's – had helped me to prepare. Dressed in a new, clean robe of white caribou skin, stitched with porcupine quills and blue beads, I had walked alone into the bush and come to a small lake. Here the men had built me a platform, a bird's nest, in the trees by placing long poles between four tall black spruce trees. Other poles, laid horizontally, created the platform on which the men had heaped boughs, their resinous scent strong in the falling sun. For three days, I had sat on there, my eyes filled with the light of the lake by day and the path of the stars by night, my palms drumming a skin drum, my mind seeking its *pawakan* guide. For three days and nights, I had fasted, only sipping water occasionally from a birch-bark container sealed with pitch.

'Kicimanitow, Great Spirit,' I had implored, 'take pity upon me, Amelia Otterchild Mackenzie, for I am an orphan.' Yet nothing came into my dreams. *Perhaps nothing wants me*, I had thought, and I had prayed harder, in desperation, reminding the Creator how I needed help to care for my little sister.

And then, at last, the *pawakan* came in human form, walking over the platform and into my dreams, the fog swirling around the pillar of its body like smoke. Its face was lean and long, and its hair was not black like the hair of my people but red, hanging down on each side of its face and with a single long lock hanging down the front, over its nose. It was dressed in a robe of red fur that I thought might be fox. Its moccasins made a strange, hollow sound on the platform poles as though they were hard – like the white man's boots – instead of soft like the moccasins of the tribes. It peered at me through the swirling fog.

'Do you know me?' it asked. 'Have you seen me

before?' And it gave a long laugh; a long, peculiar, gusting laugh.

'No,' I said, 'I don't know you,' and this was wrong, for in my vision I should have been able to recognise my own *pawakan*. Three times it asked me if I knew it and each time I answered 'No.' At last, it began to shape-shift, flashing between its human form and its true shape, but still I didn't know what my *pawakan* was, for in the swirling fog I glimpsed only flashes of vision, like the flashes of vision you get in the bush at night in the middle of a lightning storm. In those moments I saw thin, red legs running, and red hair flying. The drumming of the moccasins on the poles grew louder, it filled my ears and pounded inside my head; my heart drummed with it, leaping and rushing high in my chest. One final time I saw my *pawakan* in human form. 'Here is the song to summon me,' it said, and then, in a thin high voice, it chanted, *'Far Runner, Wind Runner, Water Runner, come to me, carry me onwards.'*

For days after returning to the lodges, I struggled to understand my vision quest dream. Without a *pawakan* I would never prosper in life; I would have no skills at healing or paddling, at hunting or trapping, at kinship or marriage. I would be taunted and jeered at by my mother's people, and would die young. Days passed but understanding failed me and a great fear, like the fear of a hare in the path of a wolverine, turned my bones to softness. Finally, I

11

sought out Betty Goose Wing where she was hanging split whitefish to dry on poles.

'I know that one does not speak to others of one's *pawakan*,' I said. 'But I need your wisdom.'

Though she listened intently, drawing deep breaths on her clay pipe and ignoring the dogs nosing around her feet, Betty Goose Wing was not able to help me. 'You must pay close attention to all your dreams each night,' she said at last. 'Perhaps your spirit guide will come to you again and you will recognise it.' But her eyes were flat and closed, and I knew that she was afraid for me, for if a dreamer could not recognise their *pawakan* during their vision quest, fasting with face painted black, seated near a lake or river, then what hope was there?

Some of my mother's people were coasters, people who lived all year near to the fur-trading fort of York Factory, hunting or fishing or gathering wood for the white men. Others of my kin were inlanders, and when the day length began to wane and the cold stalked southwards like a great white bear, these kin journeyed away from the Hayes River to hunt the moose and the bears in their dens.

'You should go into the bush,' Betty Goose Wing advised me, 'and perhaps there, where it is clean and where you are away from the white man's ways, your *pawakan* will come to you again.'

So Charlotte and I travelled into the north-west with the sled dogs, with the women carrying the lodge skins on their backs, with the hunters striding along smoking their pipes, the long barrels of their guns laid upon their shoulders and beads shining in their greased hair. At first, the winter was kind to our hunting band and the men called a grandfather, a black bear, from its den and shot it and laid tobacco in its mouth as an offering. They came back to camp quietly, without boasting. The women danced at night, asking the spirit chief of the martens to bring the martens to the trap lines, and the martens came and gave themselves to us. Their bodies were limp in the traps under their shining pelts, but their souls had gone to find new bodies and run in the bush again. We ate well, and sat around our fires talking and laughing as we repaired mittens lined with fur and hats of fox hair, and as we cured the marten skins to sell to the traders at the fort in the spring, in the grey goose moon.

Later in the winter, the bush fell silent and a great cold breathed on the land so that the tree trunks split apart, making a sound as loud and sharp as a gun being fired. The north wind blew away the snow so that the moose and the deer could run swiftly from the hunters and couldn't be killed. Day after day I set snares for the white hares but my snares lay empty and the snow was unbroken by any tracks. At night now I dreamed of nothing at all but I could feel the Witiko monster stalking our camp, moving in through the dark forest, gnawing its lips, uttering its strange, gruesome sounds, for it had no speech. At night, it sat watching our lodges, trying to catch the sparks that flew up from our fires, for each spark that it caught would be a soul that it devoured.

The cold deepened. The land seemed to die around us.

We boiled strips of willow bark in melted snow and drank the broth; we gnawed on caribou hide that filled our bellies with nothing but the memory of meat. We drummed and sang songs, hoping to entertain the animals, but they didn't come to us. The men sacrificed a white sled dog, and laid tobacco in the clefts of rocks, but still the animals stayed away, hiding, as though we had offended the spirit masters that controlled the number and movements of all the animals. What had we done to cause offence? We had hung the head of moose and bear in the trees, and decorated them with ribbons and with ochre paste. We had laid other bones upon platforms where the dirty dogs couldn't gnaw them. The dead animals had been brought to our lodges with respect, laid upon their backs, lifted inside without striking against the door posts, and given the seat of honour. We had covered their bloodstains to keep the snow clean, and had sung them songs of gratitude for the gifts of their bodies.

Yet we had somehow given offence, or a sorcerer was using his power against us, driving away the animals. We starved. A young mother died first, then two children, then a hunter with an injured leg, then my grandfather. In the lodges we lay on the spruce boughs under a pall of choking smoke, and tried to turn our thoughts away from Witiko, who would drive us crazy, and make us eat our own kin before he killed us. We were too weak now to drum or sing, too weak to make new moccasins, or to weave netting for the snowshoes that let us fly along on top of the snow's crust.

Still, the north wind blew. Sometimes, I heard the running of hard feet in my dreams or saw a flash of long red hair, but my *pawakan* didn't come to me; perhaps nothing in the spirit world felt any pity for my plight. Charlotte's heart-shaped face grew pinched and pale, her bones poking through like the wings of fledgling birds. I held her against me under a covering of Hudson's Bay Company blankets and bearskin, and waited for the moment when our hearts would grow too weak to beat in our chests, and our feet would climb the wolf road, running after our mother.

But neither Charlotte Bright Eyes nor I died in that starving moon, and when the cold lessened, the people from the fort came looking for those who were still alive: only nine of us out of a band of thirty-three. They carried us back, wrapped in blankets and laid upon sledges made of moose hide and birch-wood. The sleigh bells rang clear and bright on the dogs' harnesses. For weeks, we lay in the room at the fort that had once been slept in by Ronald McTavish, the baker, and waited for strength to return to us. I sold my marten pelts to the trading store to buy rations, and cooked for Charlotte in the labourers' cookhouse: stews of corn and pemmican, or caribou and potatoes, fried whitefish, porridge of oatmeal, tarts of cranberries and gooseberries. The plumpness returned to her cheeks and arms, and the brightness to her dark brown eyes. I braided beads into her black plaits, and began planning to make her a robe of tanned moose hide with fringes and patterns of porcupine quills.

All summer, I plucked geese before the men salted them in barrels to eat next winter. I stitched clothing for the white men at the fort: duffel socks, shirts, mittens, trousers. I washed their laundry along the shores of the Hayes River, my hands numb in the water, the tide licking in and filling the air with salt. All summer, the Blue Devil of sadness held my heart in its hand, a heavy thing, drained of joy. The white man's Blue Devil was like the Witiko monster: it turned one's heart to ice; it was a thing that was always starving. All summer, I was starving for laughter, for warmth, for all my inlander kin who had died of their hunger. When the supply ship dropped anchor at Five Fathom Hole at last, I thought that maybe Ronald McTavish would return to us on it, or that he might at least have sent us a letter and a package of tartan cloth, and some gifts from his homeland:

a brooch for me, a piece of pretty lace for Charlotte.

And so this was the true reason that I borrowed a canoe and began to paddle along the shoreline, becoming lost in the fog and tangled in a dead tree. So it was that I was expecting to drown, when the great red creature came alongside the canoe.

When it was very close, I saw the fringes of red hair inside its tapered ears. I saw the water beaded in the long whiskery hairs over its eyes. I saw how its dark eyes looked at me as though it were saying something to me, asking me a question. I was skilled in listening to animals, in understanding their natures and their spirits. The souls of animals are stronger than the souls of people, for when you kill an animal, its soul remains in this world, finding new bones to live in. I could listen to all the animals in the bush: the marten, the lynx, the beaver, the muskrat and the otter, the fox and the wolf, the grandfather bear, who has no chief over him.

Never before had I spoken to the red creature swimming alongside my canoe in the fog – yet I heard its question. I had only an instant to answer, for already the current was swirling the creature and I apart. Already the strip of churning water was growing wider, cold and dangerous, between us.

'I know who you are,' I said, and the creature swivelled its ears towards the sound of my voice. Then I kicked aside my useless paddle with a clatter, and rose without hesitation to climb out of the canoe.

Chapter 2

Aaiiiyeeee! I was falling into fire!

Its dark mouth swallowed me whole. Pain filled my body; for an instant, fire licked over the top of my scalp. My feet thrashed me to the surface of the icy, burning water and my outflung arm splashed across the ripples. I grabbed a long strand of the creature's red hair, and wrapped it quickly around my hand twice. The creature did not pause in its strong swimming. Its head was outstretched, its red-rimmed nostrils sucked air, perhaps filling with the smells of the invisible shoreline.

With a strong *pawakan*, one could survive almost anything: a drowning, the vengeance of a sorcerer, or the attack of a white bear. I could feel the strength of my *pawakan* now; it was indeed a water runner, as my song had foretold. The muscles sliding and straining in its shoulders bumped against me as I was towed alongside. Beneath the water's turbulence, I felt the stir and thrust of the creature's long legs and once a bone banged against my own dangling legs. I pulled them up, trying to make them float behind me, but they were weighted down by my soaked leggings and robe of deerskin. I stared at where the creature's back surged just beneath the water. Tightening my grip on the strands of hair, I let myself drift back from the neck, and then I stretched out my right foot in its sodden moccasin. With a lunge, I slid that leg over the top of the creature. Then I felt the true power of my *pawakan*, for its back was broad and solid, easily lifting me out of the water. Ripples creamed from the creature's neck, broke over my leggings, and fanned out into the turbulence of the Hayes' currents.

We journeyed in a silence broken only by the creature's snorting breath and, once, by the haunting laughter of a loon, a great diving bird. For a long time, we travelled through the bowl of fog with the muddy water continually sucking us downstream to the icy bay. The creature worked its way across the current at an angle. I could no longer feel my legs; even the cold burning had turned into numbness. My jaw rattled with chills. I began to wonder if we would ever reach shore, or if the fog would ever lift. Perhaps I was no longer on the Hayes River but was being carried away into some other world where the spirits lived: perhaps the world beneath the waves where Underwater Woman dwelled, or perhaps the upper air where the Thunderbirds soared, or perhaps even the world below ground where the Hairy People lived.

Suddenly, there was a sharp grating sound beneath me. The creature's back lurched. Its feet struck against small stones. From out of the fog loomed the pale sweep of a willow tree. The creature was no longer afloat now and its great body, no longer buoyant, lunged heavily from the water and on to a narrow strip of shoreline beneath a clay bank. The creature lowered its head and breathed so hard that I felt the surge of air in and out of its lungs. I glanced down. The toes of my moccasins were high above the shingle and for the first time I could see the true size of my *pawakan*. It was a massive beast; greater than a bull moose, as powerful as a bear, as elegant as a running deer. Water streamed from its sides and down the hard lengths of its slender legs, the front legs and the back legs of different shape from each other. I lay along its neck, shuddering with cold, and felt the moment when it too began to shudder, long spasms running through its shoulders.

We would die if we didn't find warmth. Although it had released us, the burning fire of that cold river might still kill us.

I slid from the creature's back and staggered, my legs buckling beneath me. When I grasped the rope trailing from the creature's harness, it began to follow me along the shoreline, heading upriver towards the lodges of the Homeguard Cree. Its hooves were not cleft in two like the hooves of a deer, or like the hooves of the white men's oxen at the fort, but were one solid piece. Those hard black hooves struck forcefully against stones, making a sound as loud as the hooves that had drummed in my vision quest, before I had seen the true form of my *pawakan*. When we crossed patches of pale sand or clay, the animal left strange marks, circular in shape but with an indented V. I had never seen this track on our land before, although I could name the tracks of many creatures in snow or mud. The white men read stories in books and newspapers sent on the ships, and I too could read, for the York postmaster had given the children lessons by candlelight. But with my mother's people I had learned another kind of reading: to understand the tracks of animals as if they were stories, the tales that the animals told about themselves.

We struggled on, shivering in our shawls of chill mist. I could feel the creature's fatigue, read it in the slump of its neck, see it in the occasional stumble over a piece of driftwood. I wondered how far it had swum to find me, to save me. Finally, a point of land that I recognised loomed up, and I turned inland and found a faint trail. We climbed it away from the shoreline, brushing through low-growing poplars. Blueberries left a dark stain on my moccasins as I strode through them. The boughs of a lone tamarack pierced the fog. I swung further inland on to a clay path worn by the feet of the Homeguard Cree as they went to and from the fort, working for the white men, bringing them fish for their sled dogs, wood for their iron stoves, wildfowl and baskets of cranberries to cure the terrible scurvy. Without help, the white men would never have survived in this world that they called Rupert's Land, named after a nephew of one of their chiefs far away in England. It was a strange thing that they could name the land, for not even the Great Creator had done so. And it was also a strange thing that this chief Rupert had never once set foot on the land that was named after him.

My *pawakan* walked steadily behind me, its warm breath gusting on the back of my neck, its hooves thumping the ground, its amazing tail swishing when it got caught in twiggy bushes. I had never seen such a tail. It was not fluffy like the tail of a fox or a skunk; it was not flat like a beaver's tail, nor long and sinuous like the tail of an otter. The tail of this red creature was like the smooth shining hair of a beautiful woman; it was so long that it brushed against the creature's ankles as it walked.

It was the dogs that first heard us coming and rushed to meet us. They swarmed around the creature and ripped up the air with their frenzied barking. The creature stopped and watched the dogs, then stretched its neck towards them. I saw that it was neither amazed by the dogs nor afraid of them, and after a moment we walked on and the dogs ran ahead into camp. I circled around the edge until I reached the pale, conical tipi where Betty Goose Wing lived. Over her fire, hung from a tripod, was a black pot containing caribou brains. When they had boiled, Betty and I would use them to tan a moose hide; the hide that she had promised to give to me for Charlotte's new robe.

I began to lead the red creature in circles around the fire, letting its heat wash and lick at both of us.

'A-aunt-auntie!' I called in Cree, my jaw seized tight with cold, my teeth chattering. She emerged from the dark triangle of the lodge doorway, a figure as round and thick as a tree stump, her face weathered like cedar bark. Her dark eyes watched us circling the fire, shaking with cold and still dripping salty water. I turned and began to circle the fire in the other direction so that we would be warmed on the other sides of our bodies.

'What have you been doing, Otterchild?' the old woman asked, tamping tobacco into her pipe with the ball of her thumb. Then she clenched the pipe's clay stem in her teeth, settling it into the groove worn there through her many winters.

'I was caught in a black spruce, drifting out to the bay in the fog,' I confessed. 'But my *pawakan* came to me in its true form and rescued me; it brought me to shore on its back. This is the creature that visited me on the platform in my vision quest. Only, Auntie, I don't know its name.'

Betty Goose Wing nodded, and the long strings of beads in her ears swung and glistened in the damp light. 'It's a horse,' she said. 'There was a horse at York Factory when you were a baby of two winters, too small to remember. It was brought on the supply ship and the men used it to ride on. It pulled sledges of firewood, and rocks from the garden. But one winter, the wolves killed it. And last summer too the white men brought a horse on the supply ship. Perhaps you didn't see it. It was when we were feasting and dancing the Round dance for your mother's spirit.'

I stared down at the toes of my moccasins, trampling in the dirt around Betty's glowing fire. Last summer had been the time to celebrate my mother's life and death so that her spirit would be free to travel to the happy lands of the west. And also, last summer, Ronald McTavish had abandoned us, sailing away on the westerly wind before ice sealed the bay shut. All I had felt was the pain in Charlotte's gentle dark eyes. So I had paid little attention to the contents of last summer's supply ship, with its bales and boxes, its kegs and livestock. Its horse, which must have been sent on to some other fort.

'So, your *pawakan* is the spirit of horses,' Betty said, her tongue thinking about the meaning of those words. 'I have not heard of this happening before. The horse is not an animal of our people, like the bear or the wolf. It is a creature of the white man's world.

24

Perhaps the horse spirit is a *pawakan* that only a half-blood like you could possess. I heard that the white men don't have *pawakans* at all, only some man they call Jesus. They all have the same man's spirit.'

She scowled at such an inexplicable strangeness, and drew hard on her pipe. 'This red horse must have come on the supply ship . . . then fallen into the river when the men were unloading. You must lead it to the fort, find out who owns it.'

'Who owns it?' A chill shook through me, but not from cold. Someone, a white man, owned my red creature, my spirit guide who had saved me from drowning! Some white man, perhaps the chief factor, perhaps the chief trader, had sent for this creature from far away and it had been brought to him across the world, so that he could ride it, and make it work for him. I was going to lose my horse, although out there in the fog we had belonged only to each other.

I was losing one more precious thing.

Pain gripped my stomach and wrung it, like a hand wringing a wet hide before it is tanned, squeezing the moisture from it. I bent over, choking on loss, grief blocking my throat. The horse came to a standstill and bent its muzzle down to nudge my head. The warmth of its breath filled my wet hair, and I felt the soft short fur around its nostrils brush my cheek. I leaned back into its shoulder and willed myself not to cry, for grief or anger were private things amongst the Cree. I would not show tears here before the children that were gathering with excited shouts, or the adults who were drifting in closer through the fog.

I felt a hand on my back. 'I will hold the horse,' Betty Goose Wing said. 'Go into my lodge and put on dry clothing before the cold eats you up. Bring out a blanket for the animal.'

I stumbled away from the staring faces and into the smoky dimness of the tipi with its familiar smells of tobacco and sweet grass, the musk of furs. Jerkily, I pulled off my robe and leggings, and pulled on some of Betty's; they were much too large for me and hung in folds from my body. Although I had recovered from the starving moon when my kin had died, I was of only medium height, stocky and strong but not plump. Still shaking with cold, I pulled a capote, a woollen blanket coat with fringes, over Betty's robe. Then I snatched up a blanket and carried it outside, where I spotted a young mother that I knew, standing amongst the circle of people exclaiming over my *pawakan*. Only they thought that it was simply some possession of a white man's.

'Jane!' I called to the young mother. 'Please, can you let me have some moss?'

She looked surprised as she turned away but when she returned she carried a large bundle of the pale grey moss. It grew all over the land beneath the tamarack and spruce trees, and the deer ate it, and the Cree packed it into babies' swaddlings.

'Thank you, Jane.' I took two large handfuls of moss and began to rub them over the horse, around and around in circles, absorbing the water from its short coat. I rubbed along its neck, across its sloping shoulders, between its front legs. The moss in my hands became limp with moisture and I turned to Jane and asked for more. 'I will gather some tomorrow for your baby,' I promised.

I rubbed the new, dry moss along the horse's spine to the base of its tail, down its back legs, under the curve of its belly.

'A fine young stallion,' Betty Goose Wing observed, watching beside me.

'Finer even than Rebecca Stonechild's new hunter!' joked someone in the crowd and there was a gust of delighted laughter amongst the women.

I ignored them and kept rubbing moss all over the horse. As his coat dried, its colour became lighter, changing from dark red to a fiery brightness. And then I saw that there were white hairs too, mingled with the red in some places like different colours of grass mingled along the shore of a pond. Down one side of his neck, across the top of his back, and spreading down towards his back legs, the horse's fire coat was silvered with white. He was like a coloured autumn leaf, touched with the lightest of first frost. I had never seen an animal with such a strange, fine pelt. Did a horse change colour with the seasons? Like the hare and fox that were brown or red in summer but white in winter, did this horse change? By the time of the snow goose moon, when the sun left us, would he be white all over? Did he know snow and darkness in his island home far away? I stared at him in wonder and ran my palms over the patches of white and red hairs. There was no white in the long hair of his tail or in the hair that grew along his neck and hung down his face. All the long hair was pure red.

Once the moss was dampened, I threw Betty's blanket over the horse and continued trampling around the fire. The people of the band drifted away into the fog, to tend their own fires and cook their evening meals. The children and the dogs ran off and finally only Betty remained, seated impassively in her lodge doorway, like a boulder, and smoking her pipe.

'You take this horse to the fort,' she said. 'Someone there will be waiting for him.'

I circled the fire in stubborn silence. *This creature is mine!* I wanted to say, but I knew that Betty was right.

'It is the spirit of horse that is your *pawakan*,' Betty said. 'That spirit is yours for life now, as long as you do what it tells you to do, when it speaks in your dreams. Your *pawakan* will not leave you just because this one horse returns to its owner. Go now, before dark.'

I slid my hand beneath the woollen blanket draped across the stallion's back. His coat steamed with warmth. 'I will wash your blanket and return it,' I told Betty and she nodded and rose, stiff but strong, to tend to her fire. Then the red stallion followed me along the beaten clay trail, as the fog began to grow thicker and darker, like a good meat broth. Somewhere in the murk, across the wide, flat land, the sun was sinking into the west. A wolf howled once and was answered by another. The stallion flung up his head, neck tensed, ears straining towards the sound. I tugged on the rope and after a moment he continued to follow me, snorting. Perhaps, I thought, there were no wolves in the land from which he had come.

My feet dragged as I approached the trading fort. In my stomach was a pain, a heaviness. I thought this was the way that the trout felt, caught on one of the white men's fancy feathered lures in Ten Shilling Creek. Every step that I took closer to the white man's world was a step closer to the moment that I would have to let go of the rope, and watch as someone else led away my red stallion.

I approached the fort's stockade from the rear, the side furthest from the river, and entered by a small gate in the tall wall of logs. Inside it, pasture drifted off into the mist and I heard the steady ripping noise of cows and oxen grazing the sparse forage. Away to my left, hogs grunted in their muddy wallow. The stallion followed me without faltering and, although his ears swivelled to take in these sounds, there was no tension in his muscles. Perhaps, I thought, he knew these animals at home, for these were white men's creatures too, brought on the supply ship each summer. Faintly, I heard the ringing of a bell to signal the evening meal.

Ahead of us loomed the pale wall of the cow byre, sided with planks that the sawyers had made from logs. The horse did not hesitate when I led him inside to a stall. The harness on his head was made of heavy leather, with a hard sheen on it; I wondered what kind of an animal it had been made from. It was secured with large buckles of bright metal. I unfastened one and slid the straps from the horse's head, then fetched him a tin bucket of water and watched as he sucked long draughts. Water dribbled from his lips and he returned my stare as if he were thinking about me. In his eye, the centre was not round like the iris of a human eye, but rectangular, and on each of his legs was a small, hard piece without hair, as rough as rock. I wondered if there was anyone at the fort who could answer all the questions that I had about this creature. Beneath the blanket, his coat was warm and dry so I slid the heavy wool from him before securing the stable door and running through the fog. Charlotte would be looking for me, and I must find someone to talk to about the horse.

I skirted the garden behind its wooden fence, and heard the sound of someone digging, throwing aside the wet, heavy soil to land with a solid thud.

'Mr Murdoch?' I called in English, and the sound ceased.

'Mr Murdoch, it's Amelia Mackenzie. Can I talk to you?'

There was a pause as I waited for the fort's postmaster to approach, moving slowly in the gloom. Although his job was to spend many hours each day writing long lists of supplies ordered, of furs shipped, of items traded, of letters received and letters sent, Mr Murdoch's joy came from the garden. He laboured on it all summer, late into the evenings when his day's work was completed and the sun lingered. He dug trenches to drain it. He hauled cow manure to it, and created raised beds on top of layers of willow wands so the air could dry the clay soil. He bent his back over the straggling rows of early turnips, potatoes, cabbages. Every year plants died from frost and of mould, but still Mr Murdoch kept trying; he said that he was an optimist. He was also kind, giving Charlotte and me hard sweets called humbugs. I'd asked if they were made from maple tree sap but he'd only laughed and said that people in England did not harvest tree sap.

Now his freckled face peered at me in the gloom, his sandy hair falling over his sweating forehead. He swiped away black flies and mosquitoes, smudging his face with dirt. 'What is it?' he asked.

He listened carefully while I recounted my story

about being adrift in the river, about being saved by a red horse. A puzzled look crept into his eyes.

'Well, it must have come off the ship, no doubt about that,' he said at last. 'But no one here ordered a horse this year, Amelia. If they had, I would have known about it. Aye, indeed. I know who ordered soap and tooth powder, who ordered a lamb's wool cravat, how many strings of beads to expect on this ship, how many hundreds of bales of fur the fort is sending back to England when the ship leaves. But there was no horse on any of my lists. Maybe some Company laddie in London decided to send us one. But it's no good here for horses; the wolves get them, they cannot get about in the deep snow, and the hay is scarce. You know how hard it is to find hay even for the oxen, and how we slaughter most of them to eat ourselves each winter. No, no, this is not a country for horses.'

'So no one here owns the horse?' I asked, a note of hopefulness creeping into my voice.

Mr Murdoch gave me a keen glance; he knew how animals fascinated me, how I had spent hours caring for an injured owl one summer, how the cats and the little dogs living in the governor's house pressed against my legs, and followed when I walked along the shore.

'Don't go getting any ideas,' he warned. 'White men's creatures always belong to someone.'

I nudged at a stone with my moccasin. 'I must go

and find Charlotte. Please will you talk to the cowman and ask him to take care of the horse? He needs something to eat but I didn't know what to give him.'

'Hay and grass, same as the cows,' said Mr Murdoch. 'Unless it's some fine, fancy animal that eats oats and corn. Off you go then, and find your sister. I'll make sure the horse gets taken care of.'

I turned as he began digging again, and ran through the misty maze of buildings: the warehouses, the tradesmen's shops – the tinsmith's, the cooper's, the blacksmith's – past the distillery, where the rum was made, past the ice house, kept cold all summer with last year's river ice. Now I was passing the storage rooms filled to the ceilings with stack upon stack of furs. All those animals had died for the white man's trade and been brought here from hundreds of miles of trap lines and rivers, inside canoes and boats, and paid for with knives, guns, kettles, blankets and beads. The buildings all looked the same as I ran past, all boarded in planks painted white and pale yellow, already peeling in the salty summer fogs and freezing winters of this land.

It was late by the time that I found Charlotte, and boiled us some caribou stew in the cookhouse, and fully dark when we went to bed at last in the room that was only ours for another day or two. An officer had told us that this room would be needed by one of the men arriving on the supply ship. Then we would have to return to the lodges and live with Betty Goose Wing.

In the morning it was still foggy, and men hung around the fort cursing the weather, yearning for news of home, for the excitement of unloading the ship. I ran to the lodges with moss for Jane's baby, then spent most of the day in the cow byre, just watching the red horse eat with a steady grinding of his jaws, or sleep standing on his feet, or flick flies away with that long, long tail. I cut a piece of old deerhide into strips and braided them together, and stitched them in a circle, then used this to rub the horse all over. He seemed to like the soft tickle; he sighed in satisfaction and turned his head to nudge me with his soft muzzle. I began to dream a waking dream; to believe that he might belong to no one at all, to be mine because we had found each other in the water, and walked to the fort together. He had been sent by my *pawakan*, spirit master of all horses.

On the second day after the ship anchored at Five Fathom Hole, the sun broke through the fog. It dazzled the eye now to look out over the blue river, to see the tiny insect of the ship out there, its three masts fine as mosquito legs. Schooners and light boats and York boats were sent out to the ship to ferry the supplies ashore. Almost everyone in the fort came out to watch, seated in the short grass along the bluff above the landing stage. Boatload after boatload came alongside. Pipers marched up the planks of the stage, the skirl and shriek of their bagpipes like the cries of shore birds. Next came what everyone was waiting for: the bales and boxes, barrels and chests, all sent from England, all filled with food, with trade goods, with books and clothing and letters from home, with seeds to grow in next summer's garden.

'I'm trying runner beans next year,' said Mr Murdoch, sitting beside Charlotte and me on the grass as the labourers hauled and heaved the supplies up the wooden ramps of the landing stage. I didn't ask what runner beans were; I was watching two goats being led onshore; their strange eyes, like glass beads, were wide with fright. And then my own eyes widened, for in the next boat being rowed alongside the jetty was a sight so strange, so improbable, that I could only stare in shock.

'Aha! Here she is then,' said Mr Murdoch. 'The owner of your stallion, Amelia. They say in the fort that she's married a trader and has come now to live with him, bringing the horse as a wedding gift. The news arrived last night, along with a packet of letters brought by a fur brigade from Oxford House. I hadn't the chance to tell you about it until now.'

I couldn't answer. *A white woman!* A woman who owned my horse!

She was helped on to the landing stage and now she was walking up it, small and short, her spine very straight, her face in shadow beneath the wide brim of a pale-coloured hat. Ribbons and feathers flew out from this hat in the stiff breeze, which sent the pleated folds of her long, blue gown snapping like a sail. Now she was being greeted by Mr Robert Miles, the governor of York Factory, dressed in a frock coat and a silk cravat instead of his usual working-day garments. Curiosity itched across my skin, demanding attention.

'Come,' I said to Charlotte and took her small, warm palm in mine; we crossed the grass where cloud shadows ran like schools of porpoise, then edged forward until we were in front of the traders watching the unloading, and watching the white woman. There were no other white women in this land, for the men of the Hudson's Bay Company came alone on their ships to trade for furs, and brought no mothers or wives or daughters with them. Instead, they married the Cree women and fathered half-blood children, like Charlotte and me. And then, when they pleased, they left us.

So there she stood, that lone white woman, in an empty space on the crowded landing stage. She was a sight as foreign, as unfamiliar, and as inexplicable, as the sight of a horse in this land. Her hands, encased in long, pale blue gloves, clenched and unclenched in the swirling folds of her gown as four boatmen, from a lighter tied up below, approached her.

'These are the men who were responsible for bringing your horse ashore,' Governor Miles told her. The men stopped at a wary distance, their red stocking caps flaring brightly in the light and the red sashes at their waists flying in the wind. Beneath the angry stare of the woman's eyes – blue as chips of spring ice – the men cleared their throats and shuffled their feet.

'Pray tell me,' she said suddenly, 'how you have lost an animal as valuable as Foxfire, a stallion of the line of Original Shales and Flying Childers. Do you dolts know what you have lost? A Norfolk Trotter, that's what, a stallion of the finest lineage, brought safely over thousands of miles of ocean in the belly of a ship. He was worth more money than you will ever earn in your entire miserable lives!'

Her voice was clear and hard despite her small size; it rose in volume as she spoke until she was almost shrieking. Everything paused on the landing stage; men set barrels down, leaned on chests, clustered along the gunwales of boats. Everyone wanted to know what would happen next. Charlotte's hand squirmed in mine and I softened my tight grip.

Beneath her hat brim, strands of the woman's hair were coming undone and blowing across her face; they were pale and bright golden, and filled with curls.

'Well, answer me!' she cried. 'How did you fools lose him?'

'Ma'am, we got him off the ship fine, in the slings, before the fog fell,' one man replied. 'You saw this with your own eyes. Then the fog came down when we was drawing closer to shore, and then the horse took fright and plunged overboard. Wasn't nothing we could do to hold him. He knocked Thomas here off his feet. Took a nasty blow to the kidneys. Then the animal was gone, into the fog. That's all, ma'am.'

'I do not give a fig about the kidneys of this Thomas!' cried the woman. 'Why did he not have a good grip on the lead rope?'

The men only shrugged and muttered.

'I will dock their rations,' interrupted Governor Miles smoothly, 'and have them all flogged.'

'That will not bring back my horse which is drowned and lying at the bottom of Hudson Bay,' said the woman. 'What will my husband say when I arrive in Red River without the horse he's expecting?'

Red River! I shook my head as though a bull fly was lodged in my ears. Red River was the place to which my father had once journeyed and from which he'd never returned. And now this tiny, furious white woman and the stallion that she called Foxfire were travelling to the same place? I gave my head another incredulous shake, and wondered what my spirit guide required of me.

When I took three steps forward, all gazes swivelled on to me. Closer, I saw with a start that this white woman was very young; her face was as smooth, pale and softly rounded as the face of a porcelain doll that had once come on the ship for someone's half-blood daughter. Closer still, and I saw the smudges of blue beneath the young woman's eyes, felt the thousands of miles that she had fretted and worried about the horse's safety and well-being in the belly of the ship. I knew how the ground, at that very moment, swayed beneath her, and how the great land stretching flat to the sky made her feel tiny and helpless.

'Your horse is safe here in the byre,' I said. 'He and I swam to shore.'

And with those words I gave him away, one more precious thing that would now leave my life, running the long wild rivers into the heart of the land without me.

Chapter 3

'What an extraordinary thing to say!' the white woman exclaimed. She did not gasp or swoon, the way that white heroines did in the novels that I borrowed from the fort's library collection. Instead, her blue eyes pierced me like a needle going into deerskin. 'Is this true?' she demanded. 'Who are you?'

'Amelia Mackenzie. I was being swept out to sea when your stallion swam past my canoe. I thought he was –' I gulped and paused. I should not talk about my *pawakan*, my spirit guide, and especially not to this strange white woman. 'I thought he was swimming to shore,' I amended. 'So I swam with him, and brought him to the fort.'

'Extraordinary!' she repeated. 'I am Orchid Sapphira Spencer, and I am for ever in your debt.' Her gloved fingers brushed across my hand in a brief, impulsive gesture before she turned to the governor. 'Please make sure that this Indian girl is rewarded,' she told him; I noticed how her lips fumbled with the word 'Indian' and how her clear glance flicked over me, puzzled and curious. I supposed she was surprised by my green eyes, my skin the colour of a dried cedar frond, the brown highlights in my hair like the highlights in the pelt of an otter. She didn't realise that I was half like her, half white; that in my veins ran the blood of men called Highlanders, from a part of that island far away that was called Scotland.

Governor Miles inclined his head but he wasn't looking at me; he frowned briefly at the four men from the lighter and shooed them away so that they turned with hasty relief, almost bumping one another off the landing stage in their rush to escape from that threat of a flogging. Men bent to their loads again, hoisting up the wooden chests of trade goods, and continued toiling with them to shore. The thunder of their feet shook the stage, and Governor Miles cupped Orchid's elbow as he steered her out of the way and guided her to continue climbing to shore.

Just as her feet, in their tightly laced shoes of thin leather with hard dainty heels, touched the bluff, she turned to glance back at me. I saw the bright flicker of her blue eyes beneath her hat's brim of woven grasses. She smiled then, brushing a strand of curly blonde hair from her face, and for an instant she didn't look much older than I was. Then she walked on beside the governor towards the fort's octagonal facade of painted planks. The wind whipped her blue dress against her short, plump body, and a feather flew out from her hat to be caught, twenty feet away, by a boatman who stuck it into his red stocking cap with a gleeful grin. He winked at me, his earring twinkling. Then he hoisted a bale of goods on to his back and adjusted the leather tumpline, the strap that went across his fore-head and held the weight of the bale.

'I'm hungry,' Charlotte said softly, and I squeezed her hand.

'I still have credit at the Company store,' I reminded her. 'Now that the ship has come in, we can buy fresh rations.'

'Maybe we can get some humbugs!' Charlotte said and her soft, dark eyes lit up.

'Maybe. Let's go now and cook something.'

She skipped beside me, her hand nestled in mine, and I felt a spasm of pity and love for her; my gentle little sister who had become an orphan even younger than I had. 'After eating, I'll take you to visit the horse,' I promised her, for the thought of the stallion pulled at me constantly; half of my mind was always with him in the cow byre.

Charlotte, however, was more interested in play-ing along the shore with some other girls and so I was alone as I crossed the pasture and opened the byre's creaking door. The horse turned his head and a gusty whicker of sound fluttered his nostrils in greeting. I approached him with slow steps, and laid my palm flat against the warm gloss of his hard shoulder. I had brought him a gift, freshly unpacked from a chest off the supply ship and given to me in the cookhouse by Samuel Beaver, who'd been given it by a Cree boy who had stolen it when no one was looking. The fruit was larger than any berry I'd ever picked, and called an apple; Mr Murdoch had told me that horses loved this fruit which grew in fields in England.

The apple was a slightly wrinkled, reddish, rounded thing in the palm of my hand. The stallion inclined his long face and I glimpsed his large teeth, square like the teeth of a beaver, as he bit into the fruit. I saw that the flesh of the apple was white. Juice oozed from the stallion's lips and his deep eyes considered me. When the fruit was all gone, he nosed at my arm, then began eating hay again. I pulled the oval of braided leather from where I'd tucked it between two beams, and began to rub the horse all over.

'Foxfire,' I murmured, remembering how the *pawakan*, entering my vision quest in human form, had worn a robe that looked like fox fur. Betty Goose Wing had said that white people didn't have *pawakans* to guide them and protect them. Perhaps in their land they didn't face the dangers that my mother's people did: the violent blizzards screaming in to bury the land; the glittering crusts of snow that broke underfoot, warning the wildlife of your approach so that they fled away over the tundra; the cramping pains of hunger eating the belly. Betty had said that the white people all shared the same spirit with the name Jesus, the spirit that sometimes a Company chaplain talked about when he climbed off the supply ship, before he journeyed inland to the other trading forts.

If this horse wasn't the white woman's *pawaka*n though, then why was he so important to her? Why had she been so crushed with fear and anger, standing there on the landing stage and berating the boatmen for his loss? She had said that he was worth a fortune in money, but what good was that here, where beaver skins were the most valuable item that a person could possess? Next to skins, a person might wish to own a good gun, or new traps, or a buffalo robe, but money was almost useless.

The barn door creaked, and sunlight sliced across the stallion's red back. I turned, a smile on my lips, for I thought that Charlotte had come to find me. Orchid stood still in the doorway, the sun burning like a flame in her uncovered hair, and a cloud of mosquitoes hovering around her face. Her cheeks were already blotchy and inflamed with bites, and needed camomile lotion. She had changed out of the blue gown and now wore a gown with wide shoulders, a scooped neckline, and puffy pale yellow sleeves. I recognised the style from copies of the *Lady's Magazine* that had arrived on last year's ship for other men's half-blood daughters. The fabric of

Orchid's gown was a thin chintz that drifted around her in gauzy folds and looked useless for life at York Factory. The gown would have torn on the smallest of twigs, and could not have been worn to pick berries or when stretching beaver skins on frames.

Despite the circling mosquitoes, a smile tugged at the corners of Orchid's lips. A sigh of satisfaction stirred the air between us, and she stepped forward and touched the stallion's forehead with her soft hand, as white as the flesh of the apple.

'You cannot believe how happy I am to see you here,' she said to Foxfire, and then she turned to me. 'You must know how to care for horses.'

'This is the first horse I have ever touched.'

Her gaze lingered on me searchingly. 'Remarkable,' she said briefly. 'In the governor's house, they tell me that you have a way with animals, that the pets follow you around.'

I inclined my head.

'I myself grew up around horses,' she explained. 'My father owned a fine stable with many mares, and one or two stallions. When I was your age, horses and flowers were all that my father talked of; horses and hounds and hunting, hothouses and growing rare species of orchids.'

Sadness hovered in her eyes, and I felt a weight press upon her shoulders. 'Now Foxfire is all that is left . . .' She trailed off, her fingers twining in the long red hair that fell from the horse's neck. Perhaps, after all, she had a horse *pawakan*, I thought, but then I recalled what Mr Murdoch had said about a bride gift.

'You are taking this horse to your new husband?' I asked, and Orchid nodded.

'My mother died four years ago,' she said. 'My father fell into deep grief; he gambled away his fortune and lost our home and lands and then he died of an excess of drinking. I was forced to become a governess, looking after other people's children, the daughters of a relation. It was a terrible blow to me.'

I watched her, puzzled. In the Cree lodges, it was an honour to take care of one's kin, and orphans were never turned away from a lodge door, from the warmth of a fire, from a pot of caribou stew or a freshly caught methy. Only a bad-hearted person would not care for their own kin yet I didn't feel darkness in this small young woman, only grief. I didn't understand what had been so terrible about being a governess but I did understand the grief of being an orphan, how one stood beneath the wolf trail of stars and felt its mournful light dance in one's eyes.

'Then one night,' Orchid said, 'there was a party in the family's London home, and I was allowed to attend once the children were in the nursery for the night. I was playing cards with a man, and he told me that he was a factor with the Hudson's Bay Company, and was home on furlough from trading furs in Rupert's Land. We were laughing and drinking

Madeira, and I asked him what he wanted most in the world. Do you know what he replied?'

Orchid's gaze flew to my face but I remained silent, caught in her story like a rabbit in a snare.

'He said what he wanted most was a large horse,' Orchid continued. 'He said that the Indian ponies in the Red River valley were all very well for running buffalo, but much too small and inferior for any other purpose. And then –'

'Ponies?' I asked.

'Small horses, mustangs and cayuses, Mr Spencer calls them; the Indians use them to hunt the buffalo.'

'What happened after he said he wanted a large horse?'

'I made a daring leap, like a horse jumping a great hedge that it cannot see over the top of,' Orchid explained. 'I asked this factor whether he would marry me and take me away from life as a governess, and make a home for me in the Red River valley, if I could grant his wish for a large horse. And he said that he would; for a moment, maybe, he thought I was joking but then he saw that I was serious. And by then, he had already agreed and couldn't, being a gentleman, go back on his word. I had a secret that he didn't know yet: when my father died and the creditors took our possessions, I was allowed to keep something that I owned personally, that my father had given to me. It was this stallion, Foxfire. I hadn't sold him, although I needed the money. I couldn't bear to part with him, for he was all that remained of my previous life, the life where I was a spoiled and indulged only child.'

The stallion shifted in the byre, his hooves rustling the bedding of wood shavings from the joiner's shop, where the chests for guns and the kegs for rum were made.

'Then what happened?' I asked Orchid.

'The man, whose name is Robert Spencer, married me, and then when his furlough ended five weeks later, he returned to Rupert's Land on the supply ship. This was last summer. I couldn't come with him because one of the children in my care was very ill and I couldn't be spared at such short notice; I felt obliged to stay. But now, this summer, I have come to join Mr Spencer, bringing with me my large horse, the thing that he said he most wanted. We are going to travel by York boat to the Red River valley, Foxfire and I, to join Robert. I hope that he will be pleased with my bride gift. We had only such a short time together, and have now been apart an entire year. I hope that he that he will not regret our agreement.'

A flicker of doubt ran over her face. I saw how she gathered her courage and resolve, how she turned her thoughts resolutely towards the vast continent that lay before her, filled with spirits that she didn't even know existed.

'What man would not be pleased with this gift?' I asked, and again, her eyes lingered on me.

She gave a short, sharp sigh, and became suddenly brisk. 'What very good English you speak.'

'I have been around white men all my life.' It was true that it was easy for me to speak the English tongue, for I had grown up hearing it, but Cree remained the language of dreams, of thoughts, and of lullabies.

'You must have questions about this animal you have not handled before,' she said. 'I will have his grooming kit brought here for you to use, his brushes and combs. You must approach a horse here, at the shoulder, on his left side. You must clean out his feet every day, using a hoof pick.'

She bent, running her hand down the stallion's front leg, and he lifted his foot from the floor and held it up for her to grasp. When she tipped it, I saw how the bottom was pale and smooth like a stone but with a spongy V-shaped piece. 'This is the frog,' she said, pointing to it.

I wrinkled my forehead in puzzlement, wondering what frogs had to do with a horse's foot; in Orchid's land, did horses live in the swamps? Or had frogs and horses made some agreement together, back in the days when the *atiokan* stories had taken place? These were the oldest stories, telling of the time when all the animals talked to one another and lived in lodges, before the trickster, Wishahkicahk, changed the world. 'Why do you clean out the feet?' I asked, for no one cleaned the hooves of deer and yet they ran fleetly over the tundra.

'Why, otherwise disease can get in, and stones can cause bruises,' Orchid replied. 'This horse, you will observe, will willingly pick up three feet. But the fourth, his off-hind foot, he is very reluctant to give to you. It was hurt once when he trod on a thorn, which had to be extracted painfully. He has been careful about the handling of this foot ever since.

'And also, every day, one must wipe around the horse's eyes with a damp sponge and clean out the nostrils. When I was a child, we had stablemen and grooms but my father made sure that I learned how to care –'

We both turned as the door creaked again, its sagging bottom board scraping against the dirt floor because the frost had heaved the old building.

'Mr Murdoch,' I said with a smile. He began to grin, the freckles standing out on his pale cheeks, but then he saw Orchid and his features rearranged themselves into formal, polite lines.

'Good afternoon, ma'am,' he said, holding himself stiff in his everyday working clothes of coarse trousers and loose shirt, and fumbling with his ink-stained fingers at a letter that he held.

'Begging pardon for the interruption,' he continued, 'but I was looking for Amelia Otterchild.'

'Pray proceed, you are not interrupting,' Orchid said in a gracious manner, and Mr Murdoch's face lit up again with a startling enthusiasm. It was the same triumphant look that he wore when he was able to harvest anything at all from the garden; once he had grown peas and had stood amongst the struggling vines, his face glowing as he picked the tiny pods.

'Amelia,' he said now, 'you know that the old octagon is going to be rebuilt? There has been talk of it for several years, and of rebuilding some of the other fort buildings too. The post office is to be rebuilt first as the work that I do there is so vital to the smooth running of the Company. So I have been ordered to clear the office out, and organise everything well, prior to the building being replaced. A boy, a new apprentice off the ship, has been given to me to help me. And we found this, Amelia, this letter!'

He flourished the paper, folded over and written upon with faded ink, his voice cracking with excitement.

'What is it?' I asked.

'A letter to your mother. Sent many years ago but never delivered. It was lost all this time, for thirteen years, Amelia, lost and lying behind a loose board in the wall of the office. But now, here, I am giving it to you!'

The paper slipped into my outstretched hand, as cool and light as the touch of a leaf. A tremor ran through me as I turned it over, and stared at the elegant sloping letters of my mother's name: *Mary Mackenzie*.

'Can she read?' I heard Orchid ask in surprise, and heard too Mr Murdoch's answer: 'Certainly she can read. I taught the evening classes myself, with free candles and paper and tea for everyone who came, be they labourers or children. It is the wish of the Company that the traders' children have a basic education. Amelia has read many of the books in the library here, ma'am.'

I ignored them both. I turned the letter over again, as though tracking an animal's hoof prints, as though walking slowly through a dream and looking for guidance. Then with infinite care, fearing the letter might fly from my grasp like a moth, I opened the paper and spread it out upon the stallion's warm, smooth back, and began to read it to myself.

18 October 1817.

My dear Mary, I trust that you and the baby are in good health as am I. Our boat brigade reached the Red River without any undue difficulty and found a fertile place. Both free traders and Métis half-bloods (who call themselves the Bois-Brûlés) have begun to settle along the river, and have both crops and cattle. The furs being brought in from the western regions are of superior quality, and the factor at York will be most pleased with them. This is a fair place and one in which I am engaged to remain as the factor wishes me to hunt for the fort's provisions. I wish you to join me here in the spring when the brigade comes west again from York Factory. I believe we can look forward to good prospects here for ourselves and our infant daughter as well as for any other children that we might be blessed with. You remain always in my thoughts. Simon Mackenzie.

The stallion shifted his weight, and the letter shifted too. I smoothed it again with the palm of my hand, smoothed those letters that my father had penned one autumn evening when I was an infant in my cradleboard, the one with the heart that my father had painted on it before leaving.

'Is something wrong? Is it bad news?' Orchid asked, but her voice came from very far away, and I didn't reply, simply went on staring at those words. *Engaged to remain . . . I wish you to join me here . . . our infant daughter.* 'Lost all this time,' Mr Murdoch had said. Lost like the light from my mother's eyes, lost like my mother whose spirit had slipped from her body in the fort at York Factory that she had never left. 'Your father went west with a boat brigade; he was a tripman, who rowed boats for the Company. He was a crack shot with a gun,' she had told me when I asked about him, but nothing more would she ever say. It was from Betty Goose Wing that I had learned of my father's broken promise and the cause of the bitterness in my mother's lips even after she had been wooed by a young chief, even after she had married another trader. Only Charlotte Bright Eyes ever brought sweetness to my mother's stern face.

I turned and brushed past Mr Murdoch and Orchid, and ran across the pasture to the small gate in the stockade wall. Faster and faster, I ran through the low bushes and the shrubby aspen poplars. On my right, the great river stretched out, swirling and sparkling. On my left side, the tundra was an enormous animal, lying down flat, splotched with shades of brown and tawny. Beneath the immense bowl of sky I fled, disturbing a ptarmigan that had been feeding on berries, so that the bird flew up in an agitated flurry of feathers.

Father! Father! my thoughts cried.

My moccasins pounded the clay trail, echoing the pounding of my blood behind my eyes. I ran with the letter clasped to my chest with one hand while the other hand paddled the air as though I were swimming against a hard current instead of cool summer wind. Pale smoke drifted from the encampment of the Homeguard Cree and the dogs ran out to meet me but I brushed through their jostling pack. Betty Goose Wing was outside her lodge, stitching lines of porcupine quills, dyed red with berry juice, on to a deerskin tobacco pouch. She straightened as I rushed to her, gasping, my heart pouring words into my mouth so fast that my lips couldn't speak them. 'Auntie, Auntie!'

'Breathe,' she told me calmly. 'What is chasing you?'

I doubled over and waited for air to suck all those words out of my mouth, while my hand holding the letter flapped in front of my knees.

'From my father – lost for thirteen winters – asking my mother to join him in the Red River valley.' I straightened. 'Why was it never delivered?' I wailed. 'Who would have lost it?'

'Hmph,' said Betty. 'It is the past chasing you.' She began to look like a woman picking medicines from the tundra grasses, like a woman setting traps, for her face was intense and still with focus. 'Thirteen winters ago,' she said at last, 'the postmaster was a half-blood named Alexander. His mother married twice. Her second husband was a chief and, later, his son became a young chief who wooed your mother.'

'It wasn't an accident?' I asked. 'The young chief wanted my mother . . . he asked his half-brother to keep this letter from her. They wanted her to think my father had abandoned her. Us.'

'Did I say any of this?' Betty asked, her gaze on me as unblinking as the dark gaze of a turtle sunning on a log. 'It is all in the past now, Amelia. You cannot mourn it any longer.' And she bent back over her stitching.

'But he might be there still, in the Red River valley! I might have kin there!'

'You still have some kin here,' Betty reminded me. 'We did not all starve.'

'The horse is going west on a York boat,' I muttered. 'The white woman is taking him to the Red River valley. Maybe this is why my *pawakan* is the horse spirit. Maybe I should travel west with the horse, Foxfire, and search for my father. Maybe there, in that valley, my father would welcome his daughter, and my sister, Charlotte Bright Eyes.'

Betty Goose Wing drew on her pipe, rubbing its clay bowl thoughtfully with one broad, callused thumb. 'There is a shaking lodge ceremony tomorrow at sunset,' she said at last, smoke drifting from her mouth. 'The inlander hunters want to ask the spirits where to travel to in the next moon, when they go into the bush to hunt. They hope to avoid another starving winter. You could come to the shaking lodge too, and ask the spirits for guidance in your choices.

'You are like your mother, Otterchild. She had one foot on the path of our people, and then she set the other foot inside the fort, into the white man's world. And now you do not know where to put your feet, either one of them. So you should come and talk to the spirits. Sunset, tomorrow,' she repeated and then rose, brushing a few stray strands of tobacco from her leggings, and stooped inside her lodge.

I wandered over the tundra, picking late-ripening blueberries and searching for grey moss for Jane's baby. Perhaps it was foolish to think that my father would welcome us, I thought, as I stooped to pick a mushroom to add to tonight's supper of fish soup. Perhaps Simon Mackenzie had forgotten us long ago, after my mother failed to join him, failed to respond to that letter. He would never have known that it was not delivered to her. It was common for the Company to move its men around, to assign them different jobs. If my father was a crack shot with a gun, as my mother said, it was not surprising that the fort in the west kept him to hunt for its provisions. The only surprise must have been that my mother failed to join him there. Now he was just another white man, another stranger. Or perhaps he might have travelled further still and become lost in the distances, lost in the great mountains. Perhaps he had even travelled to the shores of the shining Pacific ocean that Mr Murdoch had shown to us in evening class, using the terrestrial globe belonging to the governor.

Then what would become of Charlotte Bright Eyes and me, far away from our remaining kin, in a valley of free traders, and unfamiliar tribes: the Assiniboine and Salteaux bands, the Cree who ran after the buffalo on little horses? I pondered that for a moment as I tore up a handful of dry moss. Where had the tribes out west got horses from, and what kind of horses were they? Were they all red in colour, and with frogs on their feet? And how did the tribes use these horses to hunt the buffalo?

There was the big horse to consider too, the magnificent Foxfire who drew me to his burning presence like a cold person to a campfire. Perhaps he would need me on his long journey; perhaps it was for this purpose that he had saved me from the muddy Hayes River. And was it even possible, I wondered as I carried a bundle of moss towards camp, for a horse to travel in a York boat? From York Factory to the Red River valley was a journey of six hundred miles. Foxfire had already lunged overboard in the Hayes River, and the men hadn't been able to hold him, so how did Orchid expect him to travel along the wild rushing rivers, filled with rocks and waterfalls, into the heart of Rupert's Land? There was no other way to make this journey; no trail or track through the wilderness. Only in winter, the horse might have been able to walk on top of the ice. Was this creature able to withstand the cold? In his own land, did Foxfire's kind migrate south as day length waned or did their sleek coats thicken and soften with an underpelt that allowed them to endure as the moose did?

There was so much that I wanted to learn about Foxfire, and about the nature of horses. Could I risk the happiness of Charlotte for this desire? What would the spirits advise me tomorrow in the shaking lodge, when the shaman went down on his knees and sang to them, until they entered like birds and spoke to us all in different languages, Cree and English, French, Ojibwa, and Chipewyan?

Where would I place my two feet then?

Chapter 4

When I slipped into the cow byre the next morning, gulls were crying over the river where the tide rushed in to cover the muddy shoreline. Weak sunshine falling through a window illuminated the stallion's fiery back and the pale head of Orchid, his mistress. She held a tin pail that Foxfire was eating from with a steady grinding of teeth, and glanced over her shoulder as I entered.

'He is having his oats,' she said, 'and then I will turn him out into the pasture. It will do his legs good to stretch, for he was sorely cramped for ten weeks in the hold of the supply ship.'

'Oats?' I asked in surprise, thinking of porridge with caribou meat in it, and a crumbly topping for a dessert of wild gooseberries – for these were the uses we had for oats at York Factory. 'This is all that horses eat – grass and grains and fruits?'

59

'Carrots too and sometimes a root called a mangold, like a turnip. Haven't you read anything about horses in the library here?'

I shrugged, thinking. 'There were no horses in *Robinson Crusoe*. Also, I've read a detective novel and a romance called *The Road to Tralee* . . . and a book about sailing to India and trading for tea.'

There had been passing mention of carriages in some of these books – things called landaus and phaetons and mail coaches – and perhaps I had vaguely comprehended that these were drawn by horses. However, I didn't know what any of these carriages looked like and neither had I ever given thought to the animals pulling them. The truth was I did not read as well as Mr Murdoch liked to imagine that I did; it was slow, hard work finding my way through a page of words, like wading through a muskeg swamp with mud sucking at my knees. None of the words I had waded through had given me any idea of the power and beauty and nature of a real horse.

'Does Foxfire pull a carriage?' I asked now, and Orchid shook her head and set the empty pail on the floor. 'He is trained for riding on; I have brought his tack with me, his saddle and bridle, in a chest. Men ride with legs astride their horses' backs, but ladies ride side-saddle with both legs on one side of their horses.'

'Ride, on top of? It must be hard to balance.'

'It is exceedingly difficult to learn to ride this way,' Orchid conceded, 'but I have been riding since I was a small child on a fat pony with a bad temper. Despite having one's legs both to one side of the saddle, one must keep a straight spine and direct one's gaze forward. Women even hunt this way, following the hounds over rough country, through fen and bog, over fences and hedges. Hunting is the most popular pastime in Norfolk, where my father owned his lands and stables. It is a flat, wet country beside the sea; you would like it, Amelia, for it is similar in ways to your own land here, only not as bitterly cold in winter.

'Oh, it was wonderful to gallop across the fields with the sea shining along the horizon like a finger of light, with the horses fresh and eager, and the hounds giving voice like a choir! The freedom was marvellous!'

'But what were you hunting?' I asked.

'Foxes.'

'We hunt foxes too! Do you trade the pelts?'

Orchid stared at me with a mesh of puzzled lines wrinkling her forehead. 'Pelts? Oh, Amelia! We do not hunt foxes for trade but for sport, for pleasure, for the thrill of the chase. We do not skin them, nor trade the pelts, although we do cut off the brush, the tail, to keep. We leave trade to the factors of the Company here in Rupert's Land. In England we use money and not trade goods. Pelts! That is a diverting idea!' And she let out a peal of laughter, clear and sharp, so that the stallion flung up his head and watched her, the sun lustrous in his eyes.

I flushed and bit my lip, seeing myself as Orchid

must have, an ignorant girl with little learning, and little experience of the world. But then, what did she know, this white woman, about sewing a moose hide into a tent, and suspending it over a smoking fire until it had changed to a golden colour that would look wonderful decorated with blue glass beads, and stitched with coloured threads in patterns of flowers? Could she gut a speckled trout, washing it in cold water so that the innards sluiced away downstream? Could she set traps for muskrat in the springtime, using a raft of dry logs with the trap dangling beneath from a pole baited with musk?

I stepped to the open door of the byre and stared out, my back stiff, and behind me Orchid's laughter died into a silence broken only by the scrape of Foxfire's hooves as he pawed impatiently through the bedding to the ground beneath.

'Our ways are strange to one another,' Orchid said at last, when the silence had stretched taut as a rope between us. 'Do not be offended by me. Come, I will show you how to halter this horse, and you can lead him into the pasture and keep an eye on him whilst I go for breakfast in the governor's house.'

I turned back and Orchid handed me the harness that the stallion had been wearing on his head when I swam with him in the river. 'Hold it thus,' she said, 'and now reach beneath his neck and guide his head into the noseband.'

Foxfire dropped his head as I slipped the halter on

to him and fastened the metal buckle that lay along his cheek. He was not like a wild thing, I noted, that would hate straps made by man. Instead, he had been trained to accept the halter, even to welcome it. Orchid snapped the lead line into the ring beneath the horse's jaw, and handed it to me.

'Hold the line in both hands,' she said, 'with one hand near the horse. Never wrap the line around your hand or arm lest the horse bolt and drag you; you could be killed in this manner.'

Killed! I felt the power of the stallion as I led him outside; felt how puny and small I was standing at his shoulder while he flung up his great head and stretched out his neck, the breeze off the bay lifting the ends of his long hair so that it flickered around him in the light. His nostrils stretched wide, sucking at the smells of the pasture: rank pigs, oxen, young calves' sweet breath, cows' milky udders, and perhaps the smells that travelled from futher away too, of salt and mud, ice and fresh water. Presently, he dropped his head and began to rip up the sparse grass with his teeth, moving steadily along, his hooves piercing the ground and leaving semicircular marks.

'Listen, I will tell you the names of his parts,' Orchid said, and I tried to commit them to memory as she talked: the *poll* behind his ears, the *hock* where his hind legs bent like elbows, the *fetlock*, where the lowest joint of each leg flexed as he moved, the *croup* above his tail, the *shoulder* sloping towards the front legs, the *withers*, where his long hair (his *mane*) ended and his smooth, long back began.

'A good horse has correct proportions,' Orchid explained. 'You must imagine a triangle here, between the seat bone, the stifle and the hip. The sides of the triangle should be equal to one another in length. And here, the length from the fetlock to the elbow should equal the length from the elbow to the wither.

'You can see that this stallion's conformation is admirable. His lineage is impeccable, for he is a Norfolk Trotter from a long line of splendid trotters tracing back to a stallion named Flying Childers, grandson of the famous Darley Arabian himself.'

I pondered all this information. In the Cree bands, one could name one's ancestors but it was a new idea to me that one could also name the ancestors of an animal. Indeed, was not each animal only itself, over and over, being reborn into a new body after each death? Perhaps this horse before me was not merely Foxfire but was the spirit of the famous horse, the Darley Arabian, that Orchid spoke of with such reverence, reborn into the body of this red stallion.

And, had I understood Orchid correctly that there were different kinds of horses? 'Not all horses in your land are Norfolk Trotters?' I asked.

'Good gracious, certainly they are not,' Orchid exclaimed, beginning to smile but then repressing the expression as, perhaps, she remembered our previous misunderstanding. She hurried on. 'There are heavy horses that pull wagons and ploughs like the Shire and the Suffolk Punch. And there are small horses that have lived wild on the wasteland, the moors, for centuries and are called ponies. Of them there are numerous kinds: the Dartmoor, Exmoor, Fell and Welsh. There are horses bred especially for the fox hunt, and flat racing horses called Thoroughbreds and many more besides.'

After Orchid left for breakfast I walked around the pasture with Foxfire for a long time, until the bell rang for the white men's noon meal. It was a thrill to feel how he would follow me after only a slight tug on the lead rope, and a thrill to lay my hands against his warm hide. I smoothed my hands all over him, saying out loud, 'Stifle, pastern, girth, neck, quarters, chestnut,' as I touched each place. My hands began to learn the shape of that horse, every fold, every plane, every wrinkle of skin: his flat knee, the soft hair on his breast between his front legs, the mottling of silver like frost upon his redness. 'Roan,' Orchid had said this colour was called, red roan.

Suddenly, he leaped. He whirled! My hand slipped on the lead rope so that it burned across my palm. Through my line of vision he soared, a flash of muscle and white rolling eye. I spun, I jumped, I gripped on to the lead rope with my teeth clenched. His head came around towards me and he became still again, snorting. He had pulled me a yard across the slippery grass, and behind us the patterns of his hooves had dug in deeper than before. My heart pounded. I saw the quiver of his shoulder, heard the whistle of his snort. He danced sideways, as though to an invisible drumbeat, the great barrel of his body shining as the sun slid across his muscles.

I glanced around, still clinging to his lead rope, and saw that it was a kite that had frightened him, a yellow flapping kite being snatched by the wind rising up the bluff from the river as children played along the shore. The kite soared higher, and ceased its struggle with the wind to become a thing of grace and speed, climbing until it was another speck amongst the white specks of seagulls. Foxfire dropped his head and began to graze again in nervous snatches, still breathing hard and with sweat darkening his chest.

Now I had learned something about the nature of horses, I thought. He was an animal whose nature was to run; he was like the deer that lived on grass and moss, and that had no defence against wolves and lynx but their own reflexes, swift as the lick of lightning strikes. The flying blur of their slender legs raced them away from the threat of the predator. Again I wondered how this creature, this horse, would be able to travel for six hundred miles in the cramped confines of a York boat, when his nature was to flee from any threat. Who could hold him when his muscles bunched, when his legs sliced through the air, when he stretched out his neck and flew into the wind, sucking it into wide nostrils?

I ran my hands over him, soothing him as I had soothed Charlotte after our mother died; stroking her Cree hair, black as a raven's wing, stroking the backs of her small dark hands with their chubby knuckles, singing her lullabies. And sound was important to the horse too; his ears still swivelled constantly, alert for sound from any direction. I began to sing to him. I sang him a lullaby without words – *'wa wi wa way'* – and then a Cree love song, and then a song about the geese flying south in winter. Then I switched to the white men's songs that they played on their pipes and fiddles at celebrations; songs about laddies and lassies, misty mornings and unrequited love. Foxfire's breathing slowed, and the muscles in his neck and shoulders slackened as the tension left them. Soon, he began to graze steadily again, and the sweat dried on his chest. Even when the kite swooped closer, flapping again like a shot and injured bird, Foxfire merely raised his head for a moment to watch before dropping it to continue grazing.

Perhaps, I thought, something in particular had startled him in the Hayes River; perhaps he had not simply leaped overboard as the boatman had said but had been propelled into action by something frightening. If I could find out what this thing had been, I might be able to help him in his journey to the Red River valley. If, that is, I went with him . . . If I went searching for my father, who had written a letter but had never come back to find out why my mother hadn't replied, had never written again to enquire after the health and whereabouts of his infant daughter. Surely, if he had loved us, he would have come searching for us many years ago instead of waiting for us to join him in the west? What kind of a man would be so careless with what he professed to love? I yearned to hear the explanation from his own lips, to learn what the answer to the mystery was. I had thought of myself as an orphan for two winters now and it was strange to consider that perhaps I wasn't one, not quite, after all.

Would Simon Mackenzie remember calling me Otterchild, smoothing my hair with its brown highlights over the soft dome of my infant head? He had done this despite the fact that my mother, to please him, had given me a white child's name – Amelia. How Betty Goose Wing had smiled when she told me about this: each of my parents naming me for the other one's pleasure. Could a love like this have simply sputtered out, like a candle in a strong draught? Didn't he ever wonder what had become of me, whether I had survived the starving moons, the burning autumns, the fragile springs and tempestuous summers at York Factory – didn't he think about his white blood running in my veins?

I sighed, and focused my eyes back on the stallion's hard black hooves moving slowly past my moccasins. When the sun had climbed high into the sky and the kite had sunk over the bluff on to the beach, I led the stallion back into the cow byre, checked that his water bucket had been filled, slipped the halter from his head, and went to find the boatmen. It took me some time but eventually I found one of them in the boatbuilding yard where the York boats were constructed from trees dragged in by teams of lowing oxen.

'When the horse went overboard,' I asked, 'what truly happened? What frightened him?'

'Why, 'twas the white whales,' the boatman answered, scratching his hair under his cap and adjusting his spectacles on his weather-beaten nose. 'We heard the whales blowing in the fog, and then one surfaced to the side of us, his white back all sleek and ghostly in the fog. And then he blew, whoosh! And the wet and fishy air swallowed us up, and in the midst of that the horse was gone, plunged right over the side.'

'Thank you for your story,' I said, and he nodded and turned back to planing a plank so that curls of wood dropped from it as thin as sheets of paper. I paced around the perimeter of the boatshed, thinking hard. The smells of fresh cut wood – cedar and birch, spruce and poplar – tickled my nose as the breeze ebbed and flowed, swirling through the buildings of York Factory like a tide, licking at the buildings with its salty currents. Sawdust clung to my moccasins. York boats in various stages of completion or repair loomed over me, the lines of their thick hulls as swooping and graceful as the wings of shorebirds, their thick overlapping planks built to withstand the grind and bite of river rocks.

I clambered into one of the boats, tilted on its side with three broken ribs, and sat in it with the sun lying on me like a warm hand. Almost everything was carried in these boats now, although when I was younger, birchbark canoes had carried the furs and the trade goods along the vast network of rivers running through Rupert's Land like the veins in a body. Now it was the York boats that carried the chests of guns, ammunition, and sharp axes, the strings of beads and bundles of blankets, the kegs of rum for easing trade agreements. They also carried all the provisions: barrels of dried peas, oatmeal and cornmeal, sacks of pemmican made from dried buffalo meat and saskatoon berries, salted geese, salted pork, biscuits, loaves of sugar, and chests of tea.

I had seen settlers travel by York boat, after crossing the ocean because of promises made to them by a white man named Lord Selkirk, a man who had bought a piece of Rupert's Land and renamed it Assiniboia. He had convinced the Company to bring white families to live there in that land, where the Red River lazed between low hills. Company chaplains travelled by York boat at times, and so did goats: I had once seen a dog depart for the west in one, and even crates of clucking hens, but I had never seen a horse inside one. The boats were rowed by eight men wielding oars so long and heavy that they were hard to lift, and at every rapid the boat had to be unloaded and all the goods inside it had to be portaged around the rapids along narrow trails cut through the bush. The boat itself was run onshore and dragged along on rollers laid on the ground. The horse would have to climb out too, and be led through the bush – but who could induce him to climb aboard again, and would he lie in the boat or travel standing up for six hundred miles?

Whales, I thought, as the men working at the saws burst into song; their voices – rough then smooth, single then united – drifted over me and soared away into the wind like kites. The white whales swam in the bay, and into the mouth of the Hayes River, in small bands, and were hunted for blubber to feed to sled dogs. Their bodies rose from the depths like drifts of snow; silent, sleek, their bulbous snouts glimmered beneath the surface as they rose, mysterious and beautiful. But when they surfaced, they blew foul, fishy air through their holes with a gusting whoosh of sound, as the boat-man had said; it was easy to see that this would have sent the stallion plunging overboard. But what if I had been there to sing to him – would this have helped? Or what if he couldn't have seen the whales . . . if perhaps, he'd had something fastened to his halter to partially cover his eyes?

I would find Orchid and ask her about this, I thought, but first I would go to the fort's library and try to find books about horses. I clambered out of the damaged boat and brushed sawdust from my gown. The fort, as I walked through it, bustled with harried clerks and nervous apprentices, all helping to sort the items that were being unloaded from the three-masted ship at Five Fathom Hole. The goods had to be unpacked, sorted and repacked; some of the supplies would remain at York Factory but much of it would be sent on to other forts by York boat. Everything had to be packed in chests or bundles weighing ninety pounds, for this was the weight that the boatmen would carry on their backs as they staggered, almost running, along the rough portage trails. Huge quantities of furs, which had been arriving all summer in canoe brigades from places far to the west, had to be packed for sending to England.

Passing a fur warehouse, I glanced in and saw men packing the pelts into bales after they'd been flattened by a screw press. I thought of the marten pelts I had cured last winter and how they were going to travel further than I had ever been, somewhere in the hold of the ship, going to the fur auction in a city called London.

'Watch out!'

Turning from the door, I had almost collided with a group of half-blood girls of my own age, their arms filled with lengths of brilliant, patterned cloth from the Company store.

'I'm sorry,' I mumbled but one of the girls stepped forward; I didn't know her very well, although I had seen her around the fort and in the Cree camp. Her name, I remembered, was Eva.

'Amelia.' Her smooth face creased into a smooth, placid smile between her black braids and the flaps of her blue, beautifully embroidered cap with a beaded fringe. Beneath her chin, her merino gown was decorated with a row of square trade brooches, while silver thimbles and coins imprinted with a chief's head dangled from her ears. I had noticed before that she was a girl who always liked to look as fine as she could, to outshine her friends. She liked to widen her eyes at young men: boat captains in top hats with ostrich plumes, or hunters with their guns resting on their shoulders. I was surprised that her father hadn't married her to one of them yet.

'You're the one who saved Mrs Spencer's horse,' she said. 'How brave you are! I would be terrified of the creature!'

I shrugged. 'He is not so hard to manage.'

'I hope this is true. I am travelling west with him. With Mrs Spencer. Her new husband and my father traded together on the Athabasca River a few years ago. They are still friends. My father has asked Mrs Spencer to take me with her. I am going to the new school for girls, the boarding school, in Red River.'

'I didn't know.' A wave of something welled up in me; was it envy? Would Eva learn to slip a halter on

73

to the stallion's bent head, would she listen to Orchid's stories of fox-hunting and rare flowers? And in the settlement of Red River, where the Company had offered the half-blood Métis people land to farm on, would Eva ever cross paths with my father unwittingly; one more white man working in a warehouse perhaps, or rowing a boat down the river as Eva walked on the shore?

'. . . know what to take with me,' Eva was saying, 'but Mrs Spencer will help me.'

She smiled again, smoothing the folds of the fine wool shawl that was draped around her shoulders, but her eyes were dark and unreadable, fixed intently upon my face. I remembered that she was the niece of a chief, and stretched my own stiff lips in reply but Eva was already turning away to her friends. The porcelain beads and dentalia shells in her hair shone in the sun, and her leggings were deeply fringed and crusted with red beading. The girls' laughter drifted back over their shoulders as they moved around the corner of the fur warehouse.

I hurried on to the library. It was a plank-floored room with wooden shelves lining the walls, and an eclectic collection of books that the traders had sent for over the years, and magazines and newspapers. I searched for a long time but didn't find any book specifically about horses; I would have to rely on my own observations, and on Orchid's knowledge, to satisfy my curiosity. However, I did find a drawing in a magazine of horses pulling a carriage with high wheels; I bent over it, studying the web of strapping that covered the horses and fastened them to the carriage. It was impossible for me to guess the purpose of it all. I wondered if the white women made the strapping, weaving it all together the way that Cree women wove the netting for snowshoes.

Each horse, I saw, wore flat pieces of harness that covered its eyes – this was just what I had imagined for Foxfire! Wearing something like this, he would not be able to see the river water rushing along on either side of the York boat. I would suggest this to Orchid and maybe she could have something made before she left. Maybe I could persuade her to sing to the stallion in her sharp, clear voice ... but I didn't think it the right kind of voice for soothing the horse's panic. It was not a low, husky voice like my own, a voice that seemed to hold the vibration of a drum skin within it.

With a start, I realised that the sunlight had dimmed on the knotted plank floor. I laid the magazine away, for soon it would be sunset and time for the shaking lodge ceremony in the Cree encampment. I must find Charlotte and take her with me, for it was her future, as well as my own, that I was trying to decide upon, and who knew what price we might both pay if I chose to pursue the mystery of my father, and the lure of the horse, into the wilderness?

Chapter 5

Ihurried to the room that Charlotte and I had spent the summer recovering in. It was sparsely furnished with only a wooden bed that we shared, a stool, our snowshoes leaning against one wall, a fishing pole I had made from a sapling and a piece of string, my traps for catching marten, and a plain wooden chest that Ronald McTavish had left behind. In it, I kept our meagre possessions: our flannel undergarments for winter, a coat of white hare fur I'd made for Charlotte, my sewing kit with bright silks and different sizes of needles, Charlotte's baby moccasins threaded with her dried umbilical cord, and a spelling primer that I used to teach Charlotte her letters. On top lay my blanket shawl of blue and green tartan cloth threaded with bright yellow lines like the lines that connect together everything that exists, and that point to the four directions from which the animals came into the world. Charlotte had said once that my shawl matched my green eyes.

I undid the single braid that had hung all day down my back and brushed my hair, dragging at tangles in my haste. My fingers flew as I parted my hair across the centre of my head, and as I plaited it into two braids, one beside each ear. Then I coiled each braid up over an ear, and fastened it in place with a decorative covering of deerhide stitched in a zigzag pattern of yellow and white beads. I had made these hair coverings the previous winter, in the Cree lodges while the fire smoked and the cold fell. Once my hair was in place, I pulled my tartan shawl around my shoulders. In the bottom of the chest was a small bark container that I had made and carved with pictures of animals: a family of otters, a moose, a porcupine. The seams were bound together with peeled spruce roots. Inside the container lay a package wrapped in scraps of deerhide. I held it for a moment in one palm, feeling its lightness, or perhaps its heaviness.

Then, slowly, I unfolded the hide to stare at my most precious possession.

The brooch was of pure silver. Its two hearts were intertwined, decorated with diagonal score marks and round stipple marks; atop the hearts was a crown with shining points. A luckenbooth this brooch was called, designed in Scotland. Such brooches were popular in the fur trade, and copies of the Scottish ones were made in Montreal, in Lower Canada. The luckenbooth lying in my palm was from Scotland though, and was larger and thicker, of better quality, than the trade brooches. My father had given it to my mother before he paddled away into the west. When a Cree died, her possessions were buried with her; my mother had been buried with her jewellery and her traps, her axe and her cooking pots. This one thing I had kept, although guilt weighed upon my chest for many nights as I lay beneath a blanket and held tightly to Charlotte. This one thing I could not part with, not even for my mother in her grave.

Now I turned it over to trace with my fingertip the familiar inscription engraved deeply into the silver and tarnished by the salty air. *True heart is true riches. Simon and Mary.*

But if my father's heart had been so true, entwined with my mother's heart like the entwined silver hearts of this brooch, then why had he left her? Left us? Why had he brought this brooch all the way from Scotland, and pinned it on to her shawl – his hands callused from wooden paddles and the rope around bales of trade goods – and then disappeared?

I pressed my lips against the brooch's coolness and used it to pin my own shawl together before slipping outside to find Charlotte.

The sun was dipping into the west as we hurried, hand in hand, along the familiar path over the tundra towards the lazy smoke of the Cree fires. Here and there, beside the path, the leaves on blueberry bushes were already turning red as autumn approached; before long, the entire tundra would flare up, bright as fire, until quenched by snow. The last boat brigades, including the one for the Red River valley, would depart as soon as the supplies had been repacked and loaded. After that, the only travel would be over the ice of the frozen rivers.

The people were gathering around the outside of the dome-shaped tent when we arrived, and Betty Goose Wing gestured for us to join her on the women's side. Charlotte and I sat on the ground beside her, and folded our legs under us. I stared at the shaking tent and my heart fluttered twice in my chest like a bird in a snare net. Soon, as darkness fell, the spirits would enter it; soon they might talk to me. The tent was formed of deerskins wrapped around evergreen saplings, and had only been made that afternoon under the shaman's watchful eye. The dogs had been kept away from it, for if any of them peed on the materials, the tent would be too dirty for the spirits to enter through the hole in the top.

'Are you ready to speak?' Betty asked, wisps of smoke trickling from between her weathered lips. I bent my head into my hands, blocking out the laughter and conversation taking place all around me, feeling the smooth beads of my ear coverings beneath my fingertips. Did I have my question ready to speak to the spirits? But what was it that I needed most to know ... where my father was? Or whether I should travel with the horse? Were these the same thing?

A hush fell upon the Cree and I lifted my head in time to see the dark form of the shaman slip into the tent, his greased hair thick with beads and feathers, and his face painted red with ochre. Cold air poured down the back of my neck and in the silence I felt the great sky lie down heavily upon the spindly trees and the flat land, flat as a rawhide stretched upon a frame and ready to be scraped. A baby gave a fretful cry in its cradleboard but was crooned into sleepy silence. A duck flew over, high and fast, its wings whistling. Betty rocked to and fro, and the smell of sweet grass and tobacco tickled my nostrils as a slender clay pipe was passed from hand to hand until it reached me. I drew the smoke deep into my lungs and felt the land and the silence and the cold air flow into me like a tide. In the shadows, the animals were gathering; I felt their presences. My skin prickled.

Charlotte pressed against my side and I laid my cheek briefly against hers; it was as plump and smooth as an egg in a warm nest.

Inside the tent, a drum began to throb, its skin vibrating inside my ribs. The shaman's voice rang inside my head as he called upon the spirits and entreated them to come and help us, to talk with us. The sound seemed to go on all night, all autumn. My legs fused to the ground beneath me, the cool living body of our mother earth, formed after the great flood when the muskrats brought the ball of mud up from beneath the waters. With that mud, Wishahkicahk had remade the world, and then had told the animals, saved on his raft, to multiply and be good, not to hide too much when their brothers needed to eat. Pine needles pressed into my leggings, engraved their patterns upon my skin like the words that a man had once engraved into the reverse side of a silver heart brooch.

The first star climbed into the sky of my eyes.

'They are coming,' Betty hissed beside us, and I saw a quiver run through the tent's sides; it was like the quiver on the skin of a deer when the flies touch it. I strained my eyes in the gloom but the tent was still again, and all around me people held their breath and even the dogs, tied to logs on the other side of the camp, were silent. Then another quiver ran through the tent; it was as though wind had blown over a patch of grass, or a ripple had run over a pool of water. 'They are here,' Betty said, leaning forward with a grunt of satisfaction. At that moment, the harsh caw of a crow tore apart the silence inside the tent, and its tip began to swing in an arc as the other spirits entered to join Crow.

Lynx hissed and the sound ran over my skin like the rasp of a tongue. Moose bellowed as though in rut, a noise so loud that it seemed to push us backwards, further away from the tent. But then we leaned in again as Loon called to us, laughing.

A hunter stood up in the crowd on the men's side. 'My brothers, we need to know about the winter,' he called respectfully. 'We need to know where we should journey to find the deer. Can you help us?'

'He's just being nice because he wants roast meat,' a Hairy Heart sneered inside the tent; its voice was as hard and thin as new ice and I felt my bones grow brittle, ready to snap in the teeth of that cold-hearted monster. The Hairy Hearts were almost as frightening as the Witiko; they roamed the forests and the tundra in rags, gnawing on the flesh of their prey.

'Why should he have meat to roast when we are hungry?' the Hairy Heart complained. 'He should go hungry too, unless he wants to make us an offering. Maybe he'd like to make us an offering of much roasted meat.'

Beside me, Betty Goose Wing spat into the darkness; everyone knew that the Hairy Hearts were insatiably greedy, that they always wanted burnt offerings made to them. The hunter who had first spoken ignored the Hairy Heart and called out again, still respectfully, 'My brother the deer, if you are here with us, please speak to us.'

'Deer is not here!' shouted Flying Squirrel, who always spoke the opposite of the truth and so we knew that Deer had entered the shaking lodge.

'My brother, I do not know where the deer will run this winter,' said the Deer spirit suddenly, speaking in Cree, and a stifled moan arose from the people, for we all remembered the cramping pain of hunger in our bellies.

The gurgling underwater voice of Northern Pike spoke in the French tongue. 'Perhaps the men will have to catch fish instead,' translated Betty Goose Wing beside me. Another stifled moan of consternation ran through the men's side. Fishing was women's work and only in starving moons would the hunters consent to abandon the trails of big game animals and venture on to the hard sheets of river ice to chop holes and let nets down into the blackness where the currents spoke in their gurgling tongues.

'Perhaps the people have taken too much from the deer and not treated them with respect.' This thin, cruel voice from inside the tent ran over me like a flensing knife; it separated my brain from my body and my blood ran cold. It was Macimanitow who spoke, that evil being who wishes us ill, and as his words died into silence, Pakahk the skeleton rattled his bones together with a terrible dry hard rhythm like the clattering of frozen sticks.

'Hunger,' he chattered. 'Hunger is coming to the people and soon their bones will be pale and shining in the dark.'

Charlotte whimpered and pressed against me and I pulled her closer with one arm.

'I will not shine on those bones,' protested Moon in the English language.

'I do not believe the people have disrespected their brothers the deer,' interjected the voice of Wishahkicahk, the trickster hero of the ancient stories from when the world was young, for he was a man who showed kindness to our people. 'I have heard the people singing to the deer to entertain them.'

'No, no!' cried Flying Squirrel. 'They have done no such thing.'

'They have killed so many deer that the carcasses went adrift on the tide and went down Underwater,' Macimanitow said, and hunters cowered low as the cruel touch of that voice ran over their heads and whistled away into the sky's silence. 'They have wasted their brothers' gifts.'

The tent became still. Outside it we sat as still as wooden carvings for we knew that it was true; the Homeguard Cree had killed many deer as they migrated across the Hayes River, killed them for their hearts and their tongues, and let the bodies slip away on the fast current. Betty Goose Wing had complained about it, I remembered; she had said that in the bush, no animal's body was ever treated with such disrespect but that the Homeguard Cree had become dirty with the white man's wasteful ways.

Suddenly, the tent began to shake violently; the tips of the sapling poles thrashed in the air as some mighty thing entered. A cacophony of sound rose from inside as the new spirit was welcomed by a babble of languages, snorts and hoots and hisses, the crackle of ice. All fell into silence as a great growl tore apart the darkness; that growl vibrated the ground beneath me and Charlotte clapped her hands over her ears. 'It is Crooked Tail, it is Nimosom, our grand-father,' whispered the women around me, for even to name the bear – with its ability to stand on its hind legs and stretch as tall as a man, and its claws that could rip open a man's ribcage – was disrespectful.

'Grandson,' said the bear with a chuckle, speaking to the shaman down on his knees as the spirits roamed around his head, 'Grandson, we will fight. If you can throw me flat, I'll be pleased. If you can't throw me, you people won't be able to get any game this winter. Get up, Grandson, and we will wrestle. Come.'

Outside, people leaned forward, willing the shaman to wrestle that great bear to the ground, willing his *pawakan* guardian to be so strong that he might pin that hairy bear flat on to his back.

'He's winning!' shrieked Flying Squirrel in Cree.

'Push harder, grab him!' gurgled Pike in French.

'He is too weak!' cried Macimantow, and a groan escaped from Wishahkicahk.

'Again!' roared Bear. 'I will give you two more chances. We will fight three times!'

Once more, the Cree leaned forward in the dark as the tent's poles shook and the tip spun in the darkness, a pale blur as the bear and the shaman fought inside while the spirits cried and shrieked, and showers of stars littered the sky and the trees shook in the stillness of the air as though wind tore them apart. My fingernails scored marks in my palms. Sweat beaded my freezing forehead.

'Again!' roared the bear. 'Fight me again! I will give you one more chance to win.'

Sweat touched my tongue. Heavy shapes thrashed past me in the darkness; I felt the ground heave. Trees fell far out on the tundra; black spruce crashed to the ground, crushing the blueberries. The shaman heaved and struggled, his hands slipping on empty air, the bear's weight pressing a groan from his throat as he fell beneath those raking claws.

'Grandson, your *pawakan* is not strong enough,' growled Bear. 'You have lost three times, and in the moons of winter you will not sing me from my den.'

A woman wailed nearby for if the people could not lure the bears from their dens, nor catch the deer, they would starve again in the moon when the old man spreads the brush.

'Maybe the people can catch rabbits,' hissed Lynx.

'You can starve to death on rabbits,' quipped Turtle, known for his sense of humour. But it was true you could starve on rabbits for when Wishahkicahk threw all the animals, one by one, into the fatty river, he pulled rabbit out almost right away, and so rabbit has little fat on him. Bear was allowed to stay in the fat-filled river the longest, and so has the most fat on him for people to warm hearts and bellies with in the bitter cold.

Now the spirits began to argue inside the tent in tongues that no one could understand, and once Wolf howled and once Wolverine snarled.

'Ask your question,' muttered Betty Goose Wing beside me, but my tongue lay in my dry mouth like a frozen stone.

'You can do it,' whispered Charlotte, squeezing my fingers, her grave eyes fixed trustingly upon my face. I gulped and nodded but at that moment, even for Charlotte, I could not speak.

Somewhere in the crowd a woman asked the whereabouts of a missing relative and the spirits talked to her for some time; Turtle gave an impersonation of a drunk and people chuckled in response, for it was well known that this missing relative was too fond of brandy and often became lost close to home. Once, this person had spent all night staggering in circles around a grove of trees within shouting distance of camp, and had arrived home in the morning to say he had been on a far journey over the tundra.

'Maybe he thinks he is paddling across the ocean, arriving in England,' joked Turtle now. 'But maybe he is really arriving in the camp at Ten Shilling Creek!'

People laughed again, but there was a heaviness about their laughter; a heaviness on our chests and in our bellies. Yes, we could starve to death on rabbits.

'Ask,' whispered Charlotte.

My voice quivered, a poplar leaf in the wind. 'Please, tell me if I should travel west with the red stallion.'

The tent hung still and silent while the spirits considered my question; I saw them flitting around inside like tiny points of light. I shook my head and the tent was a dark cone in the deeper darkness again. Someone shuffled their moccasins in the dirt. Betty inhaled on her pipe.

'She wants to go west and get civilised,' said Moose with a snort.

'She didn't get baked long enough,' sneered a Hairy Heart. 'She's only half done.'

I flushed in the darkness; it was true that my skin was paler than the skin of full-blooded Cree. I knew the story, how the Creator had modelled people from dough and put them into the oven to bake; how he took the white people out too soon, and left the black people in too long. Only the people of our land had been baked just right, their skin a pleasing and beautiful brown.

'She needs to find her father,' said Wishahkicahk gently.

'Ah, he is wandering,' said Turtle. 'He has wandered so long that he cannot remember the way home even with a clear head. Perhaps he needs a drink!'

'Her heart is turning to ice,' said a Hairy Heart. 'If she stays here and freezes, she could follow her mother along the wolf road instead of travelling west to find her father.'

'She wants to be with the horse,' said the Moon, speaking English again. 'The horse can see in the dark; maybe his spirit can find her missing father.'

'White men do not get lost,' said Dog suddenly

with a sharp barking sound. 'They have instruments to guide them.'

'They have big noses to follow,' said Turtle and all the spirits laughed.

'Horses know how to find home,' growled Bear. 'Horses have strong spirits.'

Suddenly, the tent began to bend and shake violently again, and I felt the spirits streaming out of it, soaring away into the still, cold air, the huge sky, the flat land filled with power and living things: trees and rivers, stones and muskegs, ice and winds, Thunderbirds, stars. The world tilted crazily, the stars swinging, the trees tossing, the water crashing on the shores of the Hayes River, the ice creaking in its sheets far to the north. Then stillness settled itself over us. People sighed and shifted, got to their feet in silence. The shaman crawled from the tent and was helped to his feet and led away into the darkness, his face gouged with fatigue.

'Sleep in my lodge, it is late,' said Betty, and she hefted a sleeping Charlotte on to one hip and brushed past me. I stumbled after them and lay down on spruce boughs by the embers of a fire, pulling a covering of marten fur over me and tucking it around Charlotte's heart-shaped face.

'What did Moose mean when he said I wanted to be civilised?' I whispered. Betty's craggy profile bent over her embers and she blew on them until tiny licks of flame appeared.

'You know the Company agreed to the Red River colony,' she said. 'The Company wants the half-blood people to go and live there. After the Company merged with its enemy, the North West Company, many men lost their jobs. That was 1821. Those men were offered land in the west. And the Company decided its retired men and their Cree wives should be given land by the Red River to live on.

'The Company wants all these people to become just like white men. They think the Cree will forget their own stories, lose their own language. They think the Cree will forget the names of the stars, how to read the stories written by the animals across the land. They tell us to forget the names of the spirits, forget our own ancestors. The white man thinks we will no longer know how to talk with a drum.

'I tell you, the white men will gnaw on the Cree people like dogs gnawing on bones. This is what they mean by civilise.'

I lay on my back, shocked, as the fire sank into embers again. To call a person a dog was the worst of insults, and to allow dogs to gnaw on the bones of animal prey was the worst disrespect. The bones of deer and moose, beaver and marten and bear were usually hung in trees, or placed upon wooden platforms out of reach of the dogs.

Was my white father like a dog? The longing to know him stirred in me like a fish swimming up out of a dark pool. I remembered my envy when Eva had said she was travelling with Orchid and Foxfire: was it the journey itself that I wanted, with its rivers and rapids, its changing skies? Was it only adventure I craved? Or was it the touch of the stallion's hot shoulder – his mystery – or the sharp, bright laughter of the white woman? If I stayed here, would Charlotte and I starve because the shaman had been too weak to fight with Bear, because the people had taken the deer tongues and left the carcasses to go to waste?

'Betty?'

'Umph.'

'Whose band does Eva belong to?'

'Eva's mother is sister to Chief Joseph Many Guns. When he was younger, he sent blankets to your mother's door. She was a fool to refuse him.'

'And Eva's father?'

'A white man, a trader. He had been here for a few winters, after working on the Athabasca River.'

Eva, niece of the chief, I thought; niece of the chief who had persuaded the apprentice postmaster to slide a letter down behind a loose board in the office at York Factory so that it might lie there hidden for many years, my mother's face turning to winter while she waited for a word from my father. I wondered what stories Eva carried under her tongue, stories about a proud woman who refused a young chief, about a lost letter, about a white man named Simon Mackenzie. If I went west, would she share those stories?

'Do you think it is true? That the people will starve because they didn't respect the deer?' I asked.

Betty's reply held her scowl. 'The beaver used to be a great people,' she said. 'They used to be so wise and clever that the Transformer had to intervene. He sent the beaver to live in the water, and he took away their speech. We people have always treated the beaver with great respect. But the white man changed that. The traders wanted beaver pelts, more and more of them. We started killing the beaver, wiping out all the beavers in one lodge, not leaving any to keep the beaver families going. We took the beaver so we could have rum and guns. Now there are no more in this land around the fort, and no deer. Not even enough hare to make Charlotte another coat. That's what happens when you don't respect the beaver.'

'What do you think the spirits want me to do?' I asked after a pause, but Betty had fallen asleep; her snoring rose and fell in waves. Bear had said that horses knew how to find their way home. I already had a home here: in the deerskin lodges, inside the fort's log palisade, out on the tundra with the ducks and geese honking overhead and the tamaracks stirring in the salty wind. It would be painful to leave all this behind – and yet the people here were starving. Betty Goose Wing said we were all *ehpishhot* here now, out of balance and harmony with nature, for the coming of the white men had changed the ways that the elders had taught us. If we left all this behind us, what place would we call home if we didn't find my father? Where would we sleep at night? I needed close kin, and some kind of life for Charlotte and myself, and maybe my father could provide that. But to be civilised . . . Was this the price we would pay – a loss so great that there would be nothing left of us? That everything clean and beautiful in us would have been gnawed without respect?

I flung off the rumpled fur, then stooped to tuck it back around Charlotte. My hands ached with love, smoothing her black hair. I lifted the flap of hide over the doorway and walked out of camp and into the fort beneath the moon's grin. I found the latch on the door of the cow byre by touch alone, lifted it with a click and stepped into the sweetness of cattle. My foot nudged a pail and its handle fell with a clang; the stallion stamped a back hoof and the moon hung in his eyes. I stepped up to his left shoulder, the nearside, as Orchid called it, and his spirit encircled me like arms; a kindness, a calm pool. I pressed my forehead against his own while his breath ran over my hands.

The horse *pawakan* was a strong spirit; strong enough, I hoped, to guide me through all adversity, perhaps even through a starving moon, or perhaps through the white man's rules. It was hard to know which of these dangers to choose to walk into. I was an animal, trying to choose between two traps – which would hurt me the most, and which might I hope to escape from?

Chapter 6

I hoped that I had made the right choice.

Standing on top of the bluff, facing the Hayes River, I watched the first fingers of sunlight touch a tamarack tree; already its needles were turning golden and soon they would drop off. The moon of falling leaves was beginning. Skeins of geese flew high above, heading south to escape the cruelty of winter. Already, this morning, frost lay on the grass. The cries of the boat crews rang across the river as the sun warmed it to blueness. Men's feet thundered on the landing stage, and the York boats lay in the water below, each one packed with forty hundredweight of goods, and ready to depart for its long journey inland – each one trying, like the geese, to leave before it was too late.

Here came the men of the Portage La Loche brigade, nicknamed the Poisson blanc or Whitefish. They streamed down to their boats, the puffy sleeves of their striped shirts rumpled, their long hair dishevelled; many of them had barely fallen into bed an hour ago, after last night's ball in the carpenter's shop. Now they carried their fiddles silent beneath their arms, and buttoned their blue vests against the cold. The woven sashes knotted at their waists were bright red as cranberries. Here came their champion, Paul, massive and hairy as a bear, and nursing a black eye from a fight outside the fort's old octagon yesterday afternoon.

I closed my eyes, ignoring the bustle below as the boats filled with rowers, as oars tickled the water's surface, as the canvas sheets – oiled with whale fat – were pulled snug over the trade goods to keep them dry. I stretched my arms high to the first light and chanted a song of thanks, as Betty Goose Wing had taught me to do at sunrise. I thanked the Creator for tools, for the strength of my horse *pawakan*, for my good health, for the new morning, and for my little sister, Charlotte Bright Eyes. And here she came now, running over the white ground, dodging between men carrying long oars over their shoulders, and casks of rum slung on poles by leather strapping. Her robe of soft, fringed deerskin flapped against her legs, and the green beads on the fringes sparkled. Her moccasins left scuffed trails in the frost, like the trail left by ptarmigan feathers when the bird lands in snow.

I smiled down as she pressed against my side. 'Are you ready?' I asked, and she nodded solemnly, cradling her doll of carved wood and deerskin in her arms.

'Good. Now it is time to fetch the stallion.'

As we approached Foxfire, tied to the tamarack tree to which I had brought him at dawn, I whistled to him, a long sweet note. He strained on his lead rope, snorting, ears pricked as the boat crews laughed and cursed, and as oars clattered along gunwales. I reached into my fire bag, slung over my shoulder, and which contained dry moss and the flint I used for starting fires. Today it held something else. I pulled out the two rectangles of stiff leather that I had been stitching for several nights. Quickly, I threaded rawhide strips through the holes I'd pierced in the rectangles with a sharp awl, and then lashed the strips securely around Foxfire's halter. Now the leather rectangles – Orchid called them blinkers – partially covered the stallion's eyes so that he could see directly ahead but not all around.

'Now he cannot see whales to one side,' Charlotte said.

'Or anything else,' I replied, hoping that my plan would work. When I untied the lead rope, the stallion swung around sideways, breaking into a nervous sweat. 'Whoa, whoa, be calm,' I murmured, running my hand down his face and touching his warm nostrils. For a moment, his neck muscles slackened and he dropped his head but the next instant, as a box was dropped on the landing stage and broke open, spilling trade guns with a clatter, he snorted and bounded sideways across the grass.

'Keep back!' I warned, and Charlotte jumped away, nimble as a fawn.

I fought the stallion around, pulling his head back to my side, then led him along the bluff, waiting for the boat that would carry him away, away over the rapids and rocks into the forest and even further, over Lake Winnipeg's sheet of water, and into the grassy plains where the buffalo ran.

The boat approached the shore to one side of the landing stage; I saw Samuel Beaver's shining black face tip upwards, searching for me on the bluff. When he took off his red tam-o'-shanter and waved it in an arc, I responded with an answering wave.

'Walk on,' I said to the stallion as Orchid had taught me to, and he followed skittishly as we approached the edge of the bluff, then sank back on his hocks as we threaded a cautious descent along a narrow path to the gravel beach below. Charlotte followed, keeping well back from the reach of Foxfire's powerful hind legs that could, Orchid had warned me, kill a man with one kick. Small stones poured beneath our feet, and once the horse jumped nervously as the twigs of a shrub willow snapped against his legs.

Expertly, the men rowing the boat brought it alongside the beach, their thick arms straining at the oars that each weighed over fifty pounds. Orchid was seated in the boat, her head wreathed in a veil of gauze beneath a wide-brimmed hat to protect her from mosquitoes, and with a cloak wrapped over her gown.

'Well done, Amelia!' she called. 'Do you want help?'

'No, we are fine!'

Samuel Beaver, whose father was a black man and whose mother was a Swampy Cree, jumped into the clear cold water of the shallows along with another man. Together they hefted two heavy planks of wood, and ran them from the gunwale of the boat on to the beach. Then everyone became still, watching, waiting to see whether I could persuade the stallion to walk up those two pieces of wood, walk across empty air and sloshing water, and step into the rocking shell of a small boat.

Part of his nature, I remembered, was that he did not fear water, that he could swim even against a strong current, and that he had grown up running through the salty marshes of a place called the Norfolk Broads, along another northern sea. I led him a little way along the shore, away from the boat, and let him become accustomed to the slap of the ripples against stones, to the tickle of wavelets against his hooves. I led him into the water until his flat knees were wet; then he dropped his head and drank in that cold fire in long gulps. When he raised his head again, water dripped from his mouth, catching sunlight. His eyes grew calm and thoughtful. He swung his head around, and I laid my forehead against his own. For a long moment, we stood like this, while the seagulls soared and cried, and boats banged against the end of the landing stage, and then I led

Foxfire from the water and back towards those two planks of wood.

'You are strong and brave as a bear,' I murmured to him. 'You are going on a far journey, to a new life. I will not leave you. Come, walk on.'

I did not pause as I approached those planks; I did not allow even the thought of pausing to enter my mind; not even the shadow of pausing to cross my skin. I stepped on to the planks with a firm tread, stepped off the shore of my homeland, between the intent face of Samuel Beaver and the astonished stare of another tripman, and let my feet carry me upwards. There was the slightest of tugs on the lead rope I held in my hand.

'Walk on, heart of a bear,' I murmured, and I heard the hollow rapping of hooves as that horse's great weight was born upon the ramp of strong, short-grained tamarack planks. At the top of the planks, I stepped over the gunwale on to the platform of boards that had been constructed inside the York boat, just behind the centre, and laid crosswise between the ribbing. On three sides, this platform was surrounded by a low wall of boards, so that Foxfire would stand as though in a stall in the cow byre. The stallion paused at the top of the planks; for a long moment, he surveyed the scene: the boat's benches filled with the tripmen rowers – half-bloods and Cree, Salteaux and Assiniboine, French and Scottish. He stared at the sheets of oiled canvas laid over the boxes and bales of trade goods, the kegs of salt pork and biscuits, sugar and beans, the buffalo bags filled with pemmican. Everyone held their breath for that long moment, waiting to see if that horse would follow me onboard.

'Foxfire,' I said steadily, and tugged on the lead rope, and held out my hand with a wrinkled apple flat upon it. The stallion lifted one great black hoof over the gunwale and on to the boards. Then his other hooves followed as he stepped in after me and stood, balancing on the boards, sucking in the breeze that streamed inland from the bay, snapping the red flag on the pole outside the white fort. I fed him the apple, and tied his lead rope to a ring fastened to one of the stall walls. Then I leaned against his shoulder, stroking his neck and scratching his withers; Orchid had said that mares scratched at the withers of their foals with their teeth, and that it was calming to horses.

'Hooray!' cheered the tripmen. The steersman, standing on the platform in the boat's stern and holding on to his long oar, doffed his top hat and made me a deep bow with a twinkle in his eye.

'Oh, exceedingly well done!' cried Orchid, her voice as clear as the seagull's cries, as she clapped her gloved hands.

Samuel Beaver, who was only two winters older than me, lifted Charlotte into the boat, and settled her beside Orchid on a bench between the rowers.

Then he and the other tripman hauled the planks onboard, and took their places at the oars. With a heave and shove, our boat was pushed away from the shoreline, and sucked out into the current, swinging and surging as the wind freshened and the shoreline drifted into the distance, beyond the brigades of boats. And that was how I left it, my home on the shores of the great bay, hurrying before the leaves fell, hurrying before winter sealed it in ice, hurrying into the mystery of Rupert's great sprawling land, and of my father's life, and of the horse's journey.

There were seven boats in the Portage La Loche brigade, and six more in the Saskatchewan brigade travelling part of the distance with us; the men of that brigade were nicknamed Blaireaux or Badgers, and their champion was a dark-haired Canadian whose mother tongue was French and who had lost a tooth yesterday while fighting the other champion. The boats, laden so heavily that the gunwales were only inches above the water, crawled upstream against the current until the tide turned and swept inland, lending the rowers its aid. All that time, I stood leaning against Foxfire's shoulder, still hoping I had made the right decision while the shoreline of my home slipped away. After two hours, the men ran the bows of the boats on to the shore and smoked their pipes for ten minutes, resting the muscles of their arms and shoulders, and feeling the burn across the palms of their hands from the friction of the great oars. Samuel Beaver grimaced, holding up his hands to show me the puffy bulges of blisters ready to burst; it was his first journey as a tripman and ahead lay weeks of rowing.

'You must come now and join us on the bench,' Orchid said, and she and Charlotte moved over to make room. I ran my hand down Foxfire's neck; the horse had stood calmly so far, rocking to the rocking of the water, staring out between his blinkers into the bright light, and munching on the wilting grass that I had hung up for him, stuffed inside a fishing net. As the men resumed rowing, I sat beside Charlotte who was singing a lullaby to her doll in a husky croon; the doll's mouth, stained red with berry juice, smiled adoringly at her.

We had been able to bring so little with us for the boats were already filled to capacity. Orchid had sought permission from the Chief Trader for me to come, after I persuaded her that I – and not some tripman – should care for Foxfire. Now, somewhere on this boat, was stowed my wooden box containing our meagre possessions: a few pieces of extra clothing, a few traps, a cured moose hide that Betty had given me as a parting gift. Over my shoulder I carried my fire pouch with its strike-a-light, that piece of metal against which I could strike a flinty stone to create sparks. In a sheath around my waist, I carried my knife.

Orchid bent and extracted a flat rectangular

packet of leather from beneath her seat. 'See how I plan to pass the time,' she said, unfastening the metal clasps that held the leather together. 'I do not excel at this but nonetheless, I shall persevere, and I do believe that readers at home might find my work of interest.'

I stared as she paged through the sheets, covered in watercolour paintings of flowers and leaves, entwined decoratively, and with small, intricate drawings of the flowers' various parts beneath the main drawings.

'What do you think?' she asked. 'I rather hope to be able to draw all the flowers we find along our journey, and to write a diary to accompany them, perhaps to include poems. Or perhaps I could some-how adapt the language of flowers to the plants of this new land; it might be very diverting. Or perhaps I shall write a simple herbal, to help new settlers use the edible plants for cooking and healing. There is so much I must learn! You, Amelia, must know much about the plants we shall encounter?'

'There are bulrushes,' I said. 'The flower heads can be eaten, and the young shoots can be peeled in the spring and eaten too. And there is white cedar; we use the leaves, brewed like tea, to cure headaches. And then there is juniper; we use the dried leaves in a powder to apply to sores. But I don't think we have many flowers, not in this moon, and not like these.'

'Well, no, not like these; perhaps the wilderness

flowers will be smaller and less showy,' Orchid agreed, staring at a page filled with brilliant pink blooms spotted with purple and white. 'This is an Orchid species, my father's favourite,' she explained. 'He grew it in his hothouses.'

'It was a house where people lived, your family lived?' I asked.

'Good gracious no!' Orchid laughed. 'A hothouse is made entirely of glass, and heated by the sun's rays, and inside it my father grew many tropical species brought from far away, from hot lands.'

'Which part of the plants did you eat?' I asked. 'Or were they for medicine?'

'Just to look at,' she replied, suppressing a smile, but still I saw the corners of her lips twitch with amusement. It was a strange, unfathomable life she had led, I thought. Why would one grow plants only to admire? The Creator had filled our land with gifts that grew without help, without houses, and that appeared each in its season to provide our people with food and medicine.

'Everything here is romantic and worthy of atten- tion. I am going to begin by sketching the interior of this boat,' Orchid announced and, taking a pencil from her case, turned to a fresh sheet of paper and began to sketch – with fast, light lines – the sweeping gunwales, the bent backs of the men, and the distant flat line of the shore. It was miraculous, how the world was recreated on the paper.

'Where is Eva Many Guns?' I asked at last. 'I thought she was travelling with you to the Red River school?'

'Yes, so she is. But our boat could not take her, for already it has three passengers and a horse, so Eva is travelling in one of the other boats. She was in a state of high dudgeon when she found out.'

'She wasn't happy?'

'She was most unhappy. She said that her father would be displeased to find her place had been taken by a late arrival – that was you, Amelia. But she will share my tent tonight so I dare say that will mollify her. Oh, oh!'

I looked to see what had captured Orchid's attention and found her staring upwards to the lazy arcs that an eagle was carving on the sky; she sketched it quickly before it rose higher and became a speck against the gathering clouds that scudded westwards. By late afternoon, the rain began to fall – a warm rain that landed in large scattered drops. Orchid hastily stowed away her paper and lidded box of dry paints, and asked one of the tripmen to locate the horse's blanket in the piles of goods. Once the large oiled cloth, lined with flannel, had been found and unfolded, Orchid and I lifted it over the horse and buckled its leather straps around his belly and chest.

'I have never seen an animal wear a blanket before,' I said. 'In our stories of the earliest of times the animals lived in lodges, gathered in counsel, and spoke to each other, smoking pipes and wearing robes. Do your English cats and dogs, and cows and pigs, wear coats too?'

'Sometimes people have garments made for small, silly dogs. All well cared for horses have a blanket for cold, wet and inclement weather. It prevents them from developing skin sores or pneumonia.'

Charlotte wrapped her doll inside her own shawl. I pulled my blanket over my head and watched Foxfire doze, his bottom lip hanging slack and one hip cocked at a slant over a bent leg; his eyes grew soft and unfocused inside the blinkers, and his lids fluttered.

Orchid, who had chattered most of the afternoon, grew quiet and stared pensively across the water; perhaps she was worrying again about seeing her new husband for the first time in a year, or about what kind of a place the Red River colony was with its mixture of tribes and freemen, its buffalo hunters and French traders. I was worrying a little too, about Eva Many Guns, for there had already been enough bad blood between our families and now she was annoyed with me for taking her place in the boat with Orchid. Yet it seemed that I needn't have worried, for when the men at last ran the boats on to shore for the night, and I led Foxfire down the planks, Eva crossed the beach to find me and greeted me with a slow, placid smile.

'My mother sent me off with a pot of duck and rice soup,' she said. 'There is enough for us to share.'

Fires sprang up along the beach, one for each boat's crew, as dusk stole over the river and a loon cried mournfully. Eva hung her cooking pot from a tripod and heated the duck soup. The whine of mosquitoes filled the air, for the wet warmth brought them out in clouds. We all sat downwind of the fires and let the smoke protect us; all except Orchid, who coughed and sputtered, and finally went and sat alone inside the canvas tent that a tripman had erected for her.

'There is a strange man in this brigade,' Eva whispered, leaning against my shoulder as we slurped our soup. 'He is rowing on the boat I am in. Look, there he is.'

I glanced up, waiting for my eyes to adjust, and glimpsed a figure step into the light of another fire and sit cross-legged on the gravel to light a pipe. The man's face was long and thin, with a jutting nose burned red by the sun, in the way that the skin of white men burned, although the skin on his face was bronze. His hair was such a pale gold that it was almost silver, and hung on each side of his face in long braids. When he looked up to speak to another tripman, I glimpsed his eyes; they were pale blue as glass beads, so pale it seemed as though light shone out of them instead of into them.

'They say he is turning into a Witiko,' Eva muttered beside me. 'Now, with the winter moons approaching, we must watch him. He has been rowing all summer in the warmth, keeping his heart warm, but now his heart might be growing cold as ice. They say that sometimes he gnaws his lips and makes strange cries. These are bad signs.'

I shivered. 'Hush,' I said to Eva, for Charlotte's wide eyes had stretched round with fear. 'Do not speak of this.'

But I watched the pale-haired man with the dark skin while he drew on his pipe. Suddenly, a stripy brown cat ran from the trees and leaped nimbly into the man's lap, to settle there and begin kneading its paws with a contented expression. 'He charms it with magic,' Eva said. 'He keeps medicines for it in a little pouch and gives it to the cat to play with onboard the boat.'

I shivered again, for when an elder in our bands passed on knowledge of healing plants, it was with a strict warning to use the knowledge only from compassion, and not with evil intent. Betty Goose Wing had told me never to use hunting medicines, those that were carried in a leather pouch and used to beguile the animals, to exert an influence over them and take away their own individual power. Hunting medicines were like love medicines; they tried to wrestle away the power of another living thing and to bend it to your own will.

'I must make sure the horse is comfortable before sleeping,' I said to Eva and she smiled and rose, grace-ful and lazy, and ducked inside Orchid's tent. I could hear their voices murmuring inside while I checked the rope that held Foxfire tied to a tree, and refilled his tin pail with river water, and used a sickle to cut armfuls of grass and leaves for him to eat. I had given him oats already, when we first came to shore.

At last Charlotte and I rolled ourselves in a large piece of oiled cloth and let our bodies relax against the sand while sporadic rattles of rain fell over our backs, and the fires sputtered and pipe smoke wafted into our noses. We were close enough to the stallion that I could hear him stamping, and the whisk of his tail. Then the shore became quiet as the men rolled themselves into their blankets and only the river ripples lapped into our hearing. Darkness laid its hand upon us as the fires sank low.

'Levee, levee, levee!' a voice rang out, and my eyes opened slowly to the grey light that creeps into the sky before sunrise. A startled crow broke into a hoarse cawing and flapped overhead; distinctly, in the stillness, I heard its wingbeats before the men began groaning and protesting, rolling out of their blankets, swinging their arms to restore circulation.

'Merciful heavens,' I heard Orchid say inside the tent. 'Is this the hour at which we must rise?'

It was, and neither did the brigades eat breakfast now but simply sloshed through the shallows and climbed into the boats carrying the cooking pots and kettles from last night's dinner. Orchid was still fumbling to tie her gauze veil under her chin as a tripman dropped her tent on to the ground and folded it flat; within a minute of that, she was being carried on one of the men's backs out to the boat and hoisted over the gunwale.

'Samuel!' I called, and he hoisted Charlotte on to his back and carried her onboard while I untied the stallion and led him to and fro along the beach, letting him paw at the water's edge, and snuffle at willow trees. Finally, when all the boats but ours had departed, I led him back and up those planks on to his platform of wood, his fish net of dried grass, and his bucket of oats.

All that day we toiled up the Hayes River as the rain gathered strength and fell in grey ropy sheets that flattened the men's sodden tam-o'-shanters, and rattled on the oiled cloth covering the trade goods, and darkened the stallion's coat. Even his eyelashes quivered with raindrops, and his hooves were slick with water. He didn't seem to mind but stood stoically, gazing at the passing shoreline with its black spruce and white cedar trees. Charlotte, Orchid and I huddled under oilcloth while Orchid's hat drooped round her face like wilted petals. I could feel her sharp excitement over this adventure seeping away.

In the evening we reached the place where the Hayes River was joined by the Steel, and prepared to camp on the shore, between the water and a fringe of tall coniferous trees.

'I am going to search for interesting flora,' Orchid

announced as I gathered driftwood for our cooking fire.

'Don't wander off alone,' I warned, but when I straightened and gazed about, I glimpsed her blue gown and the stallion's red rump disappearing into the gloom of the trees. I sighed and stooped to gather more wood. I was hungry for the evening meal; our boat's cook had promised us *richeau* tonight, a rich, tasty, greasy dish of fried pemmican and one that I loved. Surely, the white woman and the big horse would be safe and, surely, Orchid would not stray far from the men's laughter.

Some time later, when I glanced around, Orchid had not returned. 'You stay by this fire,' I warned Charlotte before heading into the bush. I stopped and picked a few mushrooms to add to the *richeau*, and startled a whisky jack so that it flew off with its harsh cry. Then silence fell, and the voices along the shore became fainter.

'Orchid!' I called. 'Orchid?'

I pushed on, my moccasins silent on the floor of needles, and the light growing dim between the shaggy grey trunks of tamarack. Suddenly, a piercing scream set my teeth on edge. I ran, straight ahead, and burst through the trees into a swampy clearing; over to one side, an old beaver dam had rotted into greyness. At the edge of the swamp Orchid stood with her back to me, shouting for help.

'What?' I gasped, seizing her arm.

111

'Foxfire – there, there!'

The great horse was up to his shoulders in the muskeg; the black mud plastered his heaving chest, and spattered his rigid, straining neck. His hindquarters churned in the muck as though he were swimming, and his eyes rolled white in his upheld head. He would never get out. When the muskeg sucked you in like that, quivering around you like fat on a cold soup, you could not swim out of it. The dark ooze would take you in, deep, deeper; your bones would go down into the Underground world with the horned serpents. Reeds shook around the edges of the swamp with the horse's struggling, and patches of mossy scum broke off around his churning legs.

'We must do something!' Orchid cried, her face pale as a moth's wings and her eyes stricken.

'Do not go near him!' I said. 'You cannot help him. I will fetch the men with rope.'

I turned and flew back into the forest and there, ahead of me, something moved in the gloom – a shirt, a bright blue cloth knotted around a head of pale gold hair.

'Get ropes, get help. The horse is in the muskeg!' I shouted at the man from Eva's boat, and together we flew through the trees, dodging and gasping. The man was tall and lean; he burst on to the beach ahead of me and summoned the others, who leaped on and off boats, flinging coils of rope around their

112

shoulders, grabbing planks and canvas, and plunging through the trees. When I stumbled back into the swampy clearing, a dozen men were ahead of me, and pushing flat planks out across the surface of the muskeg towards the horse.

'I am the lightest and smallest! I will go!' I said.

'No. It's too dangerous!' Samuel protested, but as men flung a piece of oiled canvas on to the mud, I lay upon it on my stomach. Samuel knotted ropes to my wrists. The muskeg heaved beneath me. I slid a plank forward until it reached from the edge of the canvas almost to Foxfire. Then I slid another plank alongside it. Inch by inch, I shifted my body from the canvas on to the planks. I lay still for a moment, barely daring to breath, waiting for the mud to become still.

Inch by inch, I crawled forward over the planks. They tipped and twisted beneath me. Mud oozed over the edges and stained my elbows. Mud darkened my fingernails. The ropes dragged behind, still fastened to my wrists and held at the other end by the men. The swamp quivered like the skin of a horse shaking off a fly. I was the fly.

'Be still,' I murmured to Foxfire. My fingers stretched towards him. I untied a rope, breathing carefully. Then I began to dig beneath one foreleg. My fist, gripping the rope, disappeared into the black muck. Then my wrist. Then my elbow. I stopped to rest and to let the heaving muskeg subside. Then I dug beneath the other side of the same foreleg until my fumbling fingers touched the end of the rope. I pulled it through and knotted it around the leg. The men on shore let out a cheer.

Now I had to reach the offside leg and this was harder. I wriggled until I was half off the plank, my face pressed against Foxfire's chest, and only just above the mud. My spine muscles tightened, trying to hold my body out of the swamp. I panted, the horse's great neck and head hanging over me, my arms buried deep below. Sweat ran down into my eyes.

It was so quiet that I heard a breath of wind in the trees, and the suck and glop as I pulled my arm free of the mud when the second rope was tied. I shimmied back along the planks. All the way, I talked to the horse and he stayed still. I rolled off the planks on to the canvas. The men dragged it across the surface of the swamp with me inside, and I crawled off it on to solid ground. The murky taste of the muskeg filled my mouth.

Then three men got hold of each rope, and they strained and hauled, inching backwards, their boots and moccasins digging into the thin soil, tearing up blueberry bushes and mushrooms, kicking aside rotten sticks, crunching on fallen cones. Inch by inch. Inch by inch. The horse heaved and thrashed. The muscles strained in the men's necks. Their eyes bulged. They breathed in hard, short pants.

The mud sucked and gurgled. Now I could see Foxfire's flank. Now his stifle. Now his legs began to thrash free; I saw a hock, a knee. I saw white quills bristling in his muzzle, pale and black, soft and sharp. They were making him crazy, filling him with pain and panic.

'Heave! Heave! Heave!' shouted the man with glassy eyes and pale golden braids, and I saw muscles twitching in his cheek, like wind on water, and how he licked a trickle of spit from the corner of his mouth even though he was only standing watching the other men fight for Foxfire's life.

Now the muskeg gave the stallion back to us. He staggered out, shaking his head, his eyes dazed, and his breath tearing through his nostrils. His neck trembled when I laid my palm upon it. The ropes had stripped the hair from the tops of his legs.

'What happened?' I asked Orchid, waiting for the horse's panic to subside.

'Oh! It was a horrible, fearsome creature in the grass. I didn't see it. Foxfire must have heard it or smelled it, he put his nose down, it swung its tail around and stabbed him with these – these –'

'Quills, porcupine quills,' I said and Samuel Beaver suddenly turned and headed off into the bush, bent over and reading the signs. In a moment, his black skin blended into the darkness while the other men coiled up the ropes.

'When this happened, Foxfire was so startled that he plunged away from me. I lost my grip on his lead rope and he plunged into this – this – bog!'

'We call it muskeg. We must take Foxfire back to camp.'

On the shoreline, I fetched my sewing scissors and borrowed a pair of pliers from a tripman. 'Hold him very still,' I told Orchid and she gripped the stallion's lead rope with clenched knuckles. I stroked the flat of my hand down his face, murmuring to him, until he dropped his head. Quickly but carefully, I snipped at the ends of the quills, releasing the air inside them so that they would deflate and pull out more easily. With the pliers, I caught hold of a few quills and jerked them out; Foxfire flung up his head, his eyes rolling back, as those painful barbs ripped through his tender muzzle, searing him with sharp pain. Drops of blood oozed from the tiny hole where each quill had been.

'Have courage,' I murmured. 'Be still now.'

Again and again I used the pliers, and each time the stallion flung up his head, only to drop it to me again. He stood still, even though one back leg twitched nervously and his breath came in hard puffs.

'He knows that you are helping him even though it pains him,' Orchid marvelled. 'You have surely won his trust.'

Finally, no quills remained in his muzzle but all lay, still fresh and alive, in the palm of my hand. 'These must be hung in your tent by a thread,' I told Orchid, 'to show respect for the porcupine.'

'That horrible beast!' she cried.

I stared at her in shock. 'Hush! You must never

speak this way in the bush. Every creature is a gift, and has its own *ahcak*, its soul. How will we hunt and eat if we don't respect the gifts of the animals? How will Samuel catch this creature if you don't show respect?'

'Catch it?'

'He is out there now, tracking it to make a stew with. We will hope that your words were not over-heard.' I took the lead rope from Orchid and as my hand brushed hers, I realised that she was shaking. 'Come,' I said more gently. 'All is well now. I will bathe Foxfire's muzzle and give him an extra ration of oats.'

But later, lying in my oiled cloth beside Charlotte with my belly full of *richeau*, I remembered the man with the eyes like blue glass, and the pale braids on each side of his bronzed face. Why had he been out there in the bush, so close to the muskeg? Was it true, what Eva had said, that he was turning Witiko, that his heart was beginning to freeze and his mind go insane? Perhaps he was trying to fight with my *pawakan* spirit in the way that Witikos did – perhaps he was trying to overcome me using sorcery. Perhaps he had sent the porcupine to frighten Foxfire into the muskeg's quivering depths . . . Would he harm me next, or Charlotte? Or would my *pawakan* be strong enough to protect us all?

Chapter 7

D ay after day we toiled up the river against the strong current, sometimes meeting bands of Swampy Cree in birchbark canoes, going to hunt geese. At night the roar of rapids thundered in our ears, and by day the banks of trees – taller and growing more densely than any trees I had ever seen before – slid past. We left the Steel River and began to ascend the Hill River; the tundra lay far behind now with its flat horizon and dark muskeg. The York boats grew gouged and splintered from banging against rocks, and often they had to be hauled onshore and repaired, the men using chisels and hammers to pound strips of oakum into the cracks between the planks. Our oatmeal grew mouldy and our pemmican grew soggy from the water seeping into the boat; Orchid complained too that the pemmican was filled with buffalo hair and insects. It was true, I supposed, but I didn't know why she had to fuss about it. Pemmican always contained traces of hair or leaves but these didn't affect the flavour.

All day long the big red stallion stood sideways in the boat, rocking and shifting as the hull heaved over the waves. Sometimes he lay down to sleep, folding his long legs at the knee and hock and going down with a lurch and a soft grunt. His muzzle rested on the planking, wrinkling his mobile lips, and his eyelids drifted closed as his breathing grew deep and slow. At these times, I could kneel beside him and rest my forehead against his, and feel the strength running between us. I could run my hands over his huge, bent knees and use a hoof pick to clean out his upturned hooves. At other times, Foxfire stood rest-lessly in his cramped space, stamping at flies, his skin quivering and his tail swishing; strands of long red hair became snared on the rough surface of boards and dangled there, glinting in the sun. One of the men from the Blaireaux brigade liked to tease me that he would steal the whole tail some night: cut it off in the dark with his sharp knife. Then, he said, when he reached the great sheet of the mighty Lake Winnipeg, his York boat's sail would have the grand-est decorations of any boat in any brigade – for it was a fact that the Blaireaux brigade liked to decorate their sails with horsehair.

When the stallion was restless, staring at the shore, occasionally splitting the air with a ringing neigh, I would unpack his grooming kit, the one that Orchid had brought all the way from her home, and brush the tangles from his forelock, and smooth his shining coat, being careful to follow the direction of the hair growth with my brushstrokes. I would tug bits of grass seeds or twigs from the long hair at his fetlocks. When the bugs were especially numerous, I would weave fronds of cedar into his halter to keep the insects away from his eyes and face. Every evening, I used a shovel to clean off his wooden platform. I kept his tin pail filled with cold water from the river, and stuffed his fishing net with armfuls of grasses and leaves cut along the shoreline. Whenever I approached him, I whistled first and quickly he learned to recognise this call.

One morning I decided that Foxfire had grown so accustomed to riding in the boat that he didn't need to wear the blinkers any longer. Without them, Orchid had said, a horse could see almost all around itself in a circle, but for a narrow space directly ahead and behind itself. I untied the blinkers from his halter, and waited while the men brought the boat alongside a flat sheet of rock on the shore, and then led the big red horse across it. If the men could hold the boat steady against the current, using their long iron-tipped poles, Foxfire should be able to step straight into the boat from the rock. He followed me calmly, his black hooves clomping over circles of grey lichen. I stepped into the boat, over the curving gunwale, and Foxfire lifted a foreleg to follow me.

Then he tossed his head up with a snort. I turned to see what his wide dark eyes were looking at, and saw a keg of beans or perhaps of rum, tumbling and rolling downriver. It must have been lost overboard by a boat somewhere ahead of us on the river. The stallion stepped backwards away from our boat, straining at his lead rope, and snorting. I shortened the rope, and gripped his halter, pulling his head down and against me, but at that moment the keg crashed against the hull of our boat and careened onwards, knocking two men's poles from their hands so that the boat swung outwards away from the rock. At the crash of the keg, Foxfire half reared. My toes swung clear of the ground for an instant, my moccasins brushing the lichen. The stallion's hard forelegs flashed through my line of vision. Orchid shouted in alarm. Trees and green river swung dizzily across my eyes. Then the stallion's hooves hit the rock with a thud. The new shoes that the blacksmith in York Factory had nailed on to his feet – three shoes going on easily and one causing a fight – sent out a shower of sparks.

I flung myself back against the rope, fighting to keep his head down, fighting to keep him on the rock while he circled me, his legs flashing around me like lightning strikes. My toe caught in a crack in the rock and I fell forward. The stallion's momentum dragged me onwards and I staggered and found my balance again. A tripman suddenly appeared, lunging across the rock, and jumping at the stallion's head to catch his halter on the offside. Together, the man and I hauled the sweating horse to a halt and stood, all three of us panting for breath.

'Amelia, do you need these?'

I turned towards her small, solemn voice and looked into my sister's dark eyes; she stood on the edge of the rock, holding the leather blinkers in her palm.

'Maybe I do,' I said, and she began to smile, then giggle. My heart soared like a raven riding a warm current, for there was nothing sweeter in my world than Charlotte's smile. For some moons after our mother died, nothing could bring light into Charlotte's face. Now, perhaps, the red horse was leading us into happier days.

Even after I had refastened the blinkers on to Foxfire's halter, it took many tries before he would follow me onboard the boat; the tripmen were already swearing and sweating in the rising sun by the time that I had the stallion tied in his stall. Then they rowed upriver with grim concentration, silent for once when usually they sang hour after hour. Their backs rose and fell to their work and their arm muscles strained as they tried to catch up with the rest of the brigade, not stopping even for a pipe after a long spell of paddling, but simply rowing on, their shirts growing wet with patches of sweat, and sweat running down into their beards.

'It was not your fault,' Orchid said, using her paints to wash colour on to a sketch of our camp that she had completed the previous evening. I leaned against her shoulder to examine the scene. There it all was in miniature, being brought back to life under the hairs of her brush: the tripmen, in their pale shirts and bright neck scarves, sprawled around their fires, the black cooking pots dangling from tripods, the red horse eating from a pail of oats, the canvas cone of Orchid's tent, the ghostly bones of a grove of birch trees in the background.

'In England,' Orchid resumed, 'no one would dream of putting a large horse – over sixteen hands high – into a small boat. It is a miracle that you have managed this task so well.'

'Hands?'

'It is how one measures a horse from the ground to the highest point of the withers; a hand is equal to four inches.'

I took a piece of birchbark, that I had peeled from a tree last night, out of my fire pouch and laid it upon the bench at my side. With my knife, I began to cut animals from the bark's pale sheet: a moose with its great antlers, a skunk with its plume of striped tail.

'What are these for?' Orchid asked.

'For Charlotte to play with,' I replied. 'Or for me to use as patterns when I embroider designs with beads and silk thread. Tell me more about horses in your homeland, about Trotters.'

'Ah,' said Orchid, 'my father should be here to answer this question, for he could expound upon horses by the hour with great passion . . .' Her gaze became pensive, but after a moment she sighed and continued. 'Still, I suppose I can tell you what little I know in comparison. Trotters are an old, old type of horse; they can be traced all the way back to the 1300s when the King of England decided that his subjects needed horses that were powerful and had great stamina. These horses could be ridden along at a trot for many hours even when carrying a large man. Still today owners of Trotters love to race them on the roads, wagering sums of money on the outcome of the race. Foxfire himself has been known to trot seventeen miles in one hour and arrive still fresh enough to buck off his rider at the end.'

'They were all Trotters, those horses you named: Original Shales and the Darley Arabian?'

'Gracious! What a prodigious memory you have!' exclaimed Orchid, washing the sky in her painting with a mauve shade that she'd mixed from blue and red paint.

'Original Shales was a stallion born in 1755 and was exceptionally fast. He is the foundation stallion for our modern Trotters. He was by the stallion Blaze, son of a racehorse called Flying Childers, and this horse was a son – no, a grandson – of the Darley Arabian. But the Darley was not a Trotter – he was a hot blood horse, an Oriental stallion with a dished face and an arched neck, who also contributed to forming the Thoroughbred horse much used in England for flat racing at a gallop. The Arab hot blood horses have been known to exist for almost three thousand years.'

'Hot blood,' I murmured to myself; I liked the sound of these words, for a creature's blood contained life, and when I laid my hand upon the stallion's sleek hide, it seemed to pulse with both heat and life.

'Hot bloods have been imported from the Arabian desert to improve our English stock,' Orchid said. 'The Darley was smuggled from the Ottomans and brought into Britain in 1704.'

'Why smuggled?'

'The Ottoman Turks prized their horses very highly and did not wish to lose their pure bloodlines to foreign countries. In the desert, the people believe that their god, Allah, made the horse from a handful of the South Wind.'

I gave a sigh of satisfaction. 'In our land, good medicine comes to those who dream of Sawanis, spirit of the South Wind.'

Orchid mixed more purple paint to wash shadows on to the sides of the tent in her picture.

'Does everyone in England own horses?' I asked. 'Does everyone ride around at a trot?'

Orchid's wide, thin lips curled in a smile and she rinsed her paintbrush in the tin cup of water that she used for this purpose. 'It has been said that no one walks save for vagabonds and fools.'

'What will your husband, Mr Spencer, use Foxfire for?'

'He will breed Foxfire to the Indian ponies, and create a new strain of horse, one that has the toughness of the savages' mounts, and the bone and size of a Trotter.'

The point of my knife slipped a fraction when Orchid said the word 'savages'; that word rolled off her tongue smooth as a rounded stone, the kind that lames you if it gets into your moccasin when you're running fast down a trail. It rolled off her tongue so smoothly that she didn't even notice it fall, or see how the point of my knife accidentally cut off the foot of a fox that I was creating from birchbark.

'Yes,' Orchid continued, staring dreamily across the river with her paintbrush momentarily forgotten in one hand, and dripping on to her gown, 'Mr Spencer has high hopes for this stallion; he is going to create prosperity for us in the Red River colony. In coming years, many more settlers will arrive and there will be a great demand for strong, fine horses to trot on the roads, and pull the ploughs that will break the virgin prairie and allow us all to grow crops. A good horse will be worth a fortune, and foals from Foxfire will be worth more than any other.'

I stared at the stallion as he gazed at the passing shoreline of rocks and white spruce, and wondered how many beaver pelts one would trade for him, adding one more beaver pelt, one more, then another on to the pile while the white trader added brass tokens to your own pile. I thought about how you would feel, under your fingers, the toil and weariness of trapping all those creatures, the ache in your legs at the end of the long trails, the ache in your shoulders at the end of the long days carrying the lodge poles on your back, carrying the cooking pots and the babies and the beaver pelts out of the bush to the trading fort. I knew that I would never have enough pelts to trade for a horse. Perhaps I was, in Orchid's eyes, either a vagabond savage or a fool. Foxfire's life, in Red River, would continue without me to groom him or whistle to him – I would never learn the joy of riding him, but would stumble along sadly in my moccasins.

At noon, with the sun directly overhead and the trees standing in their own shadows, we ate cold bannock that I had made the previous evening from flour, water and baking soda. I had kneaded the dough, and stretched it round and flat before frying it over the fire in a long-handled iron skillet. With the bannock we ate strips of dried meat that Betty Goose Wing had shaved from a caribou and hung over poles to dry in the sun before wrapping them in scrolls of birchbark. They were chewy and dense and dark; their flavour lay for a long time on my tongue while the men continued rowing upstream, and Orchid dozed under her large grass hat, and Charlotte sang to herself and made the birchbark animals run along the gunwales of the boat, chasing each other.

Presently, the roar of rapids filled our ears and, rounding a bend in the river, we saw their white boiling fury cascading down over grey rocks and sweeping to meet us in streams of bubbles and swirling knots of fast current. Often, at rapids, I took Foxfire ashore to lighten the boat's load, and often Orchid came too for some exercise or to find something to sketch. But today, after our late start, and because the horse had been difficult, the boat captain decided that we should all stay onboard. The men pulled their oars into the boat and began instead to push the boat upstream, using their tamarack poles with iron tips to force the boat against that fast current and to thread it between the jagged teeth of the half-submerged rocks. At the front of the boat, the bows man, who had many years of experience and many miles of river running through his mind, shouted instructions. At the back of the boat, the steersman sculled with his oar, guiding the boat's slow, erratic progress.

I could feel the grip and pull of the river rushing past just feet away from me, on the other side of the boat's planking. Its thundering voice filled my head, swept away all my thoughts. Sunlight bounced and swung off the boiling water in flashes sharp as arrowheads, blinding me. The stallion snorted uneasily and

I stood to lay my hand against his face and stroke it, muttering soothing words that were barely audible above the river's great shout.

Slap! The river's hand shoved the boat, the bow swinging wildly like the needle on a white man's compass. 'Hold her straight!' roared the bows man. 'HOLD HER!'

Samuel Beaver's dark, shining face contorted with pain as he poured every ounce of his strength into the length of his pole; I saw how he gritted his teeth together, and over his shoulder, I saw the pale wooden crosses built by other brigades to remember their dead, the tripmen who had drowned in these rapids. Or perhaps some had died of hernias, their guts pushing out of their bellies from the great weight of the loads they carried around the rapids on their backs, with tumplines around their foreheads.

The boat's nose swung again and suddenly the river seized her. I felt the triumphant surge of the water as it pushed the boat around, broadside now to the current. I glanced at the steersman as he clung to his long oar, swinging on it with his entire weight, like a wolf trying to bring down a large deer by one leg. The oar became still in his hand, a dead weight. I saw the panic flee across his face as he strained to free the end of the oar from where it had wedged between two rocks.

Crash!

A shock ran through the boat. She shuddered as if

she had come alive. A jolt ran up the steering oar, and the steersman flew in an arc through the air and disappeared into the raging water; his head, sleek and wet as an otter's, was swallowed instantly by the swirling foam. I gripped a gunwale and looked over to see that the hull of our boat was lying against a ledge of dark rock and pinned there tightly by the press of the current roaring down and down, mile after mile from the heart of the great continent, roaring out to the icy bay.

I caught hold of Charlotte and gripped her to my side; her eyes stretched to fill her heart-shaped face, and the birchbark animals fluttered away from her fingers into the wind of that river's rush, and were gone.

'Hold your arms up!' I shouted and when she obeyed, I tore her deerskin robe over her head, so that it would not weigh her down when we went overboard. She pressed against me, shivering in her beaded leggings, her brass bracelets gleaming on her naked arms.

Crash!

The boat lurched, shuddered, and began to tilt on to her side; green water poured over the gunwale and burned our legs with its cold torrent. *Ride!* I thought. I lunged towards the stallion, dragging Charlotte Bright Eyes with me across the pitching planks. Foxfire's high screams of fear rang even over the river's thunder as I yanked his rope undone – it was as well, I thought in that instant, that Orchid had shown me how to tie a knot that would slip free with one jerk on the loose end of rope.

'Samuel!' I screamed. 'Get Orchid!'

He dropped his useless pole and flung himself towards her; she was clutching her leather portfolio of paintings to her chest and still clung to it as Samuel wrapped one brawny arm around her waist and pulled her to the gunwale.

I clawed my way up the side of the slanting boards, gripping Charlotte by one wrist, and caught hold of Foxfire's mane; then I slung one leg over his back and felt the heave of his muscles. As he broke free of his stall and lunged towards the water, I dragged Charlotte on in front of me, over the horse's wither, and we both wrapped our hands in his mane, coarse and strong as fishing line.

He went over the side with a jump; misty spray and the taste of fish and algae and pine needles filled my mouth. The cold river tore at my legs, slapping and pushing the stallion downstream. He thrashed against the foaming green-blue-black glinting pounding water, against the swing and roll of that river. His forelegs struck out, his hooves pulling against the current, scrabbling against rocks. His nostrils were smothered in bubbles; emerged streaming white ribbons. His soaked mane plastered itself over our legs. His shoulders ran beneath us, his tail whipped in the surges, his eyes rolled white as fish bellies.

'*Far Runner, Wind Runner, Water Runner, come to me, carry me onwards,*' I chanted, the words from my vision dream. Water splashed into my eyes, and light shimmered there in a rainbow – for an instant, in the midst of my terror, I felt a moment of pure joy. I remembered that with a strong *pawakan*, one could even lie all winter beneath the ice but rise and walk again in spring when the white bears climbed from their dens.

Then fear broke over me and I felt how the river pummelled the stallion. I felt how – like the men whose bodies were remembered with ramshackle crosses weathering on the rocky shoreline – we too might be swallowed in deep and never spat out again. Fear melted us together; Charlotte and Foxfire and I, so that we were one creature fighting for our lives in the rapids of Hill River while the sun shone bright as ice and bales of trade goods were torn from our boat and tossed downstream in the curling smash of the waves.

Fighting sideways against the current, the stallion pressed towards shore but the river was too strong for him; it swept us away, amongst the trade bales, until at last we reached quieter water far downstream. His hooves clattering against stone, Foxfire staggered on to shore and hung his head, his sides heaving. I slid off and held out my arms for Charlotte; her face was pale, and wet with tears as well as water.

'You are a brave girl,' I told her. 'And now you

have ridden on a great horse! Dry your eyes, and we will walk along the shore.'

She nodded and wiped at her eyes with her chubby bare arms, and I tickled her neck with the end of one of her black braids until she giggled, and took my hand. In my other hand, I gripped the horse's lead rope. 'Courage of a bear,' I murmured to him. 'Strength of a musk ox. Cunning of a fox. Grace of a deer.' I pressed my forehead against his, and waited until his breathing calmed; staring down, I noticed that he had knocked a chip from the wall of one hoof, and that the shoe on that foot was missing, torn loose. An abrasion on one shoulder was already beginning to swell and trickle a thin stream of his hot blood.

Presently, the three of us began to struggle along the shoreline, between groves of birch and pine, with bushes impeding our progress, and bugs circling our heads, with roots and rocks tripping us up, and one small swamp forcing us to make a detour. Finding a spruce tree, I used my knife blade to scrape off some gummy resin and smeared it over the abrasion on the stallion's shoulder, sealing the lips of the wound together and stopping the flow of blood. Then we forged on for I was worried about Orchid's safety, and the safety of Samuel Beaver and the other trip-men. I was also worried about whether my wooden box, containing my father's letter and the silver brooch, had been saved from the boat wreck.

'Hello! Hello!' shouted a voice in the woods ahead.

'We are here!' I cried, and presently a group of three tripmen, their clothes plastered to their skins and the fabric of their scarves and headbands bright against the dark pines, and their earrings glinting, toiled towards us. I saw the pale braids of the man who Eva had said was turning Witiko, saw the silver coins hanging from a chain at his throat, and the scar he bore, pale as gut string, across one forearm.

'Thanks to God that we've found you,' one of the other men said, halting before us. 'Are you unharmed?'

'Yes, and the horse. But Orchid, the white wo—' I began to ask, but the man with the pale hair and the dark face suddenly gave a wild yell. Shivers ran down my spine. I had never heard a sound like this; it was not like the shout a man gives to convey instructions or call attention to danger, nor like the whoops that the men gave at the end of their rowing songs. It was not like the cry of a wolf, nor the bellow of a moose, nor the whistle of a marten. The echoes of that strange yell seemed to hang, ringing, amongst the thick trees, and the trees themselves seemed to crowd in around us like the walls of a mysterious lodge. I struggled for a breath of air.

The man's face contorted in spasms and his mouth gaped open, silent now, drooling threads of saliva. His pale blue eyes looked right at me, through me – I knew that he was seeing far off, into a wild place, a spirit world. When his eyes rolled back in his head, Charlotte gasped in terror. Then the man fell suddenly at my feet, into the pine needles and dead twigs covered in lichen. His arms flailed the ground as though it were a drum skin. His body convulsed, jerking and squirming, and the toes of his moccasins scored marks into the grey soil. I glimpsed the pale blur of his face and saw how his teeth gnawed on his lips.

I pulled on the lead rope, backing the stallion up and hauling Charlotte with us by one arm again, until we were pressed against the base of a tall pine while the tripmen leaned over the man on the ground.

'Put a stick in his mouth!' one of them shouted, and the other man bent to obey, seizing a small dead one from the ground, but now the man's jaw was clenched and nothing could be forced between his teeth.

'He'll choke on his tongue!'

'Turn him over!'

They bent, rolling the flailing body on to its side; it continued to bend and straighten in jerks. Charlotte began to cry again, as silently as she always did, and I turned her away and pressed her face to my soaking robe, its beaded decoration imprinting itself on her cheek. The stallion began to graze, snatching at shrubbery, the fur on his face already drying.

'What is it?' one of the tripmen asked but the other shrugged, frowning.

'Damned if I know. A fever of the brain perhaps. Temporary insanity. I saw him like this once before; it is brought on by extra exertion or strain. He will be tired and confused afterwards, then back at the oars the next day.'

I stooped and meshed all my fingers together. 'Put your foot in my hands,' I instructed Charlotte and, when she obeyed, I boosted her on to the stallion's wet back. 'Don't let branches poke your eyes,' I told her, and then I tugged Foxfire's head out of a bush he was stripping of leaves, and led him in a semicircle around the tripmen. The body on the ground was still now and a low groan escaped from the man's mouth while the other men squatted on their heels beside him, muttering and looking concerned.

Fever of the brain, I thought scornfully. What did white men know of such things? Anyone could see that the pale-haired man was turning Witiko, gnawing on his own lips, losing the power of speech, uttering terrible sounds instead of words, jerking and convulsing, rolling his eyes and straining to see far away into other worlds. Now, soon, as the frosts fell at night and the winter breathed down our necks, the man's heart would turn to ice and he would begin to devour us.

I must find Eva, I thought. The man rows in her boat so I must warn her about what I have seen today; I must see if we can feed the man some melted bear's grease to warm him up inside again – to use the power of the bear's heat to stop his terrible transformation.

Ahead of us, a brown striped cat – bewitched with

medicines from a leather pouch – dropped from a tree and ran away into the bushes, yowling forlornly. I hurried on, dreading what I might find when we reached the site of the boat wreck.

Chapter 8

The shoreline was strewn with goods: broken bales of dripping cloth, boxes of guns, soggy bags of pemmican. Men were using the other boats to ferry the cargo from our wreck which still lay, listing to one side, against a ridge of rock in the river's foaming torrent. I scanned the scene, my eyes darting feverishly from man to man, boat to boat – and there! There was Samuel Beaver, bent over a keg from which he was prising the lid to check the state of the beans inside. And there! Orchid was standing on a rock, spreading out rectangles of something white! I panted with relief, and urged Foxfire through a grove of birch towards her.

'Oh, Amelia! And Charlotte! Oh, praise God you are safe!' she cried, and strode forward to stroke Foxfire's neck, and fondly pat Charlotte's dangling leg encased in soaked leggings.

'All my sketches have been water damaged, as you see.' She gestured and I realised that the white rectangles strewn upon the rock were her paintings, some reduced to mere puddles of colour on paper that was tearing apart with wetness. A few still retained a semblance of their original brushstrokes and pencil lines, although the paper was badly wrinkled.

'And your wooden chest has been brought ashore too,' Orchid said, pointing. 'Samuel laid it there, near the pile of paddles.'

My heart beat faster; I tied Foxfire to a tree and left him to graze while Charlotte helped Orchid smooth out her paintings. I hurried down to where the York boat's long paddles lay in a haphazard pile on the strip of gravel shoreline. My wooden chest with its rope handles, and the initials *HBC* stamped upon it in black, was battered and cracked along one corner. I lifted the lid and took out Betty's gift of a moose hide to spread it, soaking with water, upon a rock; hopefully, it had protected the other contents of the chest. When I plunged my hands down through our damp clothing, my father's letter was the first of my two most precious objects that I found. It was soggy and soft. Carefully, I extracted it, and peeled apart its folded layers; the ink was spreading through the wet paper, pooling into blotches. My eyes flitted over the familiar lines, finding recognisable words: *This is a fair place . . . look forward to good prospects.* With infinite care I spread the letter on a rock to dry, uncertain whether it would ever be legible again. Then I plunged my hand back into my trunk to find the luckenbooth in its wrapping of deerskin. Here was the skin, a small scrap, worn soft as goose down by age and use. My fingers fumbled with it.

It was empty.

I pulled everything from the trunk, looking for the brooch, piling spare leggings and fishing line and winter robes and my sewing kit all upon the shoreline until I was standing in a jumble of belongings. The chest was empty, its wooden bottom stained with water. My hands tore again through the clothing at my feet, shaking, unfolding, sorting. No brooch, no glint of brightness, no sharp bright sound as it fell on to the stones.

Numbly, I sorted through everything more slowly, more carefully, willing the brooch to appear magically; to be caught in a fold of tartan fabric, to be lying in the toe of a moccasin, to be trapped inside the red Morocco leather covers of my sewing kit. But it was in none of these places. I stood for a long time, oblivious to the tripmen shouting commands, rigging up rope harnesses for themselves so they could pull our wrecked boat to shore and begin repairing the broken planking. I stood in silence, trembling with the weight of such a loss. If I found my father, how would I prove to him now that I was indeed his daughter? How would I remind him of his broken promise to my mother, to me?

'Amelia!' I turned at last, focusing on Eva's smooth face as she peered at me, her arms filled with the wet, bedraggled mass of a white hare coat. 'Is something wrong?'

I stared mutely at the coins and beads swinging at her throat, at the shell discs hanging from her ears. 'I have lost something,' I said slowly at last, the words wedging themselves in my throat. 'And Eva, the Witiko man from your boat – listen, we must feed him bear's grease!'

Eva listened intently while I told her what had happened in the bush, her forehead wrinkling with concern. 'I will ask my boat's cook,' she promised. 'But you must be careful, Amelia. This is the second time that the man – his name is Angus – has followed you into the bush.'

Her eyes seemed stretched wide with concern but after a moment I realised that she was looking over my shoulder at a young Canadian, stripped to the waist and shining with sweat and river water; he was Pierre, the steersman from our boat. I was relieved to see that he had survived his plunge into the rapids, although one side of his face was swollen with a rock abrasion and he had chipped a front tooth; his grin now was jauntier and wilder than before.

'It was Pierre who brought your box ashore,' Eva explained.

'I've lost a brooch – a heart-shaped silver brooch,' I told him. 'Have you seen it?'

He shrugged and waved one hand expressively. '*Mais non, non*. Everything was everywhere in our boat,' he said. 'I collected it all, then Eva sorted through the belongings and restored them to their owners. *C'est vrai*. If your brooch is missing, what can I say? It is at the bottom of the river, *non*?'

He winked one lazy dark eye at Eva as he swung away, whistling.

For two days, we camped on the narrow strip of shore while the men hauled logs from the bush, and cut planking, planing the long timbers, then sawing the planks to length. Our boat, resting on log rollers, was propped almost on one gunwale to fully expose her ripped belly. The new planks were hammered into place, then caulked with oakum and sealed with pitch. At last, the boat was refloated, loaded with the salvaged cargo – everything torn, battered, and still slightly damp – and we began once more to ascend the long rivers and the scattered lakes.

Rain began to fall, a steady, soft, monotonous deluge that freckled the surface of abandoned beaver ponds, and drummed upon the oiled cloths in which we wrapped ourselves. Leaves along the shoreline, turning colour now, glowed dull gold and red like slow fires, in the grey air; and the tripmens' voices as they sang fell flat and small upon the dark, roiling rivers. Orchid's face was pale and pinched; the tip of her nose was red and she blew it often into a white lawn handkerchief, coughing and gasping for breath.

Her gowns were stained with clay, smoke, and leaf juice; rips and broken stitching marred the fabric along the hem. Still, when she noticed me watching her, she smiled brightly and straightened her shoulders, slumped beneath a damp, smoky blanket. A long red scratch on one cheek marked where a branch had swung back into her face as she followed a tripman over a rough portage.

Foxfire was quiet in the rain, staring at the shoreline passing by or following me docilely along trails at portages. His three remaining shoes had been removed – two coming off easily and one requiring a fight – and I had kept a nail as an amulet which I carried in a bag around my neck. Now his feet made a dull thudding sound against rocks instead of a metallic ringing. The gash on his shoulder was healing; I sponged it every evening using a baling sponge from our boat, and hot water from a kettle slung over the fire. Orchid fretted that he was losing weight on the strange diet of dying grass, leaves, and damp oats; that he was losing muscle tone from the many weeks of travelling.

Watching him as he swayed in the boat, the rain dribbling in rivulets down his legs beneath the edge of his blanket, I wondered if he felt as lost and homesick as I did; as though this great land had swallowed us in, a pike swallowing a smaller fish, so that we would never find ourselves again. Did he yearn to be with his own kind, as I yearned for the face of Betty

Goose Wing, wreathed in pipe smoke, wrinkled and kind? Did he long for the drift of salt on the wind, as I did? Perhaps he pined for the wide open spaces of his marshes along the Norfolk Broads as I pined for the sweep of Hudson Bay, the metallic light shimmering on heaving waves beneath the vast sky. Here, above the rivers, the sky seemed shrunken, ringed by the raking spires of conifers; the walls of trees on each shoreline hemmed us in so that sometimes I felt as though I couldn't breathe but was suffocating for lack of wind and space and a cold, northern light.

One night, sitting by a smouldering fire of wet wood, I asked Eva casually if she knew that her uncle had once wooed my mother, but she said that she had not heard anything about this. Then I asked whether she thought that my father might ever have sent my mother a message but she said she didn't know; it had all happened so long ago anyway so what did it matter now? Her perfect profile bent towards the fire as she spoke, her full lips curling in a smile, but when she turned her head to glance at me, her eyes were veiled and unreadable.

It was still raining, colder now, when we approached Robinson Portage, the longest stretch of trail on our trip. It was said that this portage was haunted by the ghosts of all the men who had died there of broken legs and heart attacks, as they struggled for seven days to haul the great boats overland along rollers of poplar logs, as they stumbled, half trotting, beneath the packs of goods on their backs. Songs fell into silence as we approached the long set of waterfalls, a dim white barrier glimpsed far ahead. Then the boats were run on to shore and the trip-men, with grim faces, began unloading them. For seven days, they would work beneath the threat of imminent death, kept company by the crosses leaning amongst the poplar trees.

A camp was set up, and Orchid spent hours in her tent, coughing with a deepening rattle in her lungs. Eva slipped in and out of the tent, asking Orchid for stories of her life in England, learning about balls, calling cards and town houses; about etiquette and taking the waters at the baths; about fashions in gowns and hats, and how many servants were required to run a grand house. Eva wanted to become as white as she could, I thought, she wanted to wash herself in that river of English memories until it washed the brown colour from her skin. As she murmured softly to Orchid, and as Orchid replied in her hoarse voice, Eva was learning how to change colour, like the leaves changing along the riverbanks. She confided to me one evening that she planned to find and marry a white trader while she went to school in Red River.

'Not just any white man will do,' she said thoughtfully. 'He must be a clerk with good prospects and connections, who will rise through the Company ranks to become a chief trader or factor.'

I darted her a surprised glance for she was always flirting with Pierre, who anyone could see was wild, smoking his Brazilian hard twist tobacco while light sparked on his earrings. He would never settle into civilised life or exchange his fringed buckskin jacket for a frock coat. And Eva's father would never form an alliance with him.

'What about you?' Eva asked. 'Isn't there a hunter you've had your eyes on?'

I shrugged. 'I had no one to arrange it for me, no father after Ronald McTavish left,' I said. Then I turned my face away, for there had been a hunter I liked but he had died in the starving moon, disappearing into the bitter smoke of a blizzard and never returning. Perhaps he had left moose blood lying uncovered on the snow, and had brought the blizzard upon himself.

'Ah, it is the same on both sides of the Atlantic,' said Orchid, overhearing us. 'Fathers negotiate whom their daughters will marry, for trade purposes or wealth or bonds between families. My dear departed parent would be horrified to know I am traipsing halfway around the world with no dowry but a horse.'

After a moment's reflection she added pensively, 'Yet, he is a very fine horse. And I daresay my husband's wealth is not so very great, not the thousands of pounds per annum that my father would have liked for me.'

Then she laughed, hard and clear. I was learning that this laughter was something she could hide behind like a blind, when she was hunting down her own fear.

By day, I led Foxfire to and fro through the poplars, listening to the distant shouts of the tripmen, and watching the horse's mobile lips as he foraged; it was marvellous how sensitive his lips were and how he could strip leaves from the finest of twigs and leave it upon the tree. Hour after hour I wandered with him, rain pattering on his oiled blanket, as I thought about the feel of his great back beneath me in the river. I wondered if Orchid would allow me to ride him. At last, I asked her and she had the men locate and unpack her chest containing the stallion's tack. I ran my hands over the bridle with its buckles and straps, and the smooth, cold shine of the metal bit that Orchid explained lay in a space that all horses have between their front and back teeth.

'With this, you have control over the horse's head,' she explained. 'There are many different kinds of bits but this one is a pelham with two rings. The straps attached to the rings are called reins, and there are two on each side so they are called double reins. The top rein pulls straight back from the top bit ring, but the lower rein exerts a lever-like action with the bottom bit ring, and so pulls up over the poll behind the horse's ears. This encourages the horse to drop his head and to collect his body beneath you with his spine rounded. Then his energy and his balance are under your control. '

Then she showed me the saddle; a large, heavy leather object with a shining stirrup in which to place one's foot, and with two protrusions around which a lady, who must never ride astride, might place her legs and try to balance. We tied Foxfire to a tree, and Orchid showed me how to place his saddle blanket, made from the pelt of a young sheep, on to his withers and then slide it slightly backwards in the direction of his hair growth. The saddle was placed on top, and Orchid showed me how to reach beneath the horse's belly for the girth straps of leather, and how to tighten them until the saddle was secure. 'Always check the girth again before you mount,' she said. 'You do not want to end up dangling beneath his belly if the saddle slips.'

Then she showed me how to bridle him, laying one arm along the crest of his neck and guiding the head straps over his ears while my other hand slipped the bit between his teeth.

'Mount here, on the nearside,' Orchid said.

My heart beat hard. I slipped the toe of my moccasin into the stirrup iron, and swung my weight up and over. The stallion pranced sideways, trees swayed, clouds scattered fast across the sky, and the cold wind whipped my cheeks. Joy ran through me for a moment, like the solemn joy that I felt when men played their fiddles and I danced with the other girls and women, stamping our feet to the lilting laments of their Scottish homeland. But this riding was even better than dancing; better than running through grass with the wind roaring at your back, as I used to do on the tundra when I was a small child.

From then on, I rode at least twice daily while Orchid stood patiently in the drizzle, coughing, calling commands, teaching me how to keep my hands gentle and yet strong, my body upright and yet pliant, my legs loose and yet ready to tighten so that I wouldn't fall off. Riding, I thought, was like being a weed in a river current or a tree in a strong wind – everything about horse and rider was moving, flowing, bending, and yet tenacious and powerfully alive. When the stallion trotted, he covered the ground in swinging strides, and soon I was able to bend him amongst the trees and around stones even at a trot, his whole body supple. Orchid began to teach me about leads; about which leg the stallion should lead with as he rounded rocks, and how I could feel this through the rhythm of his body. It was possible to ask the horse to change which leg he was leading with. My braids flew back over my shoulders as I rode, and my face stretched wide in a smile of delight.

On our final day at the Robinson Portage, the rain stopped and Orchid decided she wanted to go for a walk and start painting again. We left Charlotte and Eva in Orchid's tent, stringing beads, and left the horse tied to a tree, one hind leg cocked as he dozed. Orchid and I wandered off, watching squirrels scamper along logs, chipmunks stretch their faces wide with seeds, wild raspberry bushes toss in the wind, and the pale yellow tongues of willow leaves slip loose and fall to carpet the ground. Storms of yellow poplar leaves whirled around us.

A chill ran over my skin like a breath.

I could hear a great silence behind the wind and the rustling leaves; my skin prickled with the awareness of a mighty power close by. Standing stock-still, I waited, my eyes scanning every detail: a stump, a gooseberry bush, the place where a skunk had dug in the soil for roots, the place where a lynx had clawed long pale gouges into the trunk of a white spruce. Still the silence gripped me, pressed upon me.

The spirit and the power came closer.

The bear's head rose slowly from behind a screen of willows, rose until it was higher than my own head. I saw the pale brown snout, a pair of small sharp eyes, an open mouth revealing teeth sharper than thorns and as long as my hand. The bear's head swung, questing for our scent on the wind. When a gust whirled around, the bear tasted it with his open mouth and his twitching nose; he caught our smell and grunted in curiosity.

'Orchid,' I called softly. 'Stay very still. Crooked Tail is here.' Amongst my mother's people, one did not speak the bear's name aloud, but called him Crooked Tail or Galloping Along out of respect.

But Orchid did not reply and neither could I see her, somewhere to my left, meandering amongst the trees.

The bear lumbered forward, closer to me, cocking his head with questions: *Who is there? What do you want?* He rose to his hind feet, and his fore paws dangled. His tall body was as upright as a man's and rolling with thick fur, fat and mighty slabs of muscle. This was an animal that could take my whole head into his mouth and crush it like a nut, or tear my neck wide open with one swipe.

I shook with dread and awe.

Raising my arms very slowly above my chest, I took two steps backwards. I did not look into the bear's eyes, for that would have been a challenge. 'Forgive us, Grandfather,' I said softly. 'We did not mean to disturb your peace. We will leave now and let you rest.'

One more step back.

A twig snapped to my left, and the pale green of Orchid's gown flashed in the corner of my eye. The bear's head swung around, fast and heavy and blunt; I heard the woof of surprise rush between his teeth.

'Amel— oh!'

'Step away slowly, do not run,' I warned her softly and watched as she obeyed, clutching her paper to her chest, her scratched and wind-reddened face suddenly as pale as it had been on the day she walked up the landing stage at York Factory. A sneeze tore through the silence, then another. Papers flew from Orchid's hands to scatter on the ground. The bear dropped on to all fours and swung his head from side to side, growling and grinding his jaw with his rounded ears laid back. Weakness ran through my knees.

'Do not run,' I begged Orchid with a quiver in my voice. 'Talk soft –'

As she sneezed again, the bear hurtled forward, a dark blur of bone and speed like a rock crashing down a riverbank in a spring thaw, like an eagle falling from the sky upon a hare. Orchid flung herself backwards against a tree trunk. The bear covered the space between himself and her in four bounds; the light shattered on his teeth and claws into a thousand splinters that pierced us with arrowheads of terror.

I leaped forward, yelling, waving my arms, and the bear skidded to a halt, swinging around, looking for the source of this commotion. With a roar he plunged towards me; a whirling wind, a gun bullet, the darkness of death. Something crashed away through the trees behind me. A squeal of fear rode the wind. The bear halted again – he was so close to me that I could smell the sickly sweetness of dead meat on his breath – and rose back on to his hind legs. His great belly filled my vision with its luxuriant folds of fur. I stopped breathing. More crashing echoed through the trees, branches snapped, leaves whipped a large body.

'Foxfire!' Orchid cried in anguish and I glimpsed a flash of red hair. The bear dropped to all fours again and set off through the trees, chasing the fleeing horse at a flat run that ate up the ground, propelling him over the yellow fallen leaves and out of sight in a few seconds.

'Come!' I gasped. 'Come!'

I strode into the bush, my breath and my heart hurrying and churning, my eyes slow and steady, scanning every sign, every word of the story that horse and bear had left behind themselves in their flight: a hoof mark in wet soil, a claw scratch on rock, a flattened blueberry bush, a snapped willow twig, a log broken open by impact and spilling grubs on to the ground. And also: the harsh alarm call of a crow, disturbed, far ahead of us. It lifted from the canopy of trees and struggled into the wind.

I whistled until my lips felt like wrinkled berries but the horse did not neigh in return.

Behind me, Orchid slipped and stumbled, cursing beneath her breath, holding up her gown with one hand, her ankles twisting inside the tight lacing of her stiff leather boots. I was almost running now. My mind filled with visions of the bear bringing the horse down, the great wounds he would leave on Foxfire's frosted red quarters, how those claws would separate the horse's flesh from his ribs like a flensing knife, how the stallion would scream in agony as he died.

Still my eyes were careful, steady, slow, reading the land.

'Do not walk in the tracks,' I warned Orchid over my shoulder. 'And do not step across them.'

We hurried downhill between tamaracks that shed their thin yellow needles all over our shoulders and into our hair, and emerged on to the gravel banks of a small tributary creek running down into Robinson Lake. I lurched to a halt and Orchid barged into my back, panting, muttering. I laid my hand on her shaking arm.

'Quiet! Look!'

Five hundred yards ahead, the bear sat on his rump and short tail beside a carcass. Ribs protruded like the ribs of a York boat, curved and pale. Red tatters of flesh hung from them. The neck lay limp and twisted, the head bent beneath it. Long legs sprawled in the stones as though, even in death, the animal still tried to outrun the ferocity of the great bear's furious onslaught. Orchid stifled a sob.

'It's not Foxfire,' I said. 'It's an elk. Watch.'

The five wolves that had been scavenging from the bear's kill in his absence drifted along the perimeter of the trees like windblown flecks of campfire ash. Trotting in closer, from different directions, they snapped and snarled at the bear, distracting him, lunging and feinting. The long bushes of their dark tails swung in the wind, and their eyes glowed golden in the harsh light.

'When he sits, they cannot creep up from behind,' I whispered. 'Watch.'

The bear swung his great body around and from side to side, his paws whistling through the air, swatting at the wolves as though they were flies buzzing in his ears. One wolf, rashly coming in too close to snatch at a ribbon of elk flesh, was lifted half off the ground and flung sideways with a high yelp of pain; it circled away, limping on a broken foreleg. The other wolves continued baiting the bear for a few minutes but eventually trotted off and were swallowed by the forest. The bear rose to his feet, padded over to the carcass, and shoved his heavy nose inside the ribcage.

I drew Orchid back under the tamaracks. 'I am going to keep tracking,' I said. She nodded, gripping her nose to hold in another sneeze, her eyes watering with cold and fear. We made a wide detour around the bear, and waded through the frigid stream downwind of him where his keen sense of smell would not detect us. Then we worked our way back along the shoreline until I picked up the trail of the horse again and began to follow it as he plunged and zigzagged through the bush in terror.

Dusk was falling. My body was quiet now; all over me, my skin was listening; waiting to hear the wolves crying to the rising moon, or the stamp of a horse, or the padding approach of the grandfather bear who has no chief over him. I lost the trail in the gloom, circled back, picked it up, lost it again. Now it was almost completely dark beneath the pale foliage, and Orchid's rasping breath warned me that she was exhausted.

'We will have to go back,' I admitted at last, although the horse's name was crying in my mind like a lament, and my eyes bulged with the hot burn of unshed tears.

'How are we going to find our way in the dark?' Orchid cried.

'There are signs everywhere. Look here, see this aspen tree? See how its bark is thicker and whiter on one side? That side is south.'

For three miles, perhaps four, we retraced our steps while the stars climbed high, while branches slapped our faces and dead logs gave way under our feet and an owl cried somewhere to the north, like a spirit searching for us with a message. A stone pierced the bottom of my worn moccasin and bruised my foot.

Oh, Foxfire, Foxfire.

How could it be that he had journeyed so far, so many thousands of miles over sea and land and river and lake, into the midst of this vastness, and had died here without ever reaching his new stable waiting for him in the Red River valley? Was his spirit galloping now over our heads, joyous and free, along the wolf road? Or was it being reborn somewhere, in the form of a bright red colt with spindly legs and eyes like pools of water? Grief swelled in my chest, bigger and bigger, until I could barely stagger along carrying its weight.

A slanting rain began to fall, carrying a granular coldness like sleet in the core of each drop. It stung my face and eyes. My hair was plastered to my numb scalp. My wet feet slithered in the undergrowth.

There was silence behind me as Orchid stopped walking. I turned to locate the pale blur of her face. 'It is unbearable!' she cried suddenly, her high voice hard and sharp. 'I hate this country. Everything is so – so – *hostile*! The bugs, the mud, the weather, the thick trees, the – the rude uncouth men we travel with, the dark. I hate this wilderness! I am so weary of it! I cannot go on!'

Sobs racked her. I went back and put my arms around her shoulders and felt the grief and bewilderment and homesickness that poured through her like a current between the grinding power of rocks. For a long time, I held her until her outburst subsided. I wiped her eyes with a corner of her sopping shawl, as though she were a child as young as Charlotte. 'Come,' I said. 'We must get back to camp.'

We saw the bright flicker of fires at last, like stars fallen amongst the trees, and emerged on to the shoreline to stumble towards them. There was a cooking pot suspended over flames and sending out inviting smells of muskrat stew ... there were the dark piles of goods from the boats, the kegs of rum

and salt pork, the boxes of tea and soap and candles . . .
there were the men, sprawled by the fires and
wrapped in oil cloths, smoking pipes while they
waited for their evening meal . . . and here was Eva,
hand in hand with Charlotte and hurrying to meet
us, her smooth face flushed with relief and her dark
eyes glowing.

'We had just noticed you were not back yet!' she
cried, as Charlotte buried her face against my robe
and clung to me. 'When the horse came back without you, we didn't know what had happened.'

'Back?' I asked blankly.

'He strayed off; his rope must have come untied.
After some hours he returned covered in sweat and
scratches and limping on one front leg. Look, there
he is.'

I followed the line of her pointing arm, the wink
of her brass rings and bracelets, and saw the gleaming
flank turned sideways to a fire, the fall of red mane,
the elegant drooping head. Foxfire turned his face
towards me as I gave a weak whistle, and a greeting
fluttered his nostrils in return. I crossed to where he
stood tied to a sapling poplar. Flames danced in his
eyes as he lowered his face against my chest and
leaned there, breathing slow and deep in peaceful-
ness at last. Weakness poured through me, and my
hands shook, smoothing his forelock hair. I inhaled
the sweet familiar smell of his coat, then gave a silent
prayer of thanks to the Great Spirit as I went to the

river to scoop water in a tin cup. With this, I sponged the horse's nostrils clean, and washed the ragged scratches across his shoulders. I felt the heat in the tendons of his lame leg, and poulticed it with the shredded bark of a red willow.

As I worked on the leg, wrapping strips of linen around it to hold the poultice in place, I wondered about the man called Angus, who might be turning Witiko, or who might be a sorcerer. I pondered the possibility that he was wrestling with my spirit guardian, the Horse, and that he was trying to harm Foxfire. I tied the linen strips in place and went to fetch the stallion some oats and to fill his water bucket, peering along the shoreline for a glimpse of the half-blood with a bronze face and hair like drying grasses.

The next morning, before dawn, the tripmen whooped with delight, wading out to the loaded York boats and climbing onboard, hefting their paddles again, turning their faces towards the west and their backs towards Robinson Portage. Charlotte and I settled ourselves on our hard bench beside Orchid but she would not speak to me as we travelled. She stared far away, as though searching for something along the rocky shoreline with its dense walls of trees. She stared at the surface of the river as though reading a book. She bent over her sketch paper with intense concentration, as though she were praying to her Creator, asking for help from her *pawakan*, that spirit called Jesus.

Once, suddenly, as though we had been in the middle of a conversation, she said in a clipped tone, 'I don't see how you could have been so careless as to let Foxfire's rope be incorrectly tied. I thought better of your sense of responsibility, Amelia. I'm very disappointed in you.' Then she glared away over the water again, wiping at her red nose and coughing.

I did tie the rope correctly, I wanted to protest. I was sure that I did. And yet . . . how had Foxfire come untied if I had made the right knot? How had he come to be wandering in the trees alone, following us perhaps by smell and hearing, by glimpsing us with his keen eyesight? And so I didn't reply to Orchid but sat silent, gnawed by guilt and doubts, her angry accusation lying heavy on me. I huddled in my blanket, cold and as silent as she was, falling deep down into that black place that I had tumbled into when my mother died, and which it had taken me many moons to begin leaving. But now, here I was again, back in a pit of despondency, gripped by the Blue Devil of sadness. My brooch was gone, swept away by the rapids, and my father's letter was almost illegible with blots and water stains and ragged rips. And the land was so much huger than I had ever imagined, and I was so much smaller. It seemed foolish to have dreamed that I might find my father or any place for Charlotte and me to call home.

Chapter 9

The weather was wild and unpredictable as the brigades toiled onwards. Boiling white clouds threw dazzling reflections upon the water. Gusts of cold wind shook the leaves from the trees in squalls of gold. Then darkness would fall across the land as though a hand had brushed it with soot, and racing clouds obliterated the sun. Snowflakes swept over us in flurries, burning cold on our cheeks and eyelids, then dissolved as they fell on to ground or water.

I bent over the pair of new moccasins that I was making, embroidering each toe with purple thistles, that flower the Scotsmen loved. Carefully, I strung the porcupine quills and the little glass beads, along my needle even while the wind whipped against me, and Foxfire's tail streamed between his legs.

Orchid maintained her silence; her plump cheeks seemed to grow thinner, and her skin whiter, with every hour. As she breathed, I could hear the deep rasp in her lungs and I knew that she was growing sicker in her anger and loneliness, but my own tongue lay heavy in my mouth. I had done no wrong and yet she had accused me; it was hard now to break the grip of our silence, or to meet the sharpness of her blue eyes. I kept my own eyes downcast over my sewing, over Charlotte's braids as I plaited their three strands together, over our lunches of cold bannock and smoked buffalo tongue.

Misery gripped my heart so that it beat slowly and weakly, like a dying fish in the bottom of a canoe.

Although I continued to take care of Foxfire, I did not ask Orchid to have his saddle unpacked again. Instead, as the river glinted in dawn or sunset light, pearly as the inside of a shell, I found a stump or a rock to clamber on. Then I simply slid one leg over the stallion's back and sat comfortably with legs astride and dangling, feeling the horse's warmth and muscles, learning to anticipate his every move as he wandered the shoreline. He grazed contentedly while the cries of whippoor-wills echoed in the stillness, and mist smoked from the water's surface.

Since our boat's load had been lightened by the loss of goods in the wreck, Eva decided to transfer into it. She and Orchid moved to sit one bench ahead of Charlotte and me, and a small part of me felt glad. Now I didn't have to pretend to ignore Orchid any more, for when I raised my eyes from my needlework all I saw was Orchid's short back wrapped in a woollen shawl, and her stiff bonnet of grey muslin. Eva leaned against Orchid's shoulder, and they talked in monotones about England. Orchid even gave Eva some sheets of paper, and she began to learn how to use Orchid's watercolour paints, but Orchid herself did not paint or sketch; simply stared straight ahead as though nothing mattered to her now except reaching the Red River colony and clambering for ever out of this boat.

'Here I am after all,' Eva turned around to say to me once. 'I lost my place in this boat when you brought the horse onboard at York. But here I am now. And now I don't have to worry about that tripman in the other boat – you know, Angus.'

Had it offended her after all, moving to another boat to make way for me? I searched her face for a clue but she was already turning away, tossing her head so that her long braid, decorated with white ermine fur and blue beads, swung against her back. Pierre gave a whistle behind me at the steering oar but Eva pretended not to hear. Then he began to sing and the other men took up the refrain, their voices ringing clear and melodious across the river, echoing from the trees and rocks:

'Why should we yet our sail unfurl?
There is not a breath the blue waves to curl;
But, when the wind blows off the shore,
Oh! Sweetly we'll rest our weary oar.
Blow, breezes, blow, the stream runs fast,
The Rapids are near and the daylight's past!'

I knew that the men were looking forward to reaching the trading fort of Norway House and then the
great expanse of Lake Winnipeg, which would grant
them a rest from toiling up the river rapids. On the
lake they might raise the boat sails and lie dozing on
the benches while the wind carried us southwards
with the pelicans and gulls.

'Tomorrow we will reach Painted Rock Portage,'
Samuel Beaver said that evening as he helped me to
cut grass for Foxfire. 'Do you know about this place?'

I shook my head, stripping leaves from a poplar to
add to the grass.

'It's a sacred place for our people,' Sam said. 'The
ancestors have painted it with pictures. And people
go there to make offerings to the grandfather rock,
and to pray and lie on it for healing.'

He straightened with the sickle in one hand, and
gave me a steady look. 'You might find help there.'

I stared back at him, wondering if the whole
boat knew that Orchid and I weren't speaking,
that she was sick, and that my heart was heavy
and blue.

'Don't you get homesick?' I asked Samuel. 'Don't you miss the bay?'

He smiled and his dark skin gleamed above the red cloth knotted at his throat. 'The rivers are my home now. I want to follow them far to the north, to the frozen sea, and far to the west where the great mountains lie, and I want to go over the mountains and down to the shores of the Pacific! The rivers run everywhere and look – I have the hands of a tripman now!'

He held them out for my inspection and I saw that the paler skin on his palms was hard and thick from the oars, and no longer blistered or weeping.

I smiled, and turned back to the poplar tree, wondering if I too might learn to feel that the rivers were my home. But a river was not a home for a horse, although Foxfire seemed to enjoy swimming. I wondered if all horses were such strong swimmers as he was, and enjoyed wading in the shallows, snorting playfully into the water and splashing with a foreleg. If only Orchid and I were friends still, I could have asked her.

In the morning, I decided once again to try leaving the blinkers off Foxfire's halter; surely, he had been travelling by boat long enough now that he would remain calm. This time, he followed me into the boat without trouble and watched the shoreline surging past with calm attention.

'What are those?' I heard Orchid ask late in the day, and I glanced up from my needlework.

'They are *manitohkan*,' Eva replied. 'They are carvings of people's dream guardians.'

Along the shoreline, a group of trees had been cut down to leave three feet of stump, and into these had been carved the faces and sometimes the torsos of dream guardians. There was a magnificent Thunderbird from the upper air, gazing sternly across the water, and there was a moose, and there was a great northern pike with its hooked jaw. We were nearing the sacred place. I laid down my needlework to watch the shoreline and presently I saw the skull of a deer placed high in the limbs of a white cedar tree, its antlers positioned to face the rising sun, and tied with long, bright ribbons. Then I saw a package of rolled birchbark nailed to a skinny jack pine and I knew that it contained the paws of a bear, hung there to ensure good hunting in future, and after this we passed the skull of a bear, wedged into a crook in the limbs of a birch, and with its jaw decorated with loops of beads.

'It is so He that owns the chin will be respected and will give himself to the hunters again,' I muttered to Charlotte as she gazed from the boat, her wide eyes taking in every detail. Who else would help her to learn the ways of our people, if I did not pass on my knowledge? I was too young to be a wise elder, and yet my sister had no one else.

Now ahead of us lay the flat sheets of the Painted Rock, which the trade goods must be portaged around. The tripmen ran the York boats onshore beside six birchbark canoes, light and graceful as duck feathers. Their Cree owners were gathered further down the shore; the smoke from their fires and their pipes streamed sideways in the capricious wind and the fringes of their deerskin robes flapped against their legs as they danced to the slow beat of a drum. Their chanting carried to me in snatches on the wind and I knew that they had come to this sacred place to worship the Great Spirit.

While the tripmen unloaded the boats, I let Foxfire graze amongst the huckleberry bushes. Then I tied him up, and made a fresh poultice of red willow for his tender foreleg while Charlotte helped me by brushing him. She had to stand on a stone to reach his high back.

'He is always quieter for you,' I told Charlotte. 'He moves more slowly, placing his hooves carefully to avoid treading on your little feet. He understands that you are only a few moons in age.'

'I am not a baby!' Charlotte protested but I saw that she was pleased, and slid her hand lovingly along Foxfire's neck when he bent his head towards her.

I wondered if Foxfire had ever spent time in the pasture with the foals he had fathered, far away in England; if he remembered running with his mares while the foals gambled alongside. But perhaps, like human fathers, he did not cast his thoughts back-wards when he journeyed away.

It was while I was gathering firewood that I noticed the dome-shaped sweat lodge, screened by trees and huddled against the base of the sacred rock, its cracks stuffed with offerings of tobacco, tea, dried meat and even a hunting knife with a bone handle. I stared at the lodge for a long minute; it was small, and made with willow saplings covered in birchbark. A flap of deerskin hung over the low doorway. The ashes in the fire pit outside the lodge were still warm, and the grandfather and grandmother rocks placed in the centre of the pit still exuded a comforting heat.

I knew then what I must do to help Orchid's cold, and her loneliness and anger, as well as my own Blue Devil. Though I was not a wise elder, I knew some things: that warmth would speed healing, that a sweat lodge might restore harmony to troubled minds. I knew that I must bring peace to our friendship again.

Hurrying now, I dodged between the trees to the Cree fire, but the people had left, slipping away in their canoes, and so I couldn't ask permission to use their lodge. But perhaps it was here for anyone who came seeking help from the spirit world. I ran back, dodging the pale trunks of poplars in the dusk, feeling the bite of snow against my cheeks. Pulling my strike-a-light and a wad of bulrush fluff from my bag, I bent over the fire pit and struck a spark. Scraps of birchbark coaxed flames into life. With the small hatchet I kept in my belt, I chopped enough wood to get the fire roaring, creating a blaze that would send heat deep into the stones lying in its midst.

Orchid was seated outside her tent, and eating listlessly from a tin bowl of *rubaboo* stew made of pemmican mixed with flour. Her harsh coughing punctuated the laughter and conversation amongst the tripmen gathered at their fires. Charlotte was nearby, playing a game of whist with Samuel Beaver, Eva and Pierre in his tall steersman's hat with red ostrich plumes.

'Orchid,' I said softly, although I couldn't meet her stony glance with my own miserable one. 'I am worried about your health. There is a way amongst my people for healing illnesses of the heart and the body. Will you let me help you?'

For a long moment, she didn't answer but finally she nodded, stirring her spoon aimlessly around in her supper. 'I cannot take one more bite of this mess,' she muttered. 'What do you wish me to do?'

'I have some things to get ready, then I will come for you.'

It was fully dark by the time that I had gathered the items I needed, and Orchid and Charlotte followed me through the stinging air and the ghostly poplars; the peppery tang of fallen leaves tingled my nostrils. The fire I had lit was dying down. From my small leather medicine pouch, I pulled a little Brazilian hard twist tobacco and some chunks of dried caribou meat and sprinkled them on to the fire.

'What are you doing?' Orchid wheezed.

'It is an offering for the spirits,' I said, 'so they might look on us with compassion and grant our requests.'

'As in the Old Testament,' Orchid said. 'Burnt offerings for the Almighty.'

I inclined my head but didn't answer. Mr Murdoch, the postmaster who taught evening class at York Factory, had once read us a passage from the white man's sacred book, in which people brought oxen and birds called doves, and burned them with fire for their white man's Creator. Now I rolled the hot stones from my fire with a stick, and dragged them inside the lodge on a piece of deerhide, tipping them into the hole dug in the centre of the floor. 'Strip all your clothing off,' I told Orchid.

'This is madness,' she protested fiercely. 'I am ill, and it is almost freezing out here.'

'I will give you a blanket, but you won't need it soon, inside the lodge.'

'Madness,' she muttered again, breathing hard but fumbling to undo the rows of jet buttons on her gown. It seemed to take her for ever to strip; what vast quantities of strange garments the white women wore, with boning and buttons and ribbons, with lace trim and flounces! At last we stooped and entered the lodge on our knees, wrapped in blankets.

'I cannot see anything in here,' Orchid said, her voice tinged with panic.

'You don't need to see with your eyes, only with your spirit.'

The braid of sweet grass that I had lit at the fire and brought inside, glowed in the darkness. I wafted it around our bodies, letting the fragrant smoke wash us clean and prepare us for talking to the spirits.

My blanket slipped from my shoulders as I settled myself on the beaten ground strewn with white cedar fronds. When I inhaled, their sharp resinous aroma settled deep in my lungs and my mind filled with the peace and greenness of the forest, with its singing silence.

'Kicimanitow, Great Spirit,' I prayed, 'I am Amelia Otterchild Mackenzie. I come for healing for my sadness. I come for guidance to find a new home. I need your help to find it. May my *pawakan* be strong. And Mary Mackenzie, my mother, may your spirit hear me. Send strength to help me travel on without you.'

'Great Kicimanitow,' came Charlotte's voice, soft as the touch of a spring leaf against my ear. 'I am Charlotte Bright Eyes McTavish. Help me to make this great journey with my sister.'

I sprinkled cedar fronds on the fire and they spat and curled, crackling to draw the attention of the spirits to our requests. A gust of wind ran up the walls of the lodge. I heard the patter of leaves falling upon it and sliding down to the forest floor. When I touched Orchid's arm lightly, I felt her flinch in the darkness. 'You must state your name and your need,' I prompted.

'Almighty Father,' prayed Orchid, 'God of Abraham, Isaac and Jacob, I your most humble servant beseech your mercy in this hour of need –' She broke off with a racking cough, bending over from the waist.

I lifted the birchbark pail of river water and poured it on to the hot rocks so that steam billowed around us.

Orchid stifled a shriek, but her coughing subsided.

'Wake up, grandfather stones,' I pleaded. 'Wake up, grandmother stones. Send our messages to the Creator.' Then Charlotte and I began to chant while the heat and the steam from the stones pushed its fingers deeper and deeper into us, through our skin, through our organs, into our bones. It filled our heads, it pumped through our hearts. There was nothing but heat and steam and a darkness so thick it was as though the night had pressed its hand across our eyes and sealed them shut.

Our chanting voices seemed to be joined by other voices; the words of our chant rolled and sluiced around inside the lodge like stones in a bucket of water; they roared and poured against us, blocking all other sounds. Inside my head, all English words were lost, then even the words of my mother's tongue. Thoughts were obliterated. Sweat filled my mouth, poured from my chest.

Now pictures filled my mind.

I was running over the tundra of the bay, running with the wind at my back and the sparse trees bending before the blast, and the lichen a grey blur amongst the snowberry bushes. When I glanced down, I saw that my legs were not the sturdy brown legs of a girl with chubby knees but were the long, fine, red legs of a horse, slender and tough with tendons, and ending in round black hooves.

Then I was in a river's boiling rapids, fighting for breath. My lungs burned. My heart was bursting. The smother of the river went over my head but suddenly I burst skywards, in the talons of a soaring Thunderbird. But when I looked upwards, the bird had the long, elegant red face of a horse.

And one more picture: I was crawling through a dark forest, rain beating upon me, my hands covered in mud. I was lost. The forest pressed around me, leaning closer, watching me like a lynx watching a hare before it leaps upon it and kills it with one bite to the throat. Closer and lower over me that dark forest leaned, all its trees listening to my heaving breath, my feeble heartbeat. And then, beneath my hands, in the soggy dark ground, I saw the tracks of the horse: those rounded hoof prints with the indented 'V' and I knew that I was saved, and rose to my feet and began to run alongside those tracks, the trees leaning away to let sky light pour over me.

The heat was waning in the sweat lodge. The words of the chant sank low, became simply the voices of myself and Charlotte, soft girl voices. Orchid coughed.

'Mighty Kicimanitow, we thank you for all your gifts,' I said simply, and then I lifted the flap of the door and let a curl of night air lick inside the lodge. Starlight shone on the poplars. 'Wait,' I said to Orchid as she crawled towards the door. I uncapped a small glass jar that I had bought at the Company store in York Factory, and dipped my finger into the soft grease inside.

'What is it?' Orchid asked as I rubbed it over her throat and upper chest, and on the straight bridge of her nose.

'It's an ointment I made last spring. I boiled the buds of the balsam poplar in bear's grease. It is good for colds and coughs. It is from the land that you call hostile. But the land gives us everything we need for food, for clothing, for making our boats and lodges, for our medicines.'

The smell of the sticky balsam buds filled the lodge; a smell containing spring sunshine on waves, the wild song of the geese returning north, and play-ful breezes rippling new grass. A smile hovered at the corners of my lips.

'I have brought you some other clothes,' I told Orchid as she crawled from the lodge behind me. 'Your white woman's clothes are not suited to this land.' Fumblingly, she pulled on the deerskin leggings that I had been keeping in my wooden chest, and over the top a flannel petticoat and then a flannel-lined gown falling only to her knees.

'I feel half naked,' she muttered anxiously. 'I have never revealed my limbs thus in public.'

After I had handed her a Hudson's Bay blanket to wrap around her shoulders, she slipped her feet into the moccasins that I had been beading for myself; I had noticed that our feet were almost the same size. The soles of Orchid's leather boots had been wet, then dried at a fire, so often that they had cracked wide open.

'I have been beastly,' she blurted suddenly into the darkness. 'Will you please forgive me?'

When we hugged, our grip around each other's shoulders was like the grip of women being pulled from water when they cannot swim.

'We are almost halfway to the Red River colony,' I said. 'You and your horse will soon be safely at your new home. Now please will you take Charlotte back to the camp? And also, take this Labrador Tea, and brew yourself a mug. It is for healing colds.'

'But where are you going?' she asked as I handed her the small pouch of dried leaves that I had been carrying in my fire bag, and that I had picked and dried on the tundra.

'I want to lie on the rock and look at the stars,' I replied. 'I will be back soon.'

175

I saw Charlotte slip her small, dark hand trustingly into Orchid's plump, pale one, and watched their dim figures slip into the hands of the trees before I turned and climbed the flat sheet of the rock. I lay on its hard surface and felt its old spirit press against me, filled with a strength that endured all weather, all seasons. Around me on the rock were the paintings that the ancestors had made: little figures of men and animals so that their spirits too surrounded me like a great company of travellers and wanderers, hunters and all those who came in need of healing.

Orchid would grow stronger now, I thought, but what about me? Was I still going to lie in the grip of my sadness about the past? And the grip of my worry about the future?

The sky began to curl like the petals of a flower.

The light grew stronger: pale pink and deep rose against the blackness. Great waves and ribbons of light swirled across the northern sky, folding, lashing, shimmering. The stars paled in comparison. Awe stroked a light finger across my skin, and my face stretched into a smile of joy. My mother's ghost was dancing with all the other spirits. Still the sky kept changing, the colours waxing and waning, swirling and crackling with the lights that the white men called the aurora borealis, the Northern Lights. My mother, I thought, was not lost but always with me; her good heart, filled with stern fairness, kindness and loyalty, was not gone. It was not a thing like a silver brooch that could be swept downstream but was something that could survive even death. And all her teachings were alive in me: how to snare a rabbit, how to bait a fish hook, how to cure a marten pelt, how to be a daughter with a good heart of my own.

And the Bear, I suddenly realised, the Bear had come to remind me of his promise. In the shaking tent ceremony in the Cree camp at York, the Bear spirit had said that horses knew how to find home. And so the stallion had done when he was chased away from camp by the bear and I went tracking after him. The stallion had circled around after the bear stopped to eat the elk carcass, and had found his way safely back to the tripmen's camp on the shores of Robinson Lake. It was to remind me of his promise that Bear had sent Foxfire running into the bush. 'Horses can find their way home.' I savoured the words, sweet as raspberries on my tongue, while the spirits danced overhead.

My horse *pawakan* was strong, I thought, for already I had survived starvation and adversity; already it had saved me from drowning. I must keep following the roar of the rivers, and the tracks of the horse, towards my new home in the west, the home that my father, Simon Mackenzie, would provide for Charlotte and me. The home that my mother would want me to have.

The sky began to fade and the wind rose, keening in the jack pines. The last of my sadness blew away in tatters, and I stood up, feeling the hot rush of my blood, and scrambled towards the camp, where I hoped Orchid was lying peacefully with her head on the pillow I had stuffed with down picked from bulrushes.

By the time we reached Norway House two days later, Orchid's nose had stopped running, and her cough had subsided into an occasional short bark. She had filled a whole piece of paper with a painting of the goldeye fish that Samuel Beaver had given us for supper. Around the fish, she had painted water lilies, goose grass, and muskrat reeds, while I began beading another pair of moccasins. The tripmen hurled the boats across the waters of Playgreen Lake towards where the fort lay hidden behind a swell of land. The red Hudson's Bay Company flag flapped atop its high pole, and the shoreline was strewn with canoes and other York boats, for this post was an important one where brigades converged from different river systems. From here, tripmen would travel far to the north and west along the Saskatchewan, the Red Deer, and the Bow rivers to take in the trade goods and bring out the furs.

Orchid was met by the chief factor, and escorted off to his house of whitewashed planks for an evening meal, but Charlotte and I tied Foxfire in a small barn and gave him hay to eat, and then went to use the woodstove in the labourers' kitchen. It was strange to be back inside a white man's palisade after so many weeks with nothing to look at but rocks and trees; strange to see the neat rows of tilled earth in the garden, and to hear the deep lowing of oxen in the pasture.

The tripmen's champions fought that night in the midst of a roaring mob, and then the men played their fiddles and danced their reels and jigs, growing wild on rum. Charlotte and I slept, at Orchid's insistence, in the small pantry room in one of the married officer's houses; the officer even had a small wooden bed placed there for us. Unused to sleeping in its narrow confines, I stirred early and, leaving Charlotte still sleeping with her dark lashes fluttering, crept outside. It was a morning of sharp sun and glittering frost; the sky like a washed stone. The fort's buildings were bright white boxes in the hard light, and the flanks of grazing oxen steamed in the warmth.

And there! *There!* What were they, drifting along by the far wall of the palisade, behind the cattle byres?

I narrowed my eyes in disbelief, shading them with one hand.

Yes! I gave a little jump for joy, as if I were in the middle of a dance and the drum was lifting me up. Then I hurried as fast as I could walk, my old moccasins skimming along the ground without a sound, until I was closer, closer, closer ... now they were only yards away, now only feet. They raised their heads from the grass and the sun shone in the long hair of their dark forelocks. I stood before them in my green tartan blanket and feasted my eyes.

Here was only the second horse I had ever seen in my life; a tall animal, though not as tall as Foxfire, and more heavily boned. His black coat was high-lighted with mink brown, his legs were sturdy and thick, his neck and back long and smoothly curved, his shoulders strong and sloping.

And here beside him was a small mare, her coat pale golden brown like a dried cedar frond, her legs lightly feathered with longer hair, her black mane so thick it covered her neck completely. Her short wide face tapered to a small muzzle with flapped nostrils, and her ears were short and filled with hair.

I stepped closer, inhaling their scent; they had the same sweet, light smell as Foxfire did and yet each of them smelled slightly differently. If I met all three horses in the dark, I thought, I would be able to tell them apart by smell alone. The black came closer, nuzzling my arm, lipping my empty hands. His muzzle was very soft, and his winter coat was growing in thick and long, blurring the sharp edges of the white marking on his forehead. I ran my hand along the crest of his neck while the mare rubbed her face against my shoulders.

I was so engrossed with the horses, and with the song I was singing to them, that I didn't hear him approach.

'*Bonjour, mademoiselle*. You are the one they talk about in the chief factor's house,' said a voice at my shoulder. I stopped singing abruptly and swung around to see a tall, lean man gazing at me from beneath greying brows. Above the black fabric of his priest's gown, his face was pale and lined. 'You are Amelia, the young woman who brings a Norfolk Trotter all the way from York Factory. C'*est incroyable*, incredible. You have handled *les chevaux* before?'

'No, the stallion is the first horse I ever saw. And now these horses are only the second and third ones.'

'Ah.' His gaze held mine and I wondered if he was like a Cree shaman, who could talk to spirits and understand a person's deepest needs, and whether he used a drum, and what words he chanted when he spoke to his Creator. Now he pulled an apple from a pocket in his robe, and pared it carefully into sections with a small knife, then gave me half of the pieces. Together we fed the horses, and the frothy juice of the apples ran out from their soft lips.

'This black *garçon* is a Canadian horse from the valley of a *grande* river who is called the St Lawrence. The ancestors of this horse came from the stables of a French king, Louis XIV. In the year 1665, he sent stallions and mares over the sea to New France.

'But now, this horse is carrying only me, a Jesuit priest, into the wilderness to talk to the Cree about the Almighty God.'

'You brought him by York boat?'

'*Non, non*. These we do not have. We journey by schooner on the Great Lakes, to Fort William at the top of Lake Superior. Then we walk all the paths through the forest. Nothing makes his heart tremble. He walks through snow as high as his belly, through rain, through thunderstorms. I pray to serve as well. He deserves more apple; do you agree? But one is all I have.'

As if understanding his master's words, the Canadian horse dropped his head and began to crop the frosted grass again.

'And this *petite* brown mare,' continued the priest, 'she carries my baggage upon her back and follows my black horse. She is an Ojibwa pony. You know these people?'

'They live in the thick forests far to the south of York, and build lodges covered in bark,' I said. 'They travel by birchbark canoe.'

'Yes, and by pony. I bought this mare at Lake of the Woods. Some say the ponies of the Ojibwa are fathered by the Canadian horses. But their mothers are the Spanish mustangs who run with the buffalo. The people of the Sioux nation catch and ride the mustangs. You have seen them, *non*?'

Excitement caught in my throat and I heard the galloping thunder of hooves, saw hundreds of legs flashing through yellow grass, felt the wind of the mustangs' passing.

'No,' I said. 'I haven't seen them yet.'

'I am Père Baptiste. Soon, I make my travels onwards to *habiter* amongst your people. But while we rest at Norway House, *mademoiselle*, you will ride my horses. Their – how do you say it? – their harnesses, remain in the barn where the Norfolk stallion rests.'

'Thank you, oh, thank you!' I cried but already the priest was turning away, his robes swinging, and leaving me with the horses. I smoothed the mare's face with my hands, then went with a skip to fetch their bridles.

Chapter 10

The black Canadian horse had a slow, steady stride; his large unshod hooves made a wonderful dull drumming on the pasture as I trotted him in circles. I had found a saddle for him in the byre; not a woman's side-saddle such as Orchid had for Foxfire, but a man's saddle with two stirrup irons that allowed me to sit astride the horse and use both legs to feel the horse's intentions before he began to swing away to the left or the right. He did not have Foxfire's springing stride, which made him float above the earth as though his hooves ran through the air. Instead, the slope of the Canadian's heavy shoulder rocked along, comfortable and solid, while his hoof beats throbbed in my chest like the voice of a huge drum made from the stretched hide of a bull moose.

After some time riding the black, I slipped the

saddle from him and set it atop the cedar rail of the pasture fence. Then I caught the little golden mare, and bridled her, and ran my hands over the wonderful thick hair inside her daintily pricked ears. Riding her bareback, I circled the pasture, feeling the short, staccato rhythm of her strides. Her small hooves tapped the earth, sharp and fast. My toes skimmed above the melting frost, and the mare's black forelock flew backwards over her bright eyes. She circled and spun, slippery as a wet log. When I was a little child at the bay, I used to try balancing on driftwood floating in the shallow water in the brief fleeting days of northern summer. I remembered now how the wood, licked sleek by waves and without bark, would twist and turn beneath the grip of my bare feet. This little mare was like that: it took all my balance and all my concentration to stay upright on her twisting back. 'Be one with your horse,' Orchid had told me. 'Let your centre of balance sink down into the base of your spine, and always follow the horse's movements.'

Should I canter her? I had never cantered Foxfire, for there had never been stretches of ground large enough along the riverbank portages or amongst the trees when we made our evening camps. Orchid had told me though about the gaits of a horse: the walk in four-beat time, the trot in two-beat, the canter and the gallop in three-beat. She had sketched little pictures in the margins of her painting paper, showing me how the legs of a horse move differently at each speed.

'There is a heated debate,' she said, 'about whether there is a moment of suspension at the canter, when all four of a horse's hooves are off the ground and he is, for a moment, like a bird. But I am sure this must be true, for anyone who has ridden to hounds over the flat fields of Norfolk will tell you that it is like flying.'

Now I glanced down at the ground; it would not be so far to fall if I came off the Ojibwa mare. I bit my bottom lip with concentration, sat straight and felt my weight sink down to the base of my spine, felt my hands light yet strong on the reins, and nudged the mare's sides with my heels. Instantly, she surged forward in a new rhythm, I felt her back rounded beneath me, and the wonderful bounce of her canter. This was unlike anything I had ever experienced before! Around the field we flew, her black hooves a blur of sound, her body tight with energy like the spring of the pocket watch that Ronald McTavish had once taken apart and shown to me. Maybe this cantering was a little like being in a canoe and heading into the waves, feeling the canoe lift and glide over, lift and glide over. Or maybe it was like a gusty wind rushing through a thick tree so that the foliage bunched and swept forward, then subsided; bunched and swept forward again in the stream of the wind.

I laughed aloud as I rode, cantering around and

around that pasture, dodging rocks and oxen, and feeling the crisp air pour into my open mouth while sunshine glinted in the curve of the mare's dark mane.

Suddenly, I noticed a small group of figures against the far rails of the pasture. I pulled on the reins, slowing the mare into a trot and then a walk, squinting my eyes against the brightness. Charlotte was balanced on the top rail, beside the Canadian horse's saddle, and swinging her legs in their caribou leggings. Beside her stood Orchid, her long hair hanging down her back in a single braid now, instead of bundled on top of her head in a bun and pierced through with pins. And beside Orchid stood a man; I narrowed my eyes in disbelief, for beside Orchid stood – Angus, with his watery blue eyes and his pale hair the colour of oat straw! What was he doing here; was his *pawakan* spirit struggling against mine, sending his evil medicine against these horses I'd been riding? I didn't like to see him there so close to Charlotte; to note how his arms, resting atop the rail, almost touched her chubby knees, and how Orchid laughed at something he said, tilting her face to the sun. The striped cat curled around Angus's legs.

I dropped my gaze as I rode closer, then slid from the mare with my back turned to the group and smoothed my hand over her neck and face to hide my confusion. 'Thank you, golden sister,' I whispered into the flicker of her furry ears. She pressed her muzzle into my hand for a fleeting moment, so that I felt its softness, before she dropped her head and began to graze, drifting away towards her black companion whose ancestors had once belonged to the great chief of the French nation.

At last, I turned to face everyone, my eyes flying first to my little sister but she appeared unharmed, her wide eyes peaceful and contented.

'Foxfire will be growing jealous in the byre,' Orchid teased me and, as though he had heard her voice, the stallion gave a ringing neigh from inside the byre's stout wall of whitewashed planks.

'Aye, a horse lover, just like your father before you,' commented Angus softly. My whole body flinched with shock as though those words were the flick of a rawhide ox whip. I raised my eyes to Angus's gaze and noticed how pale he looked today, his face drawn with lines and one side of it mottled with a blue bruise; I supposed he had been involved in the brigade fighting the previous night. A twitch, like a shiver, ran over his skin as I stared at him, and one corner of his mouth jerked and then was still again.

'My father?' I whispered. I cleared my throat and spoke more loudly. 'You knew my father?'

'Aye. Mrs Spencer says you're Amelia Otterchild Mackenzie. If so, I knew your father, Simon. 'Twas a long time ago in Pembina, south of the Red River colony. He was for ever talking about you, his babe, and your mother, Mary. Always wondering what had become of you, when you would join him.'

I stood riveted to the spot as though my feet had grown roots and sent them down into the dry ground. The mare's bridle dangled from one hand and the sun beat hot upon my bare head.

'My father,' I said wonderingly; it seemed to be all I could say, although questions rolled around in my mouth, so many questions that they were all trapped and bunched up like caribou driven into spruce corrals by hunters.

'Simon Mackenzie could ride any horse that was ever foaled,' Angus said, and even now, after all these years, his voice was tinged with admiration. 'He had a stallion called Lightfoot, a buffalo runner. And he could shoot anything that moved. He could shoot a man's whiskers off and never mark his chin.'

'But what happened?' I cried, twisting the mare's bridle in a fierce grip, a buckle digging into my palm. 'What happened to my father?'

'Ah, lass, 'twas a long time ago. I dinna know what happened to him. I've been all over the north since then, all over the Mackenzie and the Athabasca. 'Tis many seasons since I've been to the Red River.'

'But why didn't he come back to find us?' I persisted. 'My mother waited many moons for him to return!'

Sweat broke out over Angus's face, and the corner of his mouth jerked again, a spasm that stretched the right side of his face upwards so that his eyes squinted. The tip of his tongue flickered out to catch the drool that ran from one corner of his mouth. His glance flew to Orchid and she took him by the arm.

'Enough,' she said sternly. 'We must keep our appointment with Doctor Munroe. Amelia,' she continued, her gaze steady on my face, 'Angus is not well; the celebrations of last evening have strained his nervous constitution. I have spoken to the good Scottish doctor here and he has agreed to see Angus this morning. Will you please see to Foxfire's care? They say that we will not depart for Lake Winnipeg until tomorrow for there are several boats that need repairs. You might like to exercise Foxfire this afternoon; I am told there is a pathway running along the shoreline for several miles and you may ride upon it. Come, Angus.'

'But – but wait! But, my father –' I stood with my mouth gaping, foolish as a hooked fish, as Orchid and Angus moved away across the grass in the direction of the officers' wooden dwellings clustered around the chief factor's house.

'Amelia. Amelia?'

Gradually, I focused on Charlotte's pleading eyes. I laid my arms along the rail beside her and rested my head upon them, and felt her small hands stroking my hair and patting my back consolingly. My head spun. Angus had once known Simon Mckenzie. All this time, travelling three hundred miles of wild rivers, I had been in the same brigade as a man who had once spoken to my father, who had watched him ride, who had known his horse, who had seen him – a crack shot, as Betty Goose Wing had said – fire a gun. All this time, and I had not known of it. All this time pining for some proof that my father was a real man and not merely a story. Angus could have reassured me for, in his mind, my father galloped through the grasslands, shooting the buffalo on a horse named Lightfoot. Tears blurred in my eyes.

But perhaps it was a trick? And what if Angus had used sorcery against my father, had somehow harmed him? Was this the reason that my father had disappeared, had abandoned us? Was he dead these many years, crushed beneath a falling horse and the weight of the half-blood shaman's evil medicine? Perhaps he had been burned when the barrel of his gun exploded, the powder igniting inside it, covering my father with black soot, shredding the sleeve of his robe, searing his flesh from the bone so that it turned putrid. Or perhaps he had died in the grass, gored by the savage curved horns of a great bull buffalo. There were many ways that a man might die and in my mind now my father died many times over while pain rushed through me like an incoming tide.

What more might Angus know of my father but had not admitted?

Charlotte's hand patted my back faster. 'Don't cry, Amelia,' she said. 'You still have me,' and she used the tickling ends of her braids to wipe my cheeks. I hugged her, pressing my face into the familiar smoky smell of her tartan shawl, her deerskin robe with its beaded patterns against my face. For her sake, I must be strong. I wiped my eyes with the corner of her shawl, and smiled, although her brass bracelets glittered in my tearful eyes and her heart-shaped face was a blur. 'Perhaps I could teach you to ride on this little golden mare,' I offered. 'She too is a long way from her home.'

Charlotte's solemn face lit up with the smile that had brought softness into my mother's life. 'Oh yes!' she cried, clapping her palms together, but still my eyes were drawn away to where, against the glitter of Playgreen Lake, the short bustling figure of Orchid, and the lanky shambling figure of Angus, dwindled and disappeared around the corner of a building.

All day the horses soothed my troubled spirit. I stroked my palms over the soft thickening of their coats, and lost myself in the calm depths of their eyes, and filled my nostrils with their sweetness. I hefted Charlotte on to the golden mare and led her around the pasture, then allowed her to ride alone while I went ahead on the Canadian. We braided their black manes and tails as though they were Cree women getting ready to attend a dance; Charlotte took the beads from her own hair and braided them into the mare's mane.

Afterwards I led Foxfire from the byre and he flung up his head at the sight of the two other horses in the pasture, and almost lifted my feet from the ground as he trotted to and fro, springing over the grass in his excitement and whinnying high and wild, calling to those other horses. Inside the pasture, they squealed and trotted back and forth along the rail with their tails raised and necks arched. At last, I swung on to the stallion from a rock, and pulled his head around, sending him bounding over the grass in his floating trot, and kept him to it for several miles along the shore of the lake, rushing through sunlight and dark shadow, flashing past naked little boys catching goldeye, and sending chattering chipmunks fleeing up tree trunks.

Fa-ther, fa-ther, fa-ther. Foxfire's pounding hoof beats kept rhythm with my heart as it leaped high into my throat and fell heavily into my stomach with the horse's long strides. On a straight stretch of the narrow trail, I squeezed my legs around the barrel of his ribs and he surged away from under me; his canter was not the rocking tilt of the mare's canter but was a thing of flight and power, a great sweeping through the speckled light, a soaring rush like wind and waves through the cedar-scented forest. In the headlong plunge even my father's name was obliterated and I became conscious only of speed; we were one creature, an eagle cleaving the sky, a porpoise leaping through the waves.

Later, after feeding Foxfire in the byre and rubbing him down, I went to find Angus but could find neither him nor Orchid, who was dining again in the factor's house. In the morning, though, as soon as I had tied

Foxfire into his stall on our York boat, Orchid came aboard, carried on Samuel Beaver's back.

'I need to know about Angus and my father!' I said, gripping her arm in my urgency. 'Please, Orchid, what is happening?'

Orchid seated herself on her bench, smoothing the merino gown I had given her down over her leggings, and flicking the end of her long golden braid over her shoulders.

She had given up wearing her sun bonnet and a flush of colour had stained her pale cheeks.

'The tripman, Angus, has a feverish condition of the brain,' she said. 'He was in distress on our first evening at Norway House; this much I saw when I met him on my evening stroll. Later, at dinner, I arranged with Doctor Munroe that he should assess Angus the following morning. First, however, I wanted to make sure that Foxfire was adequately stabled. That was when I saw you riding the Jesuit's horses. As we watched you, Angus asked who you were, and when I told him your name he responded that he had once known your father, as he later told you himself.'

'But I need to know more!' I released Orchid's arm as Pierre carried Eva through the shallows and lifted her over the gunwale. She seated herself beside Orchid after flashing Pierre a glance from under fluttering black lashes. He winked in return, pulled himself aboard, and stepped past us to take up the long steering oar. With a heave and a shout, our boat was pushed into deeper water, and already Norway House fort was hidden from view behind the swell of land.

'What else do you know?' I asked Orchid.

'Angus is no longer rowing with this brigade, for the doctor judged him too unwell for the rigours of the journey,' she said.

'Not with us? But – but I need to talk to him – I need to ask him more about my father!'

Orchid shook her head. 'It will not be possible. He has a nervous condition that causes convulsions.'

'He is turning Witiko. His heart is turning to ice,' I said. 'He has eaten human flesh in a starving moon, or been visited by the Witiko in his vision quest, or maybe was predestined to become a sorcerer.'

Orchid stared at me with her bright blue gaze as sharp as a knife blade, but after a moment she laughed. 'What superstitious stories,' she said, bending over to pull her sketching paper from her leather satchel. 'The poor man is simply ill.' She selected a pencil and began to sketch a bunch of feathers she had collected onshore: a grey jay's wing feather, a down feather from a goose breast.

'There was such a man of my acquaintance in Norfolk. He did no one any harm, and was perfectly sane between his periods of brain fever.'

'He uses hunting medicine to master his cat.'

Orchid stared for a moment, looking puzzled.

'Ah! In the pouch!' she realised, and began to smile. 'No, it is merely a dried plant, called catnip. Its smell is pleasurable to cats, and in England it is often grown in gardens.'

I pressed my lips together in frustration, and turned my face southwards, towards the mighty sheet of Lake Winnipeg that stretched ahead of us for about three hundred miles. The wind lifted the curls that escaped from Orchid's braid, and blew them back over her shoulders, and sent the stallion's red mane flickering around his neck. The men, rested now, were in high spirits. They broke into song as the sky suddenly stretched huge above us and the shore-lines fell away; the mighty lake shimmered from horizon to horizon, a heaving mass of waves where cloud reflections floated and fish jumped. I felt the open space and the wind swirl round me like a loud shout; it was like being home on the bay again and, despite my troubled thoughts, a smile lifted the corners of my mouth as my eyes ran to and fro over that expanse of fresh water.

When we met another brigade, the tripmen shouted challenges across the water and the boats were lined up alongside each other, the men whooping and yelling insults. Then, on a signal, oars dug into the water and the boats surged forward, racing south while arms and backs strained and the waves sloshed against our hull with the speed of our passage. On the following day, the wind swung into the north and the men raised the canvas sails, flapping at first so that Foxfire snorted nervously and shied, banging his hooves against the sides of his stall. As the sail filled with wind and grew taut, the flapping ceased and the stallion stilled again. Now the men lay on their backs on the benches or propped themselves against the bales of trade goods, smoking their pipes or sleeping, or telling stories about bear attacks and gambling debts. Eva moved to sit in the stern with Pierre, repairing a tear in his jacket with a deer's sinew, and talking to him in a low tone that the wind whipped away so that only he knew what he smiled about, twisting his earrings while he listened. I began to embroider the toe of the second of my pair of new moccasins, threading my needle through the blue beads. *Fa-ther*, the waves slapped against the hull. *Light-foot. Fa-ther*.

Day after day we travelled southwards on that expanse, the wind and the sunlight always pressing against us, the sky a vast bowl overhead. The smell of algae and pipe tobacco filled my nostrils while gulls slipstreamed overhead with their harsh, keening cries. The men fished as we travelled. In the evenings we camped onshore and fried their catches in flat pans over the fire and ate them with our bannock and our drink of weak tea made with sugar but no milk.

One morning, when we were only – so Pierre said – about twenty miles north of the lake's end and the mouth of the Red River, we awoke early to a wind blowing from the west. Its gusts lifted the shallow lake into heaving waves, thick and soupy with mud from the bottom. Briefly, the men conferred about remaining in camp until the weather improved, but they were anxious to reach the Red River and decided to set sail despite the squall. As our boat bashed southwards in the cresting waves, the men reefed the straining sail to make its canvas surface smaller. Still the wind rose. Eventually, the men took the sail down and ran out the oars. The boat rocked and jumped like a frightened horse itself so that Foxfire scrabbled in his stall, sliding, shifting. He strained for purchase on the tilting boards, and his eyes rolled white. Orchid and I balanced beside him, flung to and fro, gripping his halter and trying to soothe him. Waves splashed over the gunwales, soaking my moccasins and leggings, dashing against the stallion's red flanks so that he shied and flinched in fear, even rearing half up against the rope that held him. Soon, he was fetlock deep in water.

'We must get ashore!' Orchid cried commandingly to Pierre.

'*Oui, j'y vais.*' He swung his full weight upon the creaking oar, and the boat swung slowly into the wind so that we were heading straight into the waves, our bow swinging up, up, up into the scudding clouds and then plunging down, down, down into the next wall of rushing water. White crests formed on the waves, strangely pale in the yellow haze, and streaks of foam flew past. The wind blew hot and then cold, sending chills over me even as I broke into a sweat, struggling with the terrified horse.

'If we capsize, he will swim!' Orchid reminded me.

'But we are still far from shore!' I worried, then asked the question that I had been wondering for many days. 'Do all horses – like the water – as much?'

'Some are frightened of it! Some indifferent!' she shouted over the wind and the stallion's tossing neck. 'Foxfire learned to swim young – in the marshes of the Norfolk Broads. He has always – loved water!'

The shoreline came closer, low and flat, covered with a mixture of coniferous and deciduous trees including elm and ash. We cleared a headland to see, on its far side, a thin strip of sandy beach. 'Make for there!' the bows man cried and the men bent, wind-torn and desperate, over the oars. Their tamarack shafts groaned in the wooden oarlocks, and the boat's hull creaked and moaned as the waves twisted it. As we ran into the lee of the shore, the wind and waves subsided slightly. Gazing towards land, I noticed the tipis, covered in hides and in sheets of pale bark, and huddled amongst the trees a few hundred yards back from the beach.

'A camp!' I cried, and around me the men strained to see it. Smoke rising from fires inside the tipis was snatched away in the wind. Now I saw figures moving, and as we came closer I heard the shrieking laughter of children playing in the shallows and jumping the waves.

'It is a camp of the Métis, the half-bloods,' Pierre said behind me. 'They trade, bringing goods from Red River *peut-être*. Here they look for the Salteaux and the Cree who trap the beavers and muskrats. Here, west of Lake Winnipeg, are many swamps.'

In the shallows, the men jumped overboard and began to unload the York boats while the Métis people gathered onshore, watching us curiously. The women's brilliantly coloured calico dresses and the men's neckerchiefs were like flags in the wind. Suddenly, the stallion flung up his head and gave a shrill neigh; when I followed the line of his gaze, I glimpsed horses and oxen inside the circle formed by wooden carts with two high wheels and platforms of boards.

Samuel and another man lowered the tamarack planks into the sand in the shallows with a splash, then struggled to rest their other ends on the boat's heaving gunwale while I untied Foxfire.

'He will never walk down those,' one of the men objected, standing thigh deep in water as waves sloshed up to his waist.

'Hold the boat!' the bows man yelled. 'HOLD her steady, I said!'

The crew, all down in the water, threw their shoulders against the hull, and Pierre strained at the oar as the boat rocked in the wash of waves. I gripped the stallion's lead rope with white knuckles. 'Walk on, heart of a bear,' I crooned. 'Walk on now.'

The horse pawed at the gunwale. A wave slapped the hull and flew upwards, splattering the stallion's chest so that he snorted and flung up his head. I stepped on to a slick plank and slid one foot along it.

'*Attention!*' hollered Pierre above and behind me with a note of alarm, and simultaneously I felt the rush and the power of the stallion as he leaped over the gunwale. In a blur he was past me, his hooves ringing once on the planks before he jumped off them. I flew through the air, still gripping the rope, and the water hit me with a warm slap. My mouth filled with sand. Foxfire surged shorewards, his feet finding the sandy bottom and heaving him upwards on to the beach where I stumbled, dripping but unhurt, into the circle of incredulous Métis faces. Their hubbub of voices rose into the air as they cried and exclaimed over the stallion's huge size and strength, over his colour, over his leap from the boat, and as other voices asked after my well-being in a mixture of English, French, and a tongue that sounded like Cree and yet that I couldn't understand. Women rubbed my arms and chafed my hands in their own, and offered me hot rabbit soup with berries, and a warm fire.

'Soon,' I agreed over and over. 'Soon, but first I must care for the horse.'

A voice spoke at my shoulder in the Cree that I couldn't understand.

I swung around. And there he was, standing on

the pale beach in the hot brassy light of that wild morning: the most beautiful young man I had ever seen. A flush ran over my face and my eyes fell down the length of the stallion's legs to where his hooves pressed into the broken shells.

'Do you need help?' he repeated, this time in English.

'I am fine.'

'This horse is yours?'

I shook my head. 'No, he belongs to the white woman who travels with us. But I take care of him.'

'I am Gabriel Gunner. I have mustangs.'

My eyes rose slowly, rose over the restless shift of the stallion's shoulder, and glanced at last at the young man's face. It was all smooth brown skin and hard planes. His black eyes seemed to read every mile that I had travelled to reach this moment. Those eyes were filled with the silence of forests, the flare of campfires. They were framed by loose strands of hair, threaded through brass pipes and dentalia shells, and by two long braids. These hung down the front of his fringed buckskin coat; the fringes were decorated with orange and yellow beads, and the fire pouch hanging over his shoulder was bright with yellow beaded flowers. Hot gusts of wind lifted the black hair on his forehead, and the fringes of the red woven sash knotted at his waist.

A smile tugged the corners of his wide mouth.

'You have mustangs?' my small voice asked at last.

'They are here, grazing while my little brother keeps guard. Come, bring your red stallion and tie him up, then I will show you.'

The crowd of Métis parted as we moved up the shingle slope; children ran ahead and behind, laughing. When I glanced back, I saw that Charlotte and Orchid were already seated on the beach on a flapping blanket spread beside the piles of trade goods. Samuel Beaver leaned into the wind, bringing Orchid a handful of coloured stones to sketch later, whenever the storm blew itself out. The other tripmen used ropes and harnesses, as though they were sled dogs, to drag the York boats higher on to the shore. Orchid caught my glance and waved cheerfully.

I turned around then and stepped from the beach on to the grass, leading Foxfire and following the tall, lithe wiriness of the beautiful Gabriel Gunner, owner of mustangs.

Chapter 11

I stood still at the edge of a natural clearing awash in fine yellow grass and surrounded by thrashing poplar trees. Sucking in a mouthful of windy air, I held it in my chest. A smile of delight stretched my cheeks as I gazed at Gabriel's two grazing mustangs. Each wore a black halter of braided rope, and the lead line of each one was tied to a foreleg so that the horses were hobbled. At our approach, they tossed up their heads as far as they were able to, and gazed at us from beneath the beaded leather fringes that hung over their eyes. A nicker of welcome fluttered their black nostrils.

When Kicimanitow made these horses, I thought, *he shaped them from brown soil. Then he dipped them in wild golden honey, and then stood them by a smoking fire until a drift of mottled grey had smudged itself over their brown and honey hides.*

I let my breath out again in slow wonder.

'They are called Hard Twist and Smoke Eyes,' said Gabriel, motionless at my shoulder.

'What is their colour called?'

'Grulla,' he replied. 'It is a word from the Spanish nation.'

'Are all mustangs this colour?'

'No, a mustang can be any colour at all: brown, black, white. Maybe spotted or piebald. Buckskin. Sorrel or dappled.'

I took a step closer to Gabriel's horses, my eyes running over their compact, muscular bodies. They were smaller than Foxfire, sinewy and strong. Their hard black hooves were unshod and their long black manes and tails were luxurious, and tangled in the wind's snarl.

'This is the gelding, Hard Twist,' said Gabriel, stepping to the larger of the two mustangs and running the flat of his palm down the horse's face. 'This other is the mare, Smoke Eyes. They are brother and sister.'

I stood at the mare's shoulder and let her sniff me; her black muzzle gave my arm a gentle nudge then ran across my shoulder where she breathed gustily into my hair. Her soft lips twitched against my cheek and a giggle burst from me. Down the front of her face ran a thin wavering line of white, like the foam on a wave's crest, and between her nostrils she had a tiny white mark, shaped like a fire flint. I laid my forehead against hers, and felt the softness and the wildness of her spirit.

'She will always be your friend now,' Gabriel said, sounding surprised. 'She has never laid her face against anyone's chest before, except mine.'

I dropped my glance from Gabriel's intent gaze, and fingered the halter's braided straps. 'What is this made from?'

'Woven buffalo hair. And these fringes hanging from the band across her forehead keep the flies out of her eyes.'

I nodded, and ran my hands all over that mare, getting to know her; long after I had travelled on I wanted to be able to remember the hard bones of her black knees, the grey dapple of her belly, the golden flush on her flanks. I wanted to remember the thin, wavering whiteness of her facial pattern, the tight bend of her hocks, and the darkness of her eyes where fire smouldered, like flames beneath the softness of ashes. 'Smoke Eyes,' I whispered into the heavy fringing of her short, swivelling ears.

A sudden nudge against my shoulder made me straighten and turn; the gelding had stepped forward and pushed his muzzle against me. 'He is jealous.' Gabriel laughed. 'You need to love him too.'

I stroked my hand along the crest of Hard Twist's shaggy neck, over his low withers, down the slope of his croup. When the mare crowded in close, the gelding laid back his ears and thrust his nose towards her so that she stepped away again. 'He's the captain and makes the rules,' Gabriel said with a grin.

I glanced up in surprise. 'I have only spent much time with one horse. I don't know how they talk to each other.'

'Watch these two. They talk to each other all day long with their ears and their heads, with their bodies. Everything a horse does has a meaning – a stamp, a snort, a twitch, a sideways look. In a herd, there is a lead mare who decides where the herd will wander, where it will graze. And there is a stallion who guards the rear from attack by wildcats. He rounds up the stragglers. And all the horses in the herd have more or less power than one another.'

I had thought myself clever until now, clever because I knew how to make the big red stallion contented, how to care for him according to Orchid's instructions. Now I began to see that I knew nothing much about horses, perhaps only a tiny little pinch of everything that this smiling Métis knew. I didn't even understand where all the horses in the grasslands had come from.

'Did you buy your horses from a man of the Spanish nation?' I asked.

'No, they are from my father's herd. The Spanish came a very long time ago, across the ocean. Their country is to the south of where the Scotsmen come from, further south than the land of the French. They sent their warriors across the sea. These men brought their horses with them, many head of horses. But gradually the horses escaped, or were stolen or traded for, and gradually they spread northwards over the land. Those horses were like a flood of water, always on the move, covering the grasslands. They grew strong and tough and wild; the mares dropped many foals. Then the nations of the grassland people began to catch them and ride them. It was like being given wings! The young warriors could fight and steal over a great territory, running fast, running hard!

'The Comanche of the south had them, then their kinsmen the Shoshone to the north. The horses came east with the Mountain Crow and the River Crow. There was no name for horses in the languages of the nations; the Lakota called them Holy Dog. The Siksika called them Elk Dog. The Assiniboine called them Big Dog. In Cree too they are called *mistatim*, Big Dog. They are a sacred animal to all the peoples of the horse.'

I watched Gabriel while he talked; heard how passion fired his voice so that it soared and sang. Delight gleamed in the dark planes of his face. Even then, behind that passion and delight, I felt his stillness; the thing that attracted me to him, the place in him that contained the sure strength of the land, the trees, the sky and snow and rocks and grass. The animals.

'Your father breeds horses?'

'He freights for the Company, running brigades

of carts far north every summer, taking supplies from Red River up to Fort Carlton on the prairie trails. And my brothers go with him, trading along the way with the Assiniboine and Cree, even sometimes with the Blackfoot. My father has many horses, and many oxen.'

'Are you a trader too?'

'No, I'm a scout. I ride sometimes to Carlton, other times on the buffalo hunts in the south, in the land of the Sioux nation. The Sioux are great horse breeders. They raid our camps, stealing horses even when they are hobbled and guarded. We call it the war road, the trail leading south from the Red River colony into the land of the Sioux nation. When I'm scouting on a buffalo hunt, I ride my horse to and fro at a gallop as a signal I've found a buffalo herd. But if I have sighted a Sioux camp, or one of their raiding parties, I throw handfuls of dust into the air as a sign to those following behind.'

'What do you scout for here, on the shores of Lake Winnipeg?' I asked.

'For Cree and Salteaux camps so that the Métis traders I am with can trade for beaver and muskrat pelts. And when we are not close to the lake shore, I search for water for our oxen and horses, and also for buffalo. Both these horses of mine are buffalo runners, trained to the hunt. When they sight a herd, they will run after it and into it at a flat gallop. They will twist and turn amongst the cows by the touch of my knees alone. This leaves my hands free for loading my gun with powder. I carry the lead shot in my mouth, and spit the balls down the muzzle to reload.'

As he talked, I could feel a great door opening up. It was as though I had been living inside a smoky lodge and then a hand lifted the wide skin flap away from the entrance and outside I glimpsed a new world, a place filled with wonders and about which I knew nothing.

'I don't even know what these flowers are called!' I blurted out, staring at the beaded patterns on Gabriel's buckskin coat.

A cloud of puzzlement crossed his eyes, then he laughed. 'Flowers! I thought we were talking about buffalo running.'

'There is so much I know nothing about,' I mumbled in embarrassment, my cheeks flushing.

'These yellow ones are buffalo beans,' Gabriel said, his strong, callused fingers tracing the lines of flowers that edged the border of the beadwork. 'These pink flowers are wild roses. These other yellow ones, on my fire pouch, are sunflowers.'

My gaze skittered over his pouch as he held it up and I nodded mutely, still feeling foolish. But when my gaze flickered to his face, his eyes held no trace of laughter.

'What you have done is as brave as the deed of a warrior,' he said. 'You are far from home, from the lodges of your people. Are any of your kin with you?'

Suddenly, words began to jostle and tumble over each other in their eagerness to share with Gabriel the stories of all my moons: the birth of Charlotte Bright Eyes whom I loved like my own life, the white fathers who deserted us, the ghost of my mother walking the starry wolf road, the blizzards of the starving winter, the red stallion whom I also loved and must soon be parted from when Orchid gave him to his true owner, a white stranger in the Company's stone fort on the Red River.

'He is –' I stopped. I had almost said that the red stallion was my *pawakan*. Then I remembered not to speak this secret to this young man who was also a stranger, even though his eyes soaked in my words like dry ground soaking up water.

'Foxfire is dear to me,' I amended. 'I have – horses are – I have a special connection to them.'

'Amongst the Plains Cree, youth may dream of horses on their vision quests,' Gabriel said. He was a person who could hear buffalo far out on the plains in the silence of a gopher hole, and the silence of an enemy in the pause between two notes of a bird's song, and now he had heard the words that I had not spoken.

'Amongst the Métis, horses are precious. They are a man's wealth, and his status. Without them, how could we run the buffalo? We sell the buffalo meat and the pemmican to the Company to feed its clerks, traders, and tripmen. Without horses, how could we

211

travel the land, trading with the tribes? Horses are as good as money; you can always sell or trade them. Chiefs can get two horses for one daughter in marriage. Amongst my people on the White Horse Plain, west of the Red River, a good horse is the best gift that you can give to another person. The very best gift.

'Listen, for one good buffalo-running mare, my father will trade over twenty yards of cloth, several shirts, a few pounds of tea and tobacco, some shot and gunpowder, a few good knives, and he'll even throw in some thread and some gunflints. He knows she will repay it all with buffalo skins and fine foals.'

'Why aren't you training and trading horses instead of being a scout?' I asked.

'For scouting, I am well paid in furs or trade goods. I am saving up. Soon, the white men plan to begin building a new fort to the west in the valley of the Qu'Appelle River. One of my uncles is a Company horsekeeper. He's going to ask the Company to hire me for this new fort in the Qu'Appelle valley, and there I will be a horsekeeper too, breaking and train-ing the Company's herd. One day, I will use my money to buy land, and will have my own herds of horses and cattle.'

I thought about this for a few minutes. Gabriel's skin and eyes were as dark as any Swampy Cree's, and his black hair was worn like Cree hair, its long braids filled with shells and brass pipes. But he talked like a white man; the people of the land knew that no one could own the land, or buy and sell it. The land was our mother, and we were part of it. Only white men thought you could treat the land like a trade good, to purchase or pass on. Perhaps, I thought, all the half-blood Métis were like me, they were looking for where to put each one of their two feet. Perhaps Gabriel Gunner and I had this in common.

The mustangs had drifted away as we talked, and were ripping at the dead yellow stems of the fine grass while the gusty wind flattened their tails between their hind legs or streamed the black hair out sideways.

'Two days ago we found a small herd of buffalo,' Gabriel said. 'We killed plenty. The women in the traders' camp are drying and cooking all the meat and we will not move on yet. The men from the York boats will sit all day around our fires, waiting for the wind to drop. Would you like to ride Smoke Eyes?'

'Yes!'

Gabriel whistled piercing and sweet, and a boy of about eight suddenly jumped down from where he'd been sitting in the forks of an oak tree, hidden by the thick foliage of coppery leaves.

'Hey,' said Gabriel, 'let's fetch the horse gear!' and the boy shot off like a flushed hare, a grin lighting his face.

'But the stallion –'

'He will be fine where we left him, tied to a cart.

I'll tell my brother to guard him and bring him water,' Gabriel replied before striding after the young boy in the direction of the camp.

When they returned, they were carrying two objects of leather and beadwork, and the trailing thongs of bridles and reins. Gabriel had a gun in one hand.

'You will have to ride with a man's saddle,' Gabriel said.

'Métis women do not ride astride, but side-saddle like white women?'

He gave me a baffled look. 'Of course women ride astride. But their saddles have frames of wood or buffalo bone, and this forms a horn at the front and a cantle at the back. They can hang their babies' cradle-boards from these frames and ride with them.'

As he talked, he spread a hide over the back of Smoke Eyes. 'This is buffalo,' he said, smoothing the hide so that it lay unwrinkled with its mass of dark brown, curly hair uppermost. On top of this he hefted one of the leather objects.

'This is a saddle?' I examined it in surprise, for it was nothing like the stiff heavy side-saddle that Orchid owned for Foxfire, nor like the saddle that the Jesuit priest had owned for his black Canadian gelding. This Métis saddle was of soft rawhide that lay flat upon the buffalo skin blanket. An embroidered roll formed the front and the back of the saddle.

'Stuffed with buffalo hair,' explained Gabriel.

'These flowers embroidered here? These are fire-weed.' He flashed me a grin.

'Who embroiders all these flowers for you?' I asked, and lowered my eyes to hide my twinge of uncertainty.

'I have a home filled with sisters. Some of the tribes call us Métis the Beaded Flower People because of the needle skills of our women.'

Again, I felt that door flap lifting on my smoky lodge; outside it I glimpsed the flowers of the great grasslands waving and blooming around the legs of the running mustangs, the thundering buffalo. I too had good skills with a needle, and the men at York Factory had often asked me to embroider their moccasins with hearts and thistles, those patterns dear to their memories. But now, I could learn to name the flowers of the grasslands, and to sew them into my beadwork; already, I could see pink roses blooming on the smoked moose hide that Betty Goose Wing had given me for Charlotte's new robe. And even – yes! – I would embroider little red and yellow horses running amongst the flowers.

'But why is this a man's saddle?' I asked, as Gabriel slid the rawhide girth strap through a bone ring and pulled it tight.

'On her saddle, a women must be able to carry babies. But a man must be able to fight from horse-back with a gun, and so he uses a flat saddle without a frame. In this, he can bend over low and flat against his horse's shoulders and neck as it gallops. He can fire his gun beneath the horse's neck, or from along the neck. It's a good skill to have when you ride south on the war road to find the Sioux nation.'

He stooped and picked up a bridle from the grass, and slipped it over the mare's head. It too was lavishly decorated with a beaded pattern of fireweed and silver lines; the beadwork ran up the cheek pieces lying flat on each side of the mare's face, and across the brow band. Tassels of orange ribbons hung from the brow band, and were threaded through tin cones that chimed slightly as the mare shook her head. For a bit, Gabriel used a rope of buffalo hair, and he knotted it around the mare's lower jaw.

Then he handed me the reins, and suddenly I stopped worrying about all the things of which I was ignorant, and remembered instead that I was a girl who knew how to ride a horse. I nudged the toe of my moccasin into the bent wooden stirrup hanging on its rawhide strip, and swung up into the saddle. The mare's ears flickered ahead of me, tipped with black, flushed with gold. The wind roared overhead, and the mare jumped sideways, a step like a dance step, as though the drumming heartbeat of mother earth was tickling the bottoms of her feet. Gabriel bent against the gelding, tightening his girth. In a moment he too was mounted, the fringes on Hard Twist's bridle streaming around the gelding's head in the wind.

'Goodbye!' Gabriel shouted, but his little brother had already vanished into the trees, heading back to camp.

Gabriel nudged his moccasins into the gelding's sides and the horse leaped away into the trees with the mare hard upon his heels. Her wiry strength gathered under me. We dodged and wove through the roaring forest, crossing small clearings of withered grass, while oak and maple and elm leaves flew around us, plastering themselves momentarily against our chests or faces before being carried on in the blast. Wind filled my mouth, rushed down into my chest, hot and then cold. It stung my watering eyes. It sang in my ears, and my heart thumped.

The horses were wild with the wind. Tightening their jaws around the buffalo rope, they leaped over fallen limbs, feinted around tree trunks. Their eyes rolled white. They dodged as though bullets were pelting them, as though underground spirits were reaching up to catch their legs, as though they were turning into Thunderbirds and growing wings. The wiry muscles of that mare became mine; my body twisted and turned and bent and grasped. The hard pounding of her hooves on the ground, baked by the passing summer, drummed inside me. Prairie chickens flew up from under the horses' noses, battering at the air with their brown wings in an explosion of noise, and the mustangs jinked and shied, then flew forward even faster, dashing along a straight stretch of the track we were following. It was more the trace of a track than an actual track; it was like one skein of silk thread laid down through the trees and the clearings where purple asters flowered knee-high on swaying stems. The horses followed that track as though they had created it, and knew every bend and dip in its ghostly length.

At last, we pulled them up beside a swamp where they blew hard, their chests wet with sweat.

Gabriel ran his hand over Hard Twist's neck, and spoke to him in the language I couldn't understand, and with laughter in his voice.

'What do you say?' I asked.

'I told him in Michif that he is as fast as the chief of the antelope. Michif is what we speak at home; it is the tongue of the Métis. It is part Plains Cree, part French. But I will try to remember to speak only English to you.'

A 'V' of geese passed overhead, their calls shredded by the wind, and a flock of some other birds that I didn't recognise rose flapping into the turbulent air.

'At home by the bay, I knew the names for every kind of bird,' I said. 'But now I know how the white woman feels, in a land where nothing has a name for her, and she doesn't know any of the stories.'

'You will learn it all. Our fathers and grandfathers came from another land, and yet now this land here belongs to us.'

'Your father is a white man?'

'My father's father was white, and married a Salteaux woman after the custom of the country. So my father is Métis. My mother is also Métis, she is half Plains Cree and half French. We Métis are of this land; we know its names and its stories. Since 1816 we have been a nation with our own flag.'

'You – we – have?'

Again, I mulled over Gabriel's words. It was a strange new idea to believe that I belonged to a nation, that a half-blood like me could have her own place to stand her two feet in.

Gabriel nudged Hard Twist forward and we skirted the swamp at a walk, and came upon the faint wheel tracks made by the traders' carts. The horses broke into a trot, heading north along the wheel lines between the tossing trees.

They were there suddenly, as suddenly as images appear in dreams.

In one heartbeat I saw their shaggy dark shoulders, humped like the backs of old women, and the ragged beards hanging from their chins. The stormy yellow light lay along their curved horns. Once, in York Factory, a tripman had said that the buffalo was an animal that looked like a great damn ox wearing a rug on its back.

For that one heartbeat, the mustangs seemed to hang suspended in air, all four of their hard hooves off the ground in the manner that Orchid believed horses capable of. We were downwind, but it didn't matter now, for we had been seen. The largest of the buffalo turned to face us in the middle of the wheel tracks, and lowered his head to bellow, a roaring vibration that rattled my rib bones and hummed in my ears, and split the wind in two. Behind him, the other animals – there were about a dozen – turned to flee with their tawny calves amongst them.

'Turn around! Turn the mare around! Go back!' Gabriel yelled, wrestling Hard Twist's head sideways, and drawing his gun from its embroidered sheath that hung against his thigh. In that instant, a branch snapped from an elm tree with a sharp crack and plummeted towards the ground in the periphery of my vision. Smoke Eyes shied violently as the branch fell and I knew, even as she shied, that I had lost any control over her. When she straightened out again, she was already in a gallop and pounding down the track towards the buffalo. I heard Gabriel wheel the gelding back around to follow us.

The bull roared again, pawing the ground so that small stones and sticks flew around him. I gripped the mare with my knees, and wrapped my hands in her mane, since I didn't think there was any way, right then, for me to reach my knife. And what good would it do me against a creature that was as high as a horse at its massive shoulder, and as wide as a very old tree, and as fierce as a wolverine? An animal whose nature I knew nothing about. Even without this knowledge, I could feel the bull's obdurate rage.

Nothing but death would sever him from his cows and calves.

The mustangs were running neck and neck now and Gabriel had dropped his reins to load powder into the gun from the powder horn in his brightly woven Assomption sash. At the last moment, the bull already swivelling on his cloven hooves, the horses split away from one another to go thundering past on either side of him, and I heard the sharp crack of the gun as Gabriel fired. Then I was amongst the scattering cows with Smoke Eyes dodging between them.

The cows hurtled on. On either side of me, their shaggy darkness fled, thundered, pounded along. The mare cut a way between them, leaping past a calf, cutting under the nose of an old cow, swinging in alongside a younger cow and holding her position at the cow's shoulder. She was waiting for me to fire upon the cow, I realised, but I had no gun. We hurtled towards a bend in the track. The buffalo crowded into the bend, bunching up. Panic swelled against my lungs, pressed high in my throat.

Hold on, I told myself, *just hold on*.

One of my knees pressed momentarily into shaggy wool as the buffalo pushed us off the bend of the track. Smoke Eyes shot wide to escape, ran into the trees, dropped into a sliding halt on her bent hocks to avoid a boulder. I flew over her shoulder and hit the ground hard. Smoke Eyes charged on, running buffalo.

I lay very still on my stomach and waited for the

golden and brown world to stop spinning. I tasted my lips; no blood. I breathed in once, then out. I listened to my heartbeat. Then I climbed to my feet slowly, unfolding my joints, checking the strength and length of my bones. Nothing broken. I breathed in and out again, and began to walk back up the track towards Gabriel and Hard Twist.

When I came around the bend, the bull lay in the flattened grass, a mountain of muscle, horn, hoof and fat. His strange purple blood oozed into the dust like the juice of a flower.

'Gabriel?' I called uncertainly, and at that moment the dead bull surged into the air. He did not rise as horses do, first the front legs straightening, then the back unfolding afterwards. That bull rose straight up, unbending all four legs in one convulsive spasm that flung his great mass of flesh skywards. His tail spasmed in the wind. He swung his head, fixed his rage upon me, and began to run.

I turned to sprint. Something smoky blurred in my vision as it surged past me from behind. A horse? The force of its passing spun me around, wrenching my shoulder, before I fell. Dust filled my eyes and mouth.

'Lie still!' Gabriel shouted in a smother of hoof beats. I heard the crack of a gun again, and felt the vibrations in the ground. In my blurred vision, legs flashed past. The ground rocked. I felt the great bulk of the buffalo surge beside me, tower over me. If it fell, I would be crushed as flat as a skipping stone, my bones mashed into the dirt like berries being mashed into pemmican. Our carcasses would be inseparable. On the heels of the buffalo, I felt the swift curve of the mustang's belly flash by.

The gun rang out a third time, the sound reverberating in my ears. Trees and wind flounced around me; the whole world seemed to tremble and swing with dizzy uncertainty. For the second time, I pulled myself off the ground and looked around. The bull was lying still again. Gabriel rode around him in a circle, controlling Hard Twist with his knees, and shot the bull once more through the shoulder, a heart shot. I saw Gabriel press the gun's hot barrel to his mouth and spit a lead ball down into it to reload. I saw the mustang spin around the bull like a dancer, obeying Gabriel even when Smoke Eyes burst through the trees, wild-eyed, smothered in foam, and trailing her reins, to join them.

Gabriel snatched up his own reins one-handed and, carrying the gun in the other hand, rode to where I waited, numb with shock. He swung off the sweating horse and gripped my shoulders. 'Are you hurt?'

'No.'

I buried my face in his long braided hair, and felt the wind buffet us closer together. He kissed the parting line on my scalp, then the curve of my cheek. The two horses breathed gustily beside us. Thunder rumbled off to the west.

'What happened?' I asked at last, my voice shaking.

'You came off and the mare ran on. I didn't know this at first so I rode on past, believing the bull was dead on the track behind us. Then I saw Smoke Eyes riderless, and turned back to find you. And there you were, standing in the track with the bull getting ready to charge. Hard Twist knocked you down as we galloped past. A bull won't gore you on the ground, only if you fall off your horse on to its horns.'

'But it might have trampled me?'

'Buffalo don't step on things unless they have no choice. Same with horses.'

Thunder rumbled again. When I opened my eyes and looked over Gabriel's shoulder, the first flash of lightning split the dark sky open.

'So now you know how horses run buffalo,' he said. 'And now you have a story about this land.'

I smiled a little.

'Come on. I'm going to cut out the bull's tongue for our supper tonight.'

Unsheathing his knife, he let out a sudden whoop of laughter. 'I'll unwrap my fiddle!' he said, bending over the bull's head. 'We'll have a dance tonight, your first dance on the shore of Lake Winnipeg!'

Chapter 12

In the firelight, the horses and oxen corralled amongst the Red River carts threw bulky shadows. I followed Gabriel to a cart and waited by one of its huge wheels while he reached inside it to search through a pile of blankets.

'What is wrapped around the cartwheels?' I asked.

'*Shaganappi*, strips of buffalo rawhide. These carts are made of nothing but wood and *shaganappi*; there are no nails from the white men holding them together, and no grease on the axles. We can repair them any place we're travelling.'

As he spoke, he lifted a bundle of buffalo robe from the cart, and unwrapped a fiddle from it, checking to make sure that none of its strings were broken.

'I made this one myself from maple wood,' he said with a smile of satisfaction. 'It's a copy of a fine old one I have at home. The story was that it once belonged to a Scotsman who murdered a trader from the North West Company. But it plays a beautiful jig.'

'What was the murder over?'

'Something to do with a horse, a buffalo runner which got rustled.'

'Does that happen often?' I glanced anxiously across to where Foxfire stood, his eyes glowing in the firelight, and tied to a cartwheel.

'Horses are a man's wealth,' Gabriel said, tuning up his fiddle strings. 'Amongst the tribes, horse stealing is a glorious pleasure. Even the young men of the Métis have been known to make a horse or two disappear!'

'But how did you get the murderer's fiddle?'

'I won it at a horse race as payment for a wager. Some men will gamble everything they have on the outcome of horse races: their household goods, their tipis, even their own horses.'

'And the murderer's horse that was rustled?'

'No idea what happened to it. Long gone over the southern prairie.' Gabriel grinned, tucking the fiddle tenderly beneath his chin and running the bow lightly over the strings. 'Come on.'

We walked through the camp, past the racks of wood where strips of buffalo meat were hung to dry, past the cauldrons of bubbling buffalo meat swinging from iron tripods over the fires. Firelight washed up the sides of the pale, conical tipis. Dogs skulked in the shadows, and women chatted softly in tipi door-ways. When Gabriel began to play his fiddle, the Métis and the tripmen from the York boats drifted closer, and two other men with fiddles stepped forward to join him. Presently, a tripman pulled a harmonica from a pocket, and a Cree paddler fetched a skin drum to beat out the rhythm.

My toes began to itch as that music tugged at them. Gabriel's fiddle sang with a bounce and a lilt; even the flames in the campfires seemed to flutter in rhythm. People began to dance, their moccasins pounding the grass and flat dusty ground, their shad-ows leaping across the tipis, their eyes as bright as the sparks that occasionally burst upwards in flurries from the burning wood.

'This is the Duck dance,' said a woman beside me, bouncing her baby in her arms. 'Do you know it?'

I shook my head, watching the dancers, wishing I could join in.

The woman handed her baby to a child standing nearby. 'Come,' she said, taking my hand. 'You will learn it as you dance.'

My shadow merged with the other whirling shad-ows, separated, merged again. The pure sweet notes of the fiddles rocked me and swung me, and filled me with a wild and solemn joy. My eyes filled with the surge and flow of the dancers. Bright flashes of colour flared and then were swallowed by shadows: the fringe of a red sash, the yellow embroidery on a legging, the long strings of glass beads around Eva's neck. Pierre swung past, his hat at a rakish angle with its orange plumes of dyed ostrich feathers swaying. Charlotte danced with some other children; when I glimpsed her heart-shaped face creased with laughter, my heart bounded in my chest, over my belly filled with a stew of sturgeon fish and the root they called *askipwawa*. Orchid stood on the edge of the dancers, watching, until the fiddlers played a waltz, and then she danced it with the captain from our boat, her short plumpness bending gracefully and her feet, in the moccasins I had given her, keeping perfect time to the three-beat throb of the drum.

Then the fiddlers played a jig; 'The Red River jig' someone murmured in my ear, and Gabriel laid down his fiddle and began to dance too. I stood beside Orchid and watched as the dancers' feet flew, faster and faster, their legs a blur of motion, while the fiddles poured their song into the night. Then the fiddle notes changed, became higher. The dancers began to lift their feet in fancy steps, pirouetting, sidestepping. Knees kicked, heels thumped the ground. The spectators whistled and whooped. My eyes were fastened on Gabriel, on the flapping fringes of his jacket, the glitter of its beadwork. His long hair flew around his head. His eyes flashed and his teeth shone. Firelight ran over the hard planes of his face, over his feet that seemed to be everywhere at once, flying in one direction and then another.

At last, the fiddlers paused for a rest, and the dancers sat down to eat bowls of cornmeal pudding sweetened with wild plums. I felt shy suddenly, when Gabriel came to sit beside me, tamping wild tobacco into the stone bowl of his pipe.

Thunder rumbled far off along the western horizon, although the wind had died and the trees hung thick and clotted with stillness around the perimeter of the camp.

'Where does your father keep his horses?' I asked.

'He has a farm on the White Horse Plain, west of the Forks where the Assiniboine River runs into the Red River. It is about thirty miles from where you will be, in the new stone fort that the Company is building.'

Smoke trickled from his mouth and rose straight up, mingling with the smoke from the fires. 'Maybe you will come and visit my family,' he said softly. 'My mother would welcome you. If you cannot find your father, my family would help you.'

'*Marci*,' I said shyly, which was the first word of Métis that I'd learned that evening and which meant 'thank you'.

Gabriel smiled. 'You will soon be a true Métis.'

For a moment, our gazes locked and I felt again the stillness in his spirit, the stillness of vast skies and prairie wind, and of the long waves of the endless land.

One of the fiddlers began to tune his instrument

again, and the drummer began a slow pulsing rhythm. Gabriel knocked ash from his pipe bowl and tucked it into his sash before joining the musicians. The dancers swirled around the clearing like a school of brilliant fish in a river's whirlpool, and I felt myself sucked in and swirled around with them. We danced reels and square dances, and a dance called Drops of Brandy. We jigged, we leaped, we spun. Eva whirled past, laughing with her head tipped back, her eyes stretched wide and her lashes fluttering at a tripman with hawk feathers standing upright in his hair. Samuel Beaver's black face gleamed like polished wood as he stomped past. Pierre whirled a Métis girl in circles, and then swung her in close against his chest, winking at me when he caught my glance. He and the girl sashayed together, the hem of her bright print dress draped over his leggings while tripmen yelled and whistled, and tipped flasks of rum to their mouths.

Through the sea of dancers, I searched for Gabriel. He was dancing on the spot, bending and swaying over his fiddle, his arm sawing with the bow, his toes tapping. I heard the pure notes fly from beneath his fingers, and soar above the other notes. I caught the smile he sent me, a flash in the darkness. He laid down his fiddle in mid-tune and leaped into the dancers to catch me by one hand and swing me around, laughter shining over his skin. The fiddle notes ran through our bodies, through our joined hand, and stirred the leaves on the poplar trees so that they trembled in the smoky air. The taste of wild plums lingered on my tongue. Dancing with Gabriel was like galloping on a sure-footed horse, like swimming in the rapids of a roaring river, like running over the tundra with the wind howling in my hair.

Night and music flowed over us, poured over us, like white water over hard rocks.

Very late, when the clouds began to drift apart and reveal a sprinkle of stars, the tripmen wandered off to the York boats to sleep beneath oiled canvas. They yawned as they went, some staggering from too much rum. The Métis walked with tired legs to their tipis. The women of our brigade – Orchid, Eva, Charlotte and I – had been offered beds to sleep on inside one of the tipis. I glanced around for Gabriel but he had disappeared.

'I am going to check on Foxfire,' I told Orchid, for I remembered the time he had strayed away when his rope came undone, and how the bear had chased him, and how my friendship with Orchid had suffered as a result. I passed Charlotte's small, limp hand into Orchid's grasp, and watched for a moment as my little sister tottered away beside her.

Then I wended my way through the smouldering fires and the sleeping dogs to where the stallion stood tied to a cartwheel so that he couldn't get near the Métis mares. He had been hobbled and grazing all afternoon, in the watchful care of Gabriel's younger brother. Now he was passive, dozing with one hind foot cocked, and his head drooping. He breathed heavily in contentment as I laid my hand upon his shoulder. My head pressed against his neck and for a moment we stood, sleepy and still. *Tomorrow,* I thought, *we will reach the Company's new stone fort in the Red River valley, and our great journey together will be over. Then we will be parted, and maybe I will never ride this horse again, or run my hands over his red coat as it grows thick in readiness for winter.* Who knew what Orchid's husband, an unknown white man, would be like; whether he would allow me to care for his horse? An ache of sadness filled my throat.

'Foxfire,' I whispered, my breath stirring the coarse red hairs of his bright mane. I ran my hand down his face, and smoothed it over the softness of his muzzle. I remembered how he had swum to me out of the fog when I was being swept into the salty bay with ice chips bobbing against my canoe. My guardian spirit, my horse *pawakan* with his hard flying hooves, his noble face, his streaming red tail.

I became aware gradually of their voices, low but bulging with anger, and coming from the nearest stand of trees. The stallion's ears swivelled, taking in the sound.

'You didn't have to dance with her so many times!' Eva hissed. 'Who is she anyway? Just some wandering trader's poor daughter, that's who! She wasn't even pretty!'

'I can dance with whoever I damn well want to. *Comprends?*' I recognised Pierre's voice, a low growl with no hint of its usual mocking laughter.

'So do that! You just do that! But don't come crawling back to me afterwards!'

'Crawling? Ha, that's a new one. I do not ever crawl to you or anyone else on this trip. I'm a steersman; I make important decisions about the boat, and I earn a good income.'

'So spend it on some poor trader's daughter then! Buy her some trinkets!'

'*Oui*,' said Pierre on a long cool note. 'I will spend my money on anyone I please. But not on you, you bad-tempered witch.'

I heard the sharp snap of a twig as Eva flounced off, and dimly I saw her storm through the trees and away into the camp with the beads around her neck swinging. After he spat, Pierre was quieter, moving through the underbrush; I heard only the grate of shingle on the shore as it slipped beneath his feet. Then there was silence. A wolf began to sing to the west, and soon its cry was echoed back by its brothers as they called to the drifting clouds and the brilliant stars. I shivered, for frost was forming on the wooden spokes of the cartwheels.

As I threaded my way back towards the tipi where I was to sleep, I felt sad as well as cold. This wonderful day, filled with excitement, was over and soon dawn would flush the eastern horizon, and my last day with Foxfire would begin. And I had not even been able to say goodbye to Gabriel Gunner.

He materialised at my shoulder, a swing of deer-skin fringes, a flutter of sash. In the glow of a dying fire, he stood and looked at me.

'In the morning I am leaving early with another scout to seek the Cree,' he said. 'But I would like to see you again. When I come back from this trading trip, I would like to visit you in the stone fort. Before the first snow.'

'Yes. I would like to see you.'

'When the Métis give a gift, they lay it in the hands of the receiver. Hold out your hands. One of my cousins made this.'

He laid the bridle's straps across my palms; they were decorated with blue beads and with tassels of orange wool threaded through tin cones. 'This is so you know you will always have a horse to ride,' he said. 'Perhaps, if I don't see you at the fort, we will meet at a trotting race or a cart race in the valley. I will look for you.'

'*Marci,*' I repeated, and then shyness swallowed me and I ducked away into the entrance of the tipi where Orchid and Charlotte, and even Eva, already breathed deeply in sleep. The smells of spruce boughs and smoke and sage bit my nostrils.

'Goodbye,' I said softly, and I heard Gabriel move away into the night. Stillness fell as I pulled a buffalo robe over myself, shifting closer to Charlotte's warmth.

In the morning, I awoke with every muscle aching; there were bruises on my ribs and knees from being flung over the shoulders of the mare when she was running with the buffalo. When I rose from the bed of spruce boughs, my legs were stiff and sore from the hours of dancing. 'Wake up, Charlotte, wake.' I shook her shoulder gently and her breathing hitched, then resumed its slow rhythm. I shook her again, then knuckled my own eyes and yawned before ducking out into the cool wash of morning air. Women nearby were stirring dried buffalo meat into hot grease and dried berries to make pemmican.

Closer to the tipi, Orchid was arguing with our boat captain. 'But we cannot leave yet! I must make myself presentable for our arrival at the fort! One of your men must help me to find my belongings. I cannot possibly arrive dressed like this!'

At my approach, she turned with a determined lift of her chin. 'One of the women is going to show us where we can bathe,' she said. 'It will be cool, but we must prepare ourselves and make a decent toilette. I refuse to arrive looking like a heathen.'

'You mean dressed like a Cree woman?'

'That is exactly what I mean. It is all very well for the women of this country; they lead rough lives. But I have standards to maintain, and my husband will expect no less. Do not give me that affronted look, Amelia.'

The boat captain shrugged his shoulders helplessly.

'One hour, not a minute more. The men are anxious to reach the fort and unload the boats.'

'Thank you,' Orchid said. 'Please send a man to find my belongings.'

Charlotte's small hand slipped into mine and I bent to kiss the tip of her nose. We followed Orchid's bustling, resolute form down the shingle beach and waited while a tripman unearthed a chest from beneath the canvas-covered piles of goods. While Orchid rummaged through the chest, muttering to herself, I slid Gabriel's bridle into my own chest, and smoothed its straps flat. *I will always have a horse to ride*, I reminded myself. *Even if it's not Foxfire. I am protected by the spirit of horses, and I will not be without horses in my new life here on the prairie.*

I needed to believe this so badly that I bit my tongue in anxiety. My mouth filled with a taste like tears.

When the Métis woman arrived, we followed her around a small point of land covered with shrubby willow bushes to a rocky shoreline. While she kept watch from amongst the willows, braiding her hair, we stripped and waded into the cold shock of the water. It was clear today, still in the sunshine, lapping with a gentle wash upon the shore. Orchid's neck and face were browner than the pale folds of her body and the whiteness of her legs. She bent over, plunging her head in, her loose hair flowing around her like golden weed. She rubbed it and herself vigorously with the Métis soap of buffalo fat and wood ashes, and then handed the slimy soap to me. I rubbed myself all over, and then soaped Charlotte whose teeth were already chattering. We washed our hair, and then lay on the rocks and waited for the early sun to dry us. Gulls wheeled overhead, crying, while Orchid dressed slowly in the many layers of a white woman's costume with its lace undergarments, its petticoats, its flounces and ruffles. At last, over the top, she donned a dark green dress of a soft velvet fabric, with large puffed sleeves and a draped skirt. She pinned her masses of curly hair up into a large bun on the top of her head, and skewered it with pins, before scrutinising herself in a mirror.

'This will have to do,' she said at last, and I saw the anxiety clouding her clear blue glance.

'You look beautiful,' I offered but she gnawed her lower lip nervously.

'It is not the sort of toilette one would make at home,' she fretted. 'I do so hope it will be acceptable here. It's the best that I can manage under the circumstances. I do hope that Mr Spencer will be tolerant of this fact. I am so very brown from the sun.'

'What is wrong with sun?' Charlotte asked.

'It is not lady-like to be brown,' Orchid replied severely. 'Only women who work outdoors have brown, weathered skin.'

'Like my Cree aunties,' Charlotte agreed innocently, but I was wondering what a woman would do all day long if she didn't work outside, and what kind

237

of work she might be doing instead. In the Cree camps, the women were always working: tanning hides, drying berries, sewing moccasins, netting snowshoes, stuffing pillows with goose down. As they worked, they laughed and talked, sharing their stories, being given advice from their elders, and nursing their babies. 'Those Cree women work harder than most men of my acquaintance,' a Company clerk had said once in my hearing. I stared at my own brown skin, my sturdy legs, the muscles in my arms that had already done so much work. I remembered the story about the Creator, taking the people of the land from the oven at just the right time, when they were perfectly baked a lovely brown. I smiled then, bending my face over the ripples and seeing it hang there like an autumn moon.

Orchid lifted a large hat on to her head and pinned it in place, and then sat on a bleached log, and pushed her feet into a pair of delicate shoes of pale green leather with heels and pointed toes. With difficulty, she picked her way through the willows, and back along the beach to where the tripmen were already running out their oars and pushing the boats into deeper water. I ran to fetch Foxfire and lead him up the familiar planks of tamarack into his stall. This will be the last time, I thought, and when I sat beside Orchid on our bench, my throat was aching. I braided Charlotte's damp hair, and then my own, into two tight braids that hung down on either side of my face.

Charlotte began stringing rosehips together with a needle and a thin sinew, making herself a necklace. Behind me, Pierre leaned on his steering oar and the boat swung southwards, pointing straight to the place where the Red River ran out into the shallow vastness of Lake Winnipeg.

Orchid fidgeted beside me, pushing strands of hair back under her hat. Her jaw was set in a line of rigid tension.

'Where is Eva?' she asked suddenly.

I pointed to the boat ahead of us, where Eva's dress was a speck of brilliant purple above her leggings. 'There,' I said in a low tone. 'She isn't speaking to Pierre today so she has moved to another boat.'

'What nonsense,' Orchid said irritably. 'I hope she will behave with decorum when we arrive. She will need to lodge in Mr Spencer's house for a day or two until she begins school.'

Orchid gnawed her lower lip again. 'The stallion is looking a little thin,' she said. 'I hope Mr Spencer will understand the rigours of our long journey.'

'He has made this journey himself,' I reminded her, but I too looked anxiously at the horse. Rising from my bench, I rummaged around for his grooming kit, then entered his stall and began to smooth the brush all over him. His winter coat was roan, just like his summer one, and he still reminded me of an autumn leaf silvered with frost. I knew every swirl of his coat, every pattern. I traced a line of silver with my fingertips and wondered again whether Orchid's husband would ever allow me to ride him. I brushed his mane and tail, and with my fingers untangled every snarl created by the wind, until the hair hung smooth and straight.

'Thank you,' said Orchid, sounding calmer, when I rejoined her on the bench. 'You have done a splendid job of caring for Foxfire. I am most grateful, Amelia. I hope you will find your father but in the meantime you must treat Mr Spencer's home as your own. I am sure he will not turn you away until you have found your father. I believe him to be a kind-hearted man.'

I nodded, my stomach clenching. How long would it take me to find Simon Mackenzie? And what would I do if I couldn't find him; where would Charlotte and I go then? I hoped that Orchid was right, and that her new husband was indeed kind-hearted and would allow us to stay in his home.

The shores of the lake, which had lain along our eastern and western horizons for so many days, began to draw together like the strings of a pouch. Charlotte slipped her rosehip necklace over her head, and the York boats entered a waving expanse of reeds and bulrushes.

'See that?' asked a tripman, jutting his chin towards plants I didn't recognise. 'That's wild rice. The Salteaux women harvest it and very good it is too. There's plenty of sustenance in this land: fish and wild fowl, rice, and sugar from the maple trees. Plenty of game and wild berries.'

'Without the Salteaux, the settlers would never have survived their first years in the colony,' another man commented. 'They had a hard time of it, sure enough. All those droughts and floods, and the grass-hopper plagues in 1818. 'Twas like something from the Bible, like the plagues of Egypt.'

'True enough,' agreed the first man.

'And then the North West Company stirring up trouble,' added a third man. 'And the Métis getting restive.'

'What happened?' Orchid asked, her tone sharp again.

''Twas in 1816 when the Métis got all riled up by the men of the North West Company and killed twenty-one settlers of Lord Selkirk's, him as was so keen to get the valley carved up into farms. The Seven Oaks Massacre they called the killings.'

'And in that same year, the Métis all got together in the Qu'Appelle Valley and called themselves a nation and made their own flag.'

'Whatever for?' Orchid asked.

'Why to protect their free-roaming way of life and their buffalo land from all the white settlers coming to farm the place.'

'But they were all riled up by the other trading company, the North Westers. Now that company's been merged with the HBC, we'll have no more of their plots.'

'And no more floods either, 'tis to be hoped.'

'Was it very bad?' Orchid asked, staring overboard at the water's placid surface as though she expected it to begin rising before her eyes.

'Aye, it was bad sure enough. The old fort, Fort Garry that was, had to be abandoned afterwards. Houses and horses all got swept away downstream. Cows, chickens – they all went sailing away. The odd person too, no doubt. It's why the Company is building the new fort of stone, Lower Fort Garry they're calling it.'

The men lapsed into silence, pulling hard on the oars. Orchid kept pushing back strands of hair and adjusting the tilt of her hat with its nodding feathers and bunches of crumpled fabric flowers. Her hands shook as she smoothed the folds of her long gown. As I watched her, a tremor of anxiety shook me too, like wind stirring a tree, and I pressed my knees together to still their quaking.

I had begun to see that there were many ways my father might have died in this place.

Chapter 13

Now the bows of the York boats were free of the wild rice and bulrushes, and entered the waters of the Red River.

'*The Red River!*' I whispered to myself. Excitement and anxiety gripped the back of my neck. The Red River, to which my father had journeyed so many years ago, and where he had waited and waited for an answer from Mary Mackenzie, the Swampy Cree woman he loved, and who was far away on the shores of the great bay. I stared about, soaking in every detail of this place: the low shores with a fringe of oak and maple trees, the vastness of the prairie beyond with its waving grasses and wild flowers. The Red River's steady current eddied past, purling against the wooden hull of the York boat. My father had dipped his paddle here. My father had looked at these shores, and watched hawks and ravens ride the clouds of the sweeping sky.

Here and there, log cabins stood set back from the river's edge, and settlers in faded shirts bent over in their gardens of cabbages, carrots, potatoes and turnips. Narrow fields of barley and wheat stubble stretched away from the river, golden and rough. A man on a horse trotted along a trail running parallel to the river. Foxfire stretched out his neck, nostrils flared as he sucked in the scent of that stranger. His neigh rang in my ears, and he banged his hooves against the boards that hemmed him in.

'Fancies the local mares!' a tripman joked.

'Let us be thankful for that, since it is the reason that I brought him here,' said Orchid tartly, and the men laughed and burst into song, labouring over the oars in their haste to arrive.

'Lower Fort Garry!' shouted the captain in mid-afternoon, and the men raised their voices in shouts of satisfaction, for they had survived the cold rivers, the back-breaking portages, the rocks and dark forests, the approaching cold bringing its white storms. A Cree paddler began to thank the Creator for a safe arrival, and I closed my eyes and listened to his words, clutching Charlotte's hand and feeling my gratitude like a current, fighting with the currents of fear and doubt that swirled inside me.

When I opened my eyes, the boats were sweeping in beneath a bluff to where a wooden landing stage was crowded with Company men in striped shirts and their best vests beneath capotes with brass buttons. Briefly I remembered the moment when Orchid had stepped ashore at York Factory; it seemed so long ago, and now it was me who was stepping ashore in a strange place, my body tremulous with countless miles of wind and water.

My heart beat hard and fast, and I tried to gather up my courage.

Now we were manoeuvring alongside the stage, our gunwale at the same height as the stage's planking. Orchid rose to her feet, brushing her hands down her gown, lifting her chin. Charlotte's hand clutched my fingers so tightly that they tingled.

'I have to untie Foxfire,' I said, but Orchid shook her head.

'Leave him, Mr Spencer will have arranged for his care.' She wasn't looking at me though for her gaze was focused upon the group of men on the stage. For a moment, her teeth worried at her lower lip, then suddenly she smiled brilliantly. With head high and spine straight, she stepped from the York boat, her gloved hand brushing the outstretched hand of a man in a black frock coat and with a silk cravat tied beneath his sandy beard.

'My dear Mrs Spencer,' he said formally, and bent his balding head and his middle-aged face with thick cheeks, over her hand as he kissed it. 'Welcome to Fort Garry, such as it is in its current state. We have great hopes for its future though. I trust that you will be most happy here.'

His pale blue eyes flickered over me and then his gaze sharpened. 'Splendid!' he exclaimed. 'My dear wife, this is a most splendid animal that you have brought all this way. We must have him unloaded at once! I have had a stall prepared in the stable.'

Orchid's cheeks flushed with pleasure and relief while her husband called for a man waiting nearby with a rope.

'Bring the horse out immediately, before the unloading begins,' he ordered, and he patted Orchid's arm as she slipped it through one of his own.

'You must speak to the horse softly and –' I started to tell the man with the rope.

'He will know how to handle a horse,' Orchid interrupted.

'And pray, who is this young woman?' Mr Spencer asked.

'Amelia Mackenzie, and my sister Charlotte.'

'They have journeyed with me from York Factory,' Orchid explained. 'Amelia has made herself invaluable in caring for the Norfolk stallion. I could never have survived the trip without her assistance.'

'I am most grateful to you,' Mr Spencer said, but his eyes remained fixed upon the York boat where the other man was untying Foxfire.

'Amelia and Charlotte have come to the colony seeking their father,' Orchid explained in a breathless rush, sounding unsure of herself. 'They might need to lodge with us temporarily until they find him.'

'Indeed?' Mr Spencer seemed momentarily disconcerted, and looked directly at me for the first time.

'And here is Eva, of whom I wrote to you. You did receive my letter?'

'Certainly,' he replied, as Eva stepped forward. Her smooth smile belied the tired, sullen droop of her eyes.

'You wrote that Eva is to attend the boarding school here. She will learn to leave behind the savage ways of the Métis, to become civilised. Might I ask whether the Misses Amelia and Charlotte will do the same?'

Heat flooded my face but Orchid flashed me a warning look from beneath the upswept brim of her hat, and I swallowed my words back down. 'I do not know yet; I must find my father first,' I said.

'What a veritable bevy of young women you have brought with you,' remarked Mr Spencer, patting Orchid's gloved arm again and sounding not completely pleased. 'Yes, a veritable bevy. My modest home will be bursting at its seams. But ah – here comes the horse!'

He released Orchid's arm to hurry down the landing stage to where Foxfire was lifting first one black hoof and then another over the gunwale of the York boat and on to the hollow thump of the planking.

'Splendid! Remarkable! This fine fellow will no doubt be the talk of the colony!' Mr Spencer exclaimed, beaming and nodding so that the sun shone on his balding head and threw the creases of his face into sharper relief. I thought that he must be twenty years older than Orchid; perhaps, like the Cree, the white men sometimes married much younger women. This was good, I thought in relief, for he would have amassed enough trade wealth to be able to take care of her.

'This fellow will sire fine foals that will put the scrawny cayuses of our copper-skinned brethren to shame,' Mr Spencer continued.

An unfamiliar anger rose in me, swelling like the tide in the mouth of the Hayes River. 'The mustangs of the Cree and Métis are not scrawny –'

Orchid stepped in front of me. 'My dear Mr Spencer,' she said, 'we are in perfect accord about this stallion's abilities. I am most delighted!'

Eva stared at me, ponderingly. 'I needn't have bothered,' she muttered. 'You will spoil everything for yourself anyway.'

'Bothered with –? What do you mean?'

'You will have to hold your tongue and your temper if you want to marry a white trader.'

'I never said that I did!'

'Perhaps a Métis scout would suit you better, then you can wander around cutting up great lumps of buffalo and dragging it away in carts. I don't plan on doing any such thing. I am going to have a fine house here one day, you wait and see.'

'I don't mind what kind of house you have. You're just grouchy because Pierre – oh look, we are being left behind,' I noticed, for Mr Spencer and Orchid were climbing from the stage and ascending the track to the fort, with the stallion following on his lead rope. It seemed as though we had been forgotten, but as I took Charlotte's hand to follow, Orchid paused and glanced back over her shoulder to send me an encouraging smile.

'Welcome to the Red River!' she cried, but Mr Spencer did not turn, nor even pause in his assertive stride.

When we reached the level ground above the bluff, Mr Spencer stopped to give orders to the man leading Foxfire and presently the man walked the stallion away towards a collection of log buildings where cattle grazed. I guessed the buildings were the stables and byres for the oxen; beyond them stood a large house surrounded by a veranda, and another huge building of limestone rock.

'Our new fur loft,' Mr Spencer said proudly, waving a hand at it. 'And the Big House is the quarters for our governor, Mr Simpson, when he visits. He too has brought a white bride to this territory, my love. I am desirous that you shall soon meet her. She is a young thing herself, from London, and I fancy that the two of you will have much in common. So you shall not be starved for feminine company of the better kind.'

He patted Orchid's arm as he spoke, and gazed at her eagerly. *He wants more than her stallion,* I thought. He wants the two of them to begin their new life happily together in this colony, although they barely know each other. He is a kind man in his own way, even though he does not think that I am company of the better sort.

I hurried to catch up, realising that Mr Spencer and Orchid were moving along the cart track again. Labourers swarmed around the wooden framework of another new building, and high-wheeled carts passed us, laden with limestone and pulled by placid oxen while the whips of the bullwhackers cracked over them. Wheel tracks marred the prairie in every direction, and men shouted orders. Other oxen were chained to the trunks of oak trees which they dragged along, and in the distance I could hear the rasp of saws and the ring of hammers.

'– only room there for unmarried officers,' Mr Spencer was saying as Charlotte and I caught up to him. 'So I have arranged for us to dwell in a small cabin just to the south. Once I retire, at the end of my current contract, we shall move upstream to our own land, and I shall have us a fine house built near the Forks. Already, some grand homes are being built there.'

The small cabin to which Mr Spencer led us had been plastered in buffalo hair and lime, and its walls shone a fresh, bright white. Its small glass windows reflected the waters of the river running in the shallow valley below, and a swell of prairie folded around it, thick with berry bushes and wolf willow.

'Why, it is quite charming!' Orchid cried in delight, and a sigh of relief escaped from my lips. I had wondered, sometimes, what she expected to find at the end of her incredible journey across thousands of miles of rolling ocean, and up the wild rivers, and southwards over three hundred miles of shallow lake.

Inside, the cabin was floored with wooden planking and furnished with pieces imported from England: tall wardrobes painted green and yellow, cabinets holding china cups sprigged with delicate flowers, a bed with a walnut headboard. Paintings of ships decorated the walls, ships with three masts and billowing sails like the supply ships of the Company that dropped anchor at Five Fathom Hole. Portraits of stern white chiefs, with sashes and medals across their chests, stared out from their frames.

'It does lack a certain feminine touch that I am confident you can supply,' said Mr Spencer. 'Your luggage will be brought here once it has been unloaded. In the meantime, I must repair to the Big House for a meeting with the junior clerks, and will leave you ladies, you many ladies, to refresh yourselves after your journey. There is a cold smoked ham in the larder, and my servant will make you some tea.'

He ran a bemused glance over us all clustered in

the doorway of the parlour, and then departed with his firm stride.

We ate the ham with coarse bread, seated at the shining table with its six matching chairs, and then sipped tea from china cups as the servant, a young Cree girl, poured it. When Orchid's chests and boxes of luggage arrived on a cart, its ungreased axles squealing, we helped her to unpack her treasured possessions: silverware with her family crest on the handles, cut crystal miraculously unbroken, a bright Kidderminster carpet that we unrolled upon the drawing-room floor, dresses that she hung in the painted wardrobe. Her face shone with delight as she lifted each thing from the chest where she had packed it so many months before.

There was only one bedroom in the cabin, in addition to a kitchen, and two small rooms that Orchid called the drawing room and the parlour. She sent the Cree servant girl to the Company store, located in the fur loft, for some ticking fabric. All afternoon the five of us sewed the striped fabric into rectangles, our needles flashing along the straight seams as we sat in the thin sunlight on the bluff above the Red River. We stuffed the mattresses with dried grass and laid them on the floor of the parlour and that was where we slept that night. In the morning, Charlotte and I went walking along the shore, watching Métis children wading in the shallows, catching frogs and collecting shells. A camp of Plains Cree stood against the skyline, its tipis pale in the sunlight, its spotted horses tied to a picket line. Dogs ran past, fighting over sticks. Men drove along in carts pulled by oxen, or flashed by at a trot on sturdy mustangs.

Disturbed by canoes filled with Salteaux paddlers, two great brown birds rose from the reeds, trailing their skinny legs. Charlotte giggled. 'They are sandhill cranes,' she said. 'The same as at home, Amelia! When Wishahkicahk caught hold of a crane's legs and flew to the moon, he stretched its legs out as long as sticks!'

'Yes,' I agreed, laughing at the memory of being told this story in the camp outside York Factory when I was a child myself. Perhaps the Plains Cree also told this story . . . perhaps I did already know some of the stories of this land.

We approached a Cree boy fishing for goldeye and I tried to ask him how far it was to the White Horse Plain. The tongue of the Cree here was not exactly the same as the tongue spoken by my mother's people, and at first the boy didn't understand. Finally, he waved an arm southwards, and said the word 'thirty'. I stared into the far distance, where the land turned from golden to blue and was swallowed by sky, and thought about Gabriel's sisters, stitching sunflowers and roses on to deerskin.

When we returned to the cabin, a cart waited at the door and Mr Spencer stood beside the horse harnessed to it; a rangy black horse with one blue eye. I smoothed its forelock tenderly.

'How is Foxfire?' I asked.

'Very well to be sure, settling into his new home.'

'May I visit him in his stable? May I ride him? He needs to be exercised.'

Mr Spencer pondered my question for moment, removing his cap and running his hand through his thin, sandy hair. Sunshine shone in his pale eyelashes.

'Visit him, yes, by all means. But as to riding him, I hardly think it suitable for a young lady to ride around by herself. Not suitable at all. I shall take care of his exercise myself. I had a saddle shipped over for this very purpose.'

'But I need to look for my father and also to visit a family on the White Horse –'

Mr Spencer's glance flicked away from me as Orchid and Eva came outside. When I followed his gaze, my disappointment over the topic of riding vanished temporarily and was replaced by astonishment.

'Splendid!' cried Mr Spencer. 'My dear wife, you have worked a small miracle of transformation!'

Eva gave him her smooth, slow smile, framed now by black curls, for she had cut off her long braids, and her ringlets brushed the shoulders of her dark blue dress. It was a white woman's dress, pinned at the lace collar by an oval brooch decorated with the face of a woman shown in profile, and fastened down the front with a row of tiny pearl buttons. Her earrings of coins and thimbles had been replaced by pearl drops, and beneath the hem of the long dress her toes peeked out in pointed leather shoes. Under the dress, I knew, she would be wearing woollen stockings instead of beaded leggings.

'I am ready to go to school now,' Eva said, and Mr Spencer handed her up into the cart where a Hudson's Bay blanket had been spread upon the bench; she settled herself upon it with a flounce and waited while her small trunk was loaded and Mr Spencer climbed in and took up the reins.

'Goodbye, Charlotte and Amelia,' she said. 'I hope you will be happy here with the Métis,' and she flashed me a mocking smile. Then she faced forward as the cart drove away.

'You will have more room for sleeping in the parlour now,' Orchid said. 'I have asked Mr Spencer to make enquiries about your father's whereabouts but you must be patient. He says the colony stretches for fifty miles along the shores of the Red River, and for another thirty to the west, along the banks of the Assiniboine. If your father has retired from the Company, he could be farming anywhere along the shorelines. Or he might even be employed in the south, around Pembina.'

'Yes, thank you,' I said, but it was very hard to be patient as days, then weeks, slipped past. The ground hardened with frost, and the last leaves fell so that the trees rattled bare arms over the river's surly currents. Grey skies hung low over the new fort, where the men worked long hours trying to complete the buildings before snow fell. For hours, Charlotte and I walked along the shoreline, and wandered around the fort, waiting, watching. A slow, deep fear dragged me down into its blue depths. I scanned face after face; all those white faces with blue or green or grey eyes, all those yellow or brown beards, all those wind-reddened cheeks. Would I know my father if I looked at him, if our gazes crossed beneath the pale walls of the fur loft or the veranda of the Big House? Would some spark of recognition fly between us, or would our glances slip on by, like lures slipping past fish that didn't care to bite?

Every morning I visited Foxfire who greeted me with a gusty whicker. I leaned my face against his forehead, finding comfort. Sometimes, leaning there, I thought with longing about Gabriel Gunner dancing the jig with his long hair flying and sparks rising behind him, and sometimes I thought about Smoke Eyes with her coat of ashes and wild honey. I longed to ride her again even though I had been thrown over her shoulder; I longed to feel her bunched muscles surging through the crackling grasses. Gabriel had said he would visit me before the first snow fell but day after day dragged past, with a cold wind keening over the dull dead grass, and dark clouds scudding overhead from the west. Loneliness ached in my bones. I thought of Betty Goose Wing, seated in the doorway of her lodge, squat and heavy as a boulder, wise and enduring. I wished I could sit beside her in the camp of my kinsfolk, and listen to their stories.

I began to work for the Company, alongside the Cree women, netting snowshoes with babiche, the long strips of hide from deer and buffalo. When I worked, I lulled my fears, my hands flying with a rhythm as I wove the strips over and under, as I pulled them tight and knotted them. I began to learn the dialect of the Plains Cree people, and twice I visited their camp and borrowed a pony, which I rode along the river path, stopping at cabins to ask about my father. I would have gone more often, but I needed the work making snowshoes, and I had also unpacked my traps and was setting them for muskrat, and curing the hides to sell to the Company.

At night, as I lay on the grass-filled matress in the parlour of Mr Spencer's house, with nothing to listen to but the ticking of a tall, polished clock, my fears crowded in close like a gathering of ghosts, whispering and questioning. Where was Simon Mackenzie? Was he dead or alive? When I found him – if I found him – would he take us in? How much longer could we stay here, sleeping in the parlour, our presence growing heavy on Mr Spencer's kind heart? Had Gabriel forgotten me, had I been only an evening's entertainment? Where was he now, skimming along on Hard Twist with fiddle tunes playing in his ears?

One evening, when my fears were pinching the

edges of my sleep, I rose silently and wrapped my tartan blanket around my shoulders. On cold toes, I crept into the kitchen and dipped a tin mug into the pail of water by the enamel sink. Standing there in the darkness, sipping the water that was so cold my teeth ached, I could hear Orchid and Mr Spencer talking in the drawing room. In the evenings, she liked to sit there stitching cushion covers in something she called cross stitch, and he liked to read the newspapers that our York brigade had brought from the English supply ship. I should have covered my ears with my hands when I heard their words; I should have crept back to bed, but something held my numb toes tight against the floorboards, and prickles ran over my neck.

'– not seemly,' Mr Spencer declared in a firm tone.

I heard a log shift in the wood stove.

'She is only trying to earn some credit at the Company store so that she can provide necessities for herself and her sister,' Orchid said in a soothing tone.

'It is not suitable for her to spend her days trapping muskrat and making snowshoes with the Cree women!' Mr Spencer said. 'It is manual labour. She has a white father and if she were educated might make a good marriage to a junior clerk in the Company, and make something of her life.'

'But she doesn't want to attend school until she has found her father,' Orchid explained.

I hugged the blanket closer around my shoulders and licked my dry lips.

'I understand this, but nevertheless, it seems she is able to net snowshoes whilst awaiting him. How will she ever become civilised by pursuing this occupation? You know that it is the express wish of the Company that the Métis people be welcomed in the Red River colony as long as they forgo their savage ways and forsake their wandering lifestyle. It is of utmost importance that they become educated and Christian.'

I waited for Orchid to defend me; Orchid who had worn the moccasins I had beaded, who had sat naked with me in a sweat lodge, and waltzed in the Métis camp to the beat of a drum. But she said nothing and I understood, in the long moment of silence, that her loyalties had shifted, and that she must consider her words when talking to the white man who had provided her with a home.

'Have you heard nothing of the whereabouts of Simon Mackenzie?' Orchid asked at last.

'No one to whom I have spoken has a recollection of him. But it is thirteen years since he might have been here, and many tripmen have come and departed again in that period. Perhaps he was never here but stationed at Pembina, or perhaps he journeyed further west. But, my dear wife, you really must stop Amelia from roaming around the settlement asking questions about Simon Mackenzie. She has been wandering further and further afield, when she is not working with the babiche. She has been seen knocking at farm doors and making enquiries.'

'She is anxious to find him.'

'It is very unseemly, knocking at the doors of strangers! Does she mean to visit every farm between here and the Forks? And wandering around the fort, accosting men as they go about their work, and asking them questions! Talking even to the Cree and Métis men she meets! It is wholly indecent. If she is to live here under my roof, I must insist that this stop. I wish you to be included in the society of the wives of the Company's officers. Otherwise, you will find this place a lonely wasteland. And if you are to be included, you must not be too friendly with a girl of such disreputable habits. I have only your best interests at heart, my love. Amelia must attend school.'

'Please allow her to remain with us until Christmas,' Orchid murmured. 'It is only another few weeks. After that, if she has heard nothing, we will send her to school.'

'As you wish,' Mr Spencer replied grudgingly. 'But after that, I will take Charlotte to the school myself; I will make sure that she, a young innocent, is educated. Amelia can do as she pleases.'

I moved so fast that my foot knocked against an empty bucket which fell with a clang, rolling away as I rushed out of the kitchen and into the drawing room.

'No!' I shouted. 'No, you cannot separate

Charlotte and me! She is an orphan and she will stay with me. And I do not want to go to your white man's school and be shut up inside its walls, reading books. I can already read the stories of the land, and that is all I want!'

Orchid sat as though frozen, her needle poised in mid-air and motionless over her stitching. A dark flush ran over Mr Spencer's face, and even the top of his balding head glowed as though rubbed with berry juice.

He half rose to his feet. 'This is insolence!' he said, his words tight and clipped as though cut off with a knife. 'You are nothing but an ungrateful half-breed who –'

Orchid shot to her feet in a rustle of gown, her lips quivering. 'Robert, be quiet,' she snapped, her eyes flashing. 'Amelia is nothing of the sort. Without her help, you would never have received your precious stallion. It was Amelia who kept him in good condition. How dare you speak to her like this?'

Orchid's chin lifted, and her eyes blazed like chips of spring ice. The newspaper rustled in the tension of Mr Spencer's grip. My teeth chattered with shame. I was causing difficulties here, in this home where I had been sheltered, and causing distress in Orchid's new marriage; because of me, her loyalties were being stretched out fine as a tendon in two different directions. If those tendons tore apart, we would all feel the pain.

'I am sorry,' I muttered, speaking softly, although blood thundered in my ears and my pulse raced. I stared down at my toes which seemed very far away.

'Go back to bed,' Orchid said. I heard the rustle of her gown as she seated herself, and the whisper of the newspaper like dead leaves. My legs seemed to belong to someone else as they carried me back to the parlour. I lay down beside Charlotte, and let my tears stream over my cheeks in silence to be absorbed by my grass bed. I gripped one of Charlotte's braids as though I were afraid we'd be torn apart in our sleep.

In the morning Orchid said nothing of what had happened but asked me to stay at home and help her to finish embroidering a set of cushion covers. I jabbed my needle in and out of the coarse canvas, threaded with a dull green shade of wool. I stitched inside a pattern that Orchid had drawn on the canvas with pencil, a pattern of leaves and strange flowers whose names I didn't know, and didn't ask for. A light as cold as pewter lay on our laps, and the cold crept across the floor, although the wood crackled in the stove. Below the bluff, the river had frozen into a sheet of steely ice, and the cold wind whistled over the cabin roof and away across the dark land. Still, it didn't snow.

Sometimes I laid my stitching aside and went to stand at the window, gazing out as though the force of my longing could make a strange white man stride to the front door, calling my name, or as though I could pull Gabriel Gunner and his mustangs over the empty horizon. But the only person who arrived was Mr Spencer, his nose running with the cold and his eyes bright with alarm.

'The horse is gone! Rustled!' he shouted, slamming in the front door with the wind flowing past his trousers and flapping the edges of Orchid's embroidery.

The wind whipped his words against me and I leaped in shock. 'What horse?' I cried, but even before he answered I knew what his reply would be.

'His stable door is locked every night, but they picked the lock and stole him away. Those filthy Cree or thieving Métis are behind this! Fetch me my gun, Orchid!'

'Foxfire?' she asked, her face pale as bleached wood.

'Of course, the Norfolk stallion! But I have hired a tracker from the Salteaux, and we are setting out now with dogs and a few men to find the horse and bring him back. Fetch my gun, if you please.'

The cushion cover fell from her lap as she rose and went without a word to bring it to him; its smooth barrels and polished stock were dull in the dark light. Briefly, he kissed her and then turned back to the door. 'Don't wait for me at dinner, I might be late. But we will find the horse – this tracker I have hired can find anything!'

I stood in the door and watched him depart, mounted on one of the mustangs that the Company kept in a herd near the fort. Its black hooves hammered on the ground, which was frozen hard as rock; ground that held no hoof prints, nothing to tell the story of a horse's disappearance.

I was plummeting, plunging, falling. I was in the bottom of a deep pit. My heart was turning to ice like the heart of a wild Witiko, dying of hunger, howling alone.

Chapter 14

For three days Mr Spencer and his tracker and dogs searched for a trace of Foxfire but found nothing. I myself persuaded Samuel Beaver to ask for time away from his tasks at the fort, and we too searched, beating through bushes and looking for even a strand of red hair blowing in the cold wind, or for a white crescent scraped upon a rock by a passing hoof. We walked gingerly along on the river ice, sliding our moccasins over its dull sheen and searching for the V-shaped indentation of a foot pressed into the frost. But there were no signs anywhere to tell us where the horse had gone. It was as though the Thunderbirds had descended and carried him into the air.

'Otterchild, I am sorry about your horse,' Samuel said on the evening of the second day as the light drained from the sky and the prairie turned its back on us like an animal hunkering down into hibernation. 'I cannot help you search any longer. The Company is sending me up to Norway House tomorrow. But have you heard that there is a big wedding feast planned by the Métis on the White Horse Plain?'

I shook my head as the wind gusted at the edges of my blanket. I pulled it more snugly around my shoulders, and turned away from the wind. Samuel's bent face was almost completely black in the fading light.

'The men have been talking about it as we work. A free trader is marrying a Cree chief's daughter in the week before Christmas; they say there will be horse racing and dancing and feasting for days. Perhaps you might ask there about your horse.'

'Perhaps,' I muttered. 'Thank you, Samuel. And – goodbye.'

He hugged me briefly. 'Goodbye, Otterchild. I hope you find what you're looking for.'

Then he was gone with his callused hands and his shining face, a bulkiness in the rising dark, the memory of shared apples, bannock, miles of river. Soon, there was only the sound of receding footsteps on the hard ground. It was like listening to my past walk away, all those days at York Factory when my mother had still been alive, when Charlotte had been a gurgling baby in a cradleboard painted with Scottish hearts. I stifled a sob as I trudged back to Mr Spencer's cabin.

For a few more days, I continued searching on my own, although I knew that by now the horse was probably many miles away. I searched along the shoreline, whistling and waiting for a neigh in reply. I looked for holes broken through the ice by hooves as I set my muskrat traps. I searched around the stable, fingering the cold flatness of the picked lock that dangled uselessly from its bolt. I stood for long moments, lost in sorrow, in Foxfire's empty stall, remembering how beneath his red forelock the hair swirled in a pattern like a river current, and how the white hairs lay over his flanks like frost. Tears blurred the pale rectangle of the open stable door, and the silence was a burden on my back.

At home in the evenings, in Orchid's parlour, I laid out the moose hide that Betty had given me, and cut the pieces for Charlotte's winter coat. From birchbark, I cut templates of roses and horses. The strings of seed beads, brought all the distance from York Factory in my chest, lay shining in my lap like droplets of water as I worked, threading them upon my needle, laying them flat upon the moose hide. *Tick, tock, tick, tock.* The tall polished clock seemed loud in the silence for the wind had died. Beyond the window, the land brooded, vast and cold and empty, waiting for the snow that was so late in falling.

I was quiet at suppers, not speaking unless spoken to, making sure that Charlotte and I both had hands and faces scrubbed clean and hair neatly braided so that Mr Spencer could find nothing to object to. I was glad to see that, although the horse was missing, Mr Spencer still spoke kindly to Orchid and called her 'my love', his face grave and tender in the flickering light from the lantern on the wall. He treated us all with courtesy, and no more was spoken about school.

Yet I knew that he had not forgotten about his plan or changed his mind; I could see this in the set of his mouth and the cool paleness of his forehead with its straight, sandy eyebrows. He was not a man who changed his mind easily about anything. And the feast of Christmas was coming closer, closer, with every swing of the clock's round pendulum inside its walnut case. Christmas . . . and no Simon Mackenzie, no Gabriel Gunner, no rumour of a red horse. And after this, school for Charlotte and even for me, school with walls that shut out the vast sky, the touch of wind, the taste of snow or rain, the smell of animals crossing the horizon. School with its clocks that cut time up into smaller and smaller pieces – hours, minutes, seconds – like a knife chopping meat finer and finer. This was not time as I knew it, time measured by shadows stretching, by the moon waning, by water rising and ebbing, by birds flying north or south and rending the sky with their music.

Bent over my beadwork, I felt the white man's trap closing slowly. The beads quivered in my fingers and blood sprang from the accidental jab of the needle. I knew then what I must do – but not whether to tell Orchid. Yet how could I leave her without saying goodbye, after the hours we had spent seated in the York boat, our eyes running along the stallion's red back, the slope of his croup, the bend of his neck? Those hours had tied us together like a tie of kinship. I decided that I would have to risk saying goodbye, for I was almost grown and she couldn't stop me from carrying out my plan.

I waited until the last morning and then I rose in the dawn greyness and went into the kitchen where Orchid was struggling to rouse the fire in the belly of the black stove. As I entered, she wiped her hand across her cold face, smudging it with soot. I bent to blow on the embers, adding small twigs and a curl of birchbark until the flames leaped up.

'I am leaving,' I said.

Her blue eyes widened. 'What are you talking about?'

'I am going to the White Horse Plain with a Métis family. They are giving Charlotte and me a ride in their schooner. I am going to a wedding feast to listen for rumours of Foxfire. I might spend the winter there.'

'Don't be ridiculous!' Orchid cried, pushing back strands of hair and rubbing her chilled hands together before holding them to the flames. 'Mr Spencer has not been able to find any clues about the stallion. You cannot go off on a wild goose chase, a girl travelling without a chaperone! It is not suitable and Mr Spencer would not condone it!'

'He is not my husband or my chief,' I said evenly. 'And this is not my lodge, although you have made me welcome here.'

'But – surely, you will return? Amelia, what has possessed you?'

'I am not a child. I have travelled six hundred miles to this place, and now I am travelling on and you cannot stop me, Orchid.'

She looked at me for a long drawn-out moment, and those six hundred miles sat between us, a truth as round and solid as a grandfather stone. The weight of that stone was like the weight of loyalty to kin, and Orchid surely felt it lying between us. Her gaze softened and she pulled me against the flannel nightrobe that she had not yet changed out of. Her hands gripped my back

'Oh, Amelia,' she said brokenly, and nothing more for a long time. Behind us the fire crackled, taking hold of the maple wood, and I felt the stove's heat against my legs.

'We must eat and then leave,' I said gently at last, and Orchid sighed and stepped away, wiping her eyes before becoming brisk again.

'Have you got everything packed? Look, you must take this cold venison from the pantry, and this salt pork. And here is the bannock you baked last night; I will wrap it in a cloth. And have some oat porridge now, before you leave.'

She pulled her robe tighter and bustled around, placing things in my open trunk that I had dragged to the door while Charlotte, yawning sleepily, crouched by the stove to get warm.

'I hope you won't get into trouble on account of this,' I muttered.

'Perhaps, but I will take care of it,' Orchid replied with her customary determination, her chin lifted. We smiled then, and hugged for the final time as the schooner creaked to a halt at the door, and the faces of the Métis children peered out from beneath the wagon's canvas awning. The wife lifted Charlotte onboard, and her husband swung my chest up before he climbed on to his seat and sent his whip cracking out over the oxen's red backs. I scrambled up, the wheels already beginning to turn, and waved to Orchid as she stood in the doorway of her cabin, a woman who knew even fewer stories of this land than I did myself. The swell of the prairie folded her in. I felt the tug of our parting, and then I turned my face towards the south. It was hard to keep saying goodbye to people I had journeyed with.

For a day, we followed the river trail past the settlements of Lord Selkirk's people, and the homes of retired Hudson's Bay Company men, and the cabins of the Swiss and German farmers. The ribbon of river lay beside us, a cold sheen, until we reached the Forks where the Assiniboine flowed in from the west. Here there were grander homes, some of stone and others of board upon stone foundations, and a general store and a blacksmith's shop. We turned west and began our second day's journey along the banks of the Assiniboine, the trail winding amongst willow and cranberry bushes all bare of leaves.

The family we travelled with were in high spirits, anticipating the festivities. Around me, they sang and laughed, but I hunched in my blanket and thought about the family of Gabriel Gunner. Should I try to find them? It was humiliating, I decided, to stand knocking at their cabin door, an orphan with no kinship claim upon them, a girl who had only danced for one evening with one of their sons. I set my jaw and pushed my wounded pride down into one of those places inside me that were like birchbark rogans, sealed with pitch. Things could be stored in those containers for a very long time. Even liquid things. Even tears.

We approached the settlement of St François Xavier that evening, on the White Horse Plain.

'Are there white horses here?' Charlotte asked Louise, the Métis woman, as the schooner bumped along on the uneven ridges of the frozen track.

'Tell us the story of the *blanco diablo*,' one of the Métis children cried immediately. The other children crowded against their mother, who was nursing a baby at her breast. Even Charlotte snuggled closer. Curiosity got the better of me and I let my blanket slip from my ears so that I too could listen to Louise's words.

'This is a story that my mother heard from her mother, and she had heard it from her own mother. About one hundred and forty years ago, as the white man reckons them, only the people of the tribes wandered the great land, riding their horses over the waving grasses. It was summer, the larks sang in the blue sky, the roses bloomed, the thoughts of the young turned to love. A Cree chief from Lake Winnipegosis came riding south to ask for the daughter of an Assiniboine chief camped here on the plains. The young man promised a bride gift of a pure white horse, called a *blanco diablo* in the tongue of the Spanish nation. This horse was from the famous white horses in the country far to the south, called Mexico. The horse could outrun anything it raced against. It could journey for four days longer than any other horse, and go without food or water all that time. It was nimble and swift.

'So the Assiniboine chief and his daughter accepted the Cree suitor's marriage gift, and a time was arranged for a wedding ceremony. But in the Assiniboine camp was a sorcerer who remembered that the Cree and the Assiniboine had once been enemies and not allies. It was wrong, he felt, for the chief's daughter to be given to this Cree man even though he came with a *blanco diablo* horse as a gift. And this sorcerer sent word to the camp of the Sioux to the south, where another young man wanted the same daughter for his wife.

'On his wedding day, the Cree chief arrived mounted on a grey horse and leading the *blanco diablo*, the pure white horse that could fly like the wind over the land. The wedding commenced with

273

feasting and dancing but then a cloud of dust was seen in the distance. Sioux warriors were galloping over the prairie! The bride's father cried to his daughter to mount the white horse and flee, and her Cree bridegroom must flee also. The two young people rode hard over the prairie, doubling back, hiding behind trees and bushes. They rode along ridgelines like smoke from a forest fire in a strong wind. They clattered down the banks of creeks. But no matter how hard or fast they rode, the Sioux followed them, for they could glimpse the white horse from many miles away.

'At last, near St François Xavier – which is where we are going now – the young couple were shot. The arrows of the Sioux killed them both. The grey horse was caught. But the white horse, the *blanco diablo*, escaped. Wild and free, it roamed the plains. It was never caught.'

'But what happened to it?' asked Charlotte, her eyes stretched wide in her heart-shaped face.

'Sometimes it is still seen, a ghost horse, slipping into a hollow in the summer grass. Some people have glimpsed it, swirling in the falling snow.'

Louise changed her nursing baby to the other side. One of the little boys began to whittle a flute from a willow branch, and Charlotte began to braid a girl's hair. I stared ahead, out of the opening in the schooner's canvas awning, and pulled my blanket tighter around my head again. Chills ran up and down my back. The story's sadness seemed like an omen, like a bad sign on a hunting trail. Two lovers dead. A horse that no one could ever catch, that ran wild for ever until it became a ghost horse, lost in the tall grass, the drifted snow. A horse that could disappear again as though the Thunderbirds had lifted it into the clouds. I shivered.

We reached the settlement of St François Xavier shortly after this, and slept in the schooner surrounded by Métis farms, clusters of carts and wagons, groups of dogs running half wild, lowing oxen and whinnying ponies. To the north-west lay a long, low ridge which the Métis woman told me had always been a gathering place for the people of the land, a place where they held Dog Feasts and Sun dances. Tonight, against the stars, I saw the glow of the Cree campfires scattered on the ridge and sending their flickering light over the tipis and the horses.

In the morning Charlotte and I roamed the banks of the Assiniboine, the ridge of land to the north-west, and the flat expanse of the White Horse Plain amongst the celebrating crowds. The frosty air vibrated with the throb of drums and chanting from the Cree and Salteaux encampments. Horses neighed, sometimes shrill and sometimes challenging. Dogs barked and ripped up stolen hides or fought viciously over offal. Buffalo haunches roasted over fires, spitting grease, warming my nostrils with their thick, dark aroma. Métis men squatted in tent doorways and against the sides of schooners, playing cards, drinking firewater from jugs, cursing and singing. Fiddles and mouth organs made me walk with a bounce, and jigs tugged at my toes.

Horses of all shapes and colours filled my eyes; they breathed their sweet, grassy breath over my hands as I stroked their flanks, or smoothed their forelocks from their eyes. Métis women rode in saddles with swells of padded hide at the front and back, and I remembered Gabriel telling me that these cantles and horns were carved from wood or even bone before being covered with hide. Babies with eyes as small and round as berries hung from saddle horns, strapped inside their cradleboards. Very small children were tied to their mother's backs with blankets, while older children sat astride the horses and held on to their mother's back, or rode ahead of her, hanging on to coarse strands of mane.

There were horses with white coats covered in brown spots, and horses with brown coats covered in white patches; there were horses wearing bridles made of nothing but one piece of rope cleverly twisted around their jaws and up over their heads, and other horses wearing fancy bridles intricately decorated with beautiful beadwork, with quills and tassels and coins. There were horses tied to picket lines, and horses hobbled by their own rein tied to a foreleg, and horses rolling in the dead grass, tossing their legs over the pale swells of their bellies. At all hours of the day, there were horses being raced, sometimes at a gallop and other times at a trot. The cheering and jeering of the crowds roared in my ears like waterfalls. Money and trade goods, weapons and wagons changed hands hour after hour as men won and lost their wagers.

The entire plain seemed to seethe with horses and dogs, with people in buffalo robes, capotes and Hudson's Bay Company blankets; with headdresses of feathers; with faces painted in yellow and green stripes. The brightness of all the beads and earrings and bracelets seemed to shine in my eyes long after I lay down in the schooner, surrounded by snoring Métis, to sleep beside Charlotte. In my sleep, I seemed to mutter the same questions all night, over and over, as I had done all day, asking for rumours of a red horse, or news of a man called Simon Mackenzie. All night long my questions fell into a well of dark silence, and every day they were absorbed into the crowd's roar and swept away from my mouth, from my aching ears. No one could answer me.

On the third day, a young boy walked past me leading a horse, a grulla gelding. I narrowed my eyes. Hard Twist? My breath caught. When the gelding swung his head to glance in my direction, I was sure of it. My gaze shot around the vicinity, ricocheting off a horse pulling a pole-framed travois loaded with kettles and pans, off men rolling dice and women braiding each other's hair. Nowhere did I see Gabriel

Gunner but still I rushed away as fast as I could walk, my heart hopping like a hare. *I do not want to see him*, I thought. *I will not speak to him if I meet him accidentally*. I waited, fearful, hopeful, for his voice calling my name but only drumming and laughter filled my ears.

On the fourth day of the feasting and racing, as the crowds grew still thicker on the plain, and as the drumming rose higher in the Cree camp, I left Charlotte playing with other children and wandered off between a group of Assiniboine tents. My feet ached from the hard, cold ground. My ears ached from the surge of noise, and my belly growled with hunger. I paused to rest against a wagon wheel, slumping in my blanket. A line of picketed horses stood with heads drooping as they dozed in the thin sunlight. Their breath smoked white in the cold air. There was a scrawny black with a large head and a kind eye, a bright chestnut with a blonde mane, and two horses beneath layers of blankets. One had legs of muddy brown, and a black tail, while the other was a pale, sandy buckskin. The two blanketed horses were tall, especially the muddy brown. On its head it wore a mask made of hide, and bright red and yellow feathers; tassels hung down over its nostrils in a luxuriant fringe.

My eyes wandered on across the scene; women were husking heads of corn and dropping them into an iron pot, suspended over a fire, to boil. The pot's steam curled up and mingled with the plumes from the horses' nostrils. A group of young women on one side of the fire were roasting marrow bones and then cracking them with stones and sucking out the fat; their mouths shone with grease as they giggled and chatted.

Two men sat on stones nearby and played a game of change hands while a small crowd of spectators gathered to watch. The man wearing a hat of grey badger hair held one knuckle bone in the palm of one hand, and two knuckle bones in the other hand. He closed his fingers over the bones and swayed back and forth. His hands darted beneath the blanket draped over his legs, then waved in the air above his head in a blur of motion as fast as a bird's wingbeats. Finally, he crossed his arms behind his back. The man in a red fox hat, who was his opponent, leaned forward, his eyes darting after the waving hands like the eyes of a hawk watching the scurrying of a mouse.

'Haw, haw! Haw, haw!' the onlookers shouted, trying to guess which hand the bones had been changed over into, and who would win this round of the game. At the men's feet lay their wagers: a folded blanket, a buffalo horn for carrying gunpowder in.

'The two bones are in your left hand. The one bone is in your right!' cried the man beneath the fox hat.

A shock jolted through my slumped body and my eyes, drooping with fatigue, flew wide open. I stepped forward, skirting the fire, brushing past the reaching nose of a picketed horse.

'Pierre?' I said, squatting to see beneath his hat.

The steersman's face tilted towards me; his grin gleamed mockingly. '*Oui, c'est moi,*' he said. 'Who is asking? Ah, *c'est la jolie fille,* Amelia.'

'What are you doing here?'

'The Company sent me to trade,' he said nonchalantly. 'What are you doing here yourself, heh? I haven't seen your Métis man, your Gabriel.'

'I don't care where he is!' I said hotly but Pierre only winked.

'My next wager!' he called to his opponent. He thought for a moment. Then he reached into a pocket of his capote and pulled out something silver that he tossed on to the ground. Its twin hearts shone on the trampled stems of dead prairie grass, and the crown above the hearts was speckled with points of light.

'It is my brooch!' I shouted in astonishment.

Pierre's hand shot out and closed over the luckenbooth. 'Prove it,' he said. 'Many people own brooches. What does it say, the writing on the back?'

'*True heart is true riches. Simon and Mary,*' I recited. Pierre grinned again, and opened his fingers, turning the brooch over. I leaned down, breathing hard as though I had been running. The girls with the marrow bones crowded around, and all of us could see the deep, spidery score of the lettering, of those words that my father had given to my mother, those words forming a promise that was broken.

'It is my brooch,' I repeated, and Pierre caught hold of my hand and laid the silver's coldness on my palm, and wrapped my fingers over it, grinning.

'Where did you get this?' I demanded, my voice fierce with shock.

Pierre shrugged, his eyes suddenly sullen. He spat into the fire, beneath the pot of boiling corn. 'Eva gave it to me. She did not say it was yours.'

'What? Eva? Why?'

'She gave it to me in payment for untying the red *cheval*. At Robinson Portage. She wanted to get you in trouble with the white woman.'

My mind reeled back to that terrible evening of rain and sleet, when the grandfather bear had chased the panic-stricken stallion away from our camp, thrashing aside the underbrush. I recalled how afterwards, Orchid had not spoken to me for many days and how Eva, instead of me, had sat on the bench beside her and how they had murmured together, bent over the sketching paper.

'I don't understand,' I said. 'I thought it was the Witiko man, Angus, who kept causing trouble for the horse.'

Pierre shrugged again. 'Eva was jealous of you. Bad blood between your families in the past, *non*? She wanted revenge.'

'She found my brooch after the boat wreck and stole it?'

'Perhaps.'

'But why are you telling me this?' I asked, although I already knew the answer, for I had heard Eva and Pierre arguing on the edge of the Métis camp, the day that I rode with the buffalo.

Now Pierre's red lips curled in a sneer and he bit on to the end of a marrow bone so that it gave a sharp crack. 'What do I care for her and her secrets and her revenge?' he said. 'I care nothing,' and he spat a piece of bone on to the ground.

'But what about the stallion?' I demanded. 'Didn't you care about him? Didn't you think that something bad could have happened to him running free in the woods?'

Pierre spread his hands. 'Nothing happened. *Allez!* Take your brooch and go before I ask for it back!'

I glared at him for another moment but he ignored me, until finally I turned and walked off, awash with anger and shock.

On the fifth day, the day before the white man's feast of Christmas, I awoke in the schooner as usual amongst a heap of sleeping children. It was very early yet; only a hint of light softened the canvas roof above me. I lay still and thought about Pierre's confession. It was to impress Eva that he had carried out her suggestion and not merely for the payment of a brooch. But it had done him no good in the end for

Eva had her sights set on marrying a Company clerk and one day having a stone house. I thought about how I had misjudged Angus, and how Eva had clouded my judgement with her sly whispers about Angus's heart turning to ice.

If only I had known sooner that Angus had known my father. Then I might have been able to find out more. Instead, I had avoided him because of Eva's hints of danger. Eva, I thought now, was like an ermine in winter. Its coat is all white but the tip of its tail is black, and it twitches this tip so that birds of prey notice it. When the bird goes for that tip, the ermine leaps away unscathed. Eva had used Angus like a black tip.

Simon Mackenzie could ride any horse that was ever foaled, Angus had said. *He had a stallion called Lightfoot, a buffalo runner.* Now I treasured these words as though they might bring me closer to the man who had fathered me and then disappeared into the silence of the land.

As I lay there in the schooner, the memory of the muddy brown horse that I'd seen the day before returned. My mind drifted away on to other things but that horse's memory kept bothering me, like a black fly tangled in the hair around my ears. I didn't know why I kept thinking about that horse, about how tall it had been, about the wide nostrils beneath the fringe of bright feathers on its face mask. Finally, I decided to throw off my blanket and slip quietly from the schooner to see if I could find that horse again on its picket line. I didn't know why I was doing this. I just had a feeling in my belly like the feeling I got when it was time to check my trap lines or my snares; that feeling that there was something I needed to pay attention to.

By now other people were stirring in the camps. Women were rousing flames from banks of embers and smoke rose into the dawn sky. My breath puffed before my mouth. I pulled a piece of dried meat from the pouch I carried, and sucked its dark sweetness as I wandered around, wending between travois and tents and schooners. A man shaved over a basin of water, the razor's blade a gleam in the rising sun. A girl carried armloads of hay to a spotted pony that nickered in pleasure.

'Amelia!'

I swung around at the voice.

His eyes were still and dark, and filled with wind and sky that I fell down into. Then I ducked my head and looked away. All I felt was shame because Gabriel Gunner had thought so little of me that he'd broken his promise to visit me at the stone fort and was here, instead, at a wedding feast.

I broke into a fast walk, dodging around the spotted pony snatching up mouthfuls of hay, leaping aside as a dog pack rushed by.

'Amelia!' he called again but I didn't turn. I broke into a trot, my face flaming. He was nothing to me, I thought. He was just one more broken promise. Just another man who disappeared.

Chapter 15

Gabriel's moccasins beat the ground behind me. His hand caught me by one arm and slowed my rush. I kept my arm as stiff as a branch in his grasp.

'What's the matter? Don't you remember me?'

'You're the one who's forgotten! You promised you'd come and see me at the stone fort!' My lips were stiff as frostbitten fingers.

'But I am coming! I only reached St François Xavier two days ago from the trading trip around Lake Winnipeg. Then my father asked me to stay here and race his horses. I could not go against my father's wishes. I told him I would race for the last time today and then ride north tomorrow, to find you.'

I allowed my eyes to flicker back to his face. In his own eyes there was no shadow of a lie; they were clear as water over stones.

'What are you doing here?' he asked.

'I'm looking for Foxfire – he has been stolen.' I tugged against his hand on my arm, turning away again, but his grip held me fast.

'When did this happen? I will help you search for him!'

'Let me go!'

His hand jumped off my arm, and I turned and began to walk on, staring at the toes of my moccasins. 'When was he stolen?' Gabriel persisted, falling into step beside me as I continued heading for the brown horse's picket line.

'Two weeks ago,' I explained. Suddenly, words poured from me like a spring torrent. I told Gabriel about my meeting with Pierre, and how I had learned of Eva's treachery. I pulled the brooch from my pouch, and unwrapped it from its covering of deer-hide. It lay in Gabriel's broad palm, licked by morning sunshine. When he bent over it, his long hair swung forward, and the dentalia shells threaded on the strands laid their cool touch against my cheek. He turned the brooch over and read the inscription while I waited, gazing over his shoulder.

Beyond him, on its picket line, stood the muddy brown horse still blanketed and wearing the feathered face mask.

'It is strange,' said Gabriel, his brow furrowed. 'I have a fiddle at home with these same words upon it.'

'What words?'

'*True heart is true riches*. There is a small metal piece screwed to the back of the fiddle, with these words upon it. Is it a proverb from the Scottish nation?'

'I don't know. Maybe so. Or maybe it is from one of their stories. Or their heroes.' My mind flashed quickly over stories that the Scotsmen had told around the stove in the long winter evenings in York Factory while my mother sat sewing mittens; stories about strange creatures called kelpies which were half woman and half seal, and about giants, and standing grandfather stones, and *manitous* of the land that the men called wee folk.

'I must go and get the horses ready,' Gabriel replied, handing the brooch back to me. 'My father wants some of them to go in the trotting races.'

He glanced up and scanned the sky for the position of the sun. 'I must go,' he repeated. 'Amelia, my family's farm is three miles west of here, at a bend in the Assiniboine. If I cannot find you after the race, will you meet me at the farm? There is a cabin of peeled logs, a stable and a small herd of horses. It is the only farm at the river's bend.'

'Yes,' I said, a smile tugging at my mouth and at Gabriel's mouth too. The dark brown fur of his buffalo hat flared reddish in the sun. Beyond this nimbus of light, the muddy brown horse at the picket line stamped a hind hoof beneath the hem of his blankets,

287

and shook his head inside the feathered mask. Something about the movement caught my attention.

My gaze sharpened. My eyes ran along the horse's back – 'the top line' as Orchid called it – beneath the covering of blankets. I considered the black tail. I stared at the hard, dark legs, the flatness of the knees, the shape and size of the hooves. I thought about the arc of the blanketed neck. There was no forelock hanging between the ears for it had been braided and tied back. The horse's muzzle was muddy brown beneath the mask's fringe of feathers. I stared at the size and shape of the nostrils.

'What is it?' Gabriel asked, turning to look.

I whistled, low and sweet. Once, twice. The horse had fallen back into a doze beside the blanketed buckskin. I whistled a third time. The horse's head swung up; I saw the shine of eyes inside the holes in the mask. His ears flickered towards me.

Into my stomach leaped the feeling that I got when I found something big in one of my traps, some animal larger and with a better pelt than I could have hoped for.

'When is the trotting race?' I asked, gripping Gabriel's arm.

'Very soon. Look, already the horses are gathering. I must go and get mine ready.'

I followed the line of his pointing arm to see, beyond the wagons and tents, a knotted bunch of horses gathering on the main track leading through the settlement. They pawed and stamped, their mouths foaming with excitement, and sweat dampening their necks.

'I am racing. Please help me!' I said, and pulled him close. 'That mud-coloured horse in the mask? I am riding him in the race. Just before it starts, I am going to jump on that horse. I need you to cut his picket line with a knife. Then I need you to do something here by his owner's tent. Delay the chase.'

He stared at me incredulously. 'I have a horse you could ride if you –'

'I think he's Foxfire. That brown horse. I am going to steal him back. Help me.'

He grinned in sudden delight. 'Ah, it is the highest honour! Amongst warriors, it is the highest honour to steal a hobbled horse from the enemy camp.'

Gabriel slid his knife out from its sheath inside his buffalo coat. The look he gave me was steady and shining; it held the solemn joy that I felt when I danced, stomping my feet to the drum. It was a joy that raised bumps along my skin.

'Charlotte is with the family of Jean-Paul and Louise Laval,' I said. 'Whatever happens, will you find her and take her to your mother?'

Gabriel nodded. 'Don't worry about her; I will keep her safe.'

Shoulder to shoulder, we stared at the line of gathering horses being held in check behind a stretched rope that two men held across the track.

'That man will start the race.' Gabriel pointed to a tall white man in a rawhide jacket who stepped forward with a raised gun.

'Now!' Gabriel said into my ear; I felt the tickle of his lips.

When we lunged forward, the picketed horses all shied in alarm like a school of frightened fish. I saw the flash of Gabriel's knife arcing towards the picket rope, and I grasped the blankets and dragged them backwards over the horse's tail, dodging to avoid the lash of a hind foot. As the blankets laid the horse's neck bare, I saw his black mane was hogged off short. At this strange sight, a wave of panic washed through me. I was making a terrible mistake. But it was too late now to stop.

I sprinted forward and flung myself upward, clawing that horse's muddy side, up that familiar height of muscle and ribs. I flung my leg over as Gabriel threw the severed line from the halter rope to me. The end of it stung across my face like a whip before I snatched it from the air and hauled the horse's head around to face an opening between the tents. Two men were crowding out through a tipi doorway, pushing aside the flap of buffalo skin, shouting angrily. One of them raised his gun and fired it into the air. The picketed horses leaped again, and beyond the wagons the horses gathered for the trotting race leaped forward too, spooked and running too soon, plunging into the rope that was quickly dropped to lie beneath their thundering hooves. I glanced back in time to see Gabriel throw himself around the knees of the man with the gun and bring him crashing to the ground.

I dragged on the halter rope, bringing the horse around to face the main track where the trotters were already darting away, their manes billowing. A snort shook my horse's ribcage. He swung around a tent, a child, two dogs, a horse pulling a travois of branches loaded with blankets and kettles. His stride smoothed out; his legs became sweeping arcs of sinew and bone. Those flashing legs swung us on to the track. His hooves hammered the frozen ground. Breath streamed from his nostrils in one long, uninterrupted, white plume. His neck stretched out, his ears strained forward. His eyes bulged and sparked in the mask holes; he sucked in the sight of the hindquarters rising and falling ahead of us. His hind legs thrust against the ground's resistance. His front legs disappeared under his belly with each stride. His back and front hooves breezed past each other; only a sliver of space existed between them.

He was a horse, I was sure, who could trot seventeen miles in one hour.

There were more gunshots behind us in the camp; and then the sound of galloping hoof beats and shouting. The spectators lining the track jeered and yelled. I glanced over my shoulder. The galloping horse was the buckskin that had been picketed under blankets.

He pounded after us, a tiny struggling figure far back down the track.

We swept on. I pummelled my mount with my heels but he wouldn't break stride, for he had been trained to hold a trot in a race. Now we were catching up to the knotted mass of other trotters, now we were pushing our way through. Bridles, wild eyes, knees clad in wool and leather, brass tacks decorating saddles, feathers in forelocks, braided tails – they all surged through my vision. Now we were through, breaking free, forging ahead.

The river snaked and looped to one side. Far out on the ice, men were running a sleigh race; the crack of whips carried like gunshot in the still air. Behind us, the buckskin had reached the trotters and was blocked there, as I had anticipated. Behind it another horse, a bay, swept on at a gallop. Unsettled, panicked, the trotters began to break stride and gallop too; suddenly, they were all bunching up behind me, wild and out of control, their bits lying useless in their wide-open mouths. Men whooped and cheered. A bullet whistled high overhead and I ducked as though it would have clipped me.

Now my horse, pressed from behind, broke stride at last; the rhythm changed as he galloped on with the other racers pounding after him. Another gunshot. I lay along the hogged mane, and rode the surge of his neck like a porpoise riding the incoming tide in the mouth of the Hayes.

Three miles, I thought. *A bend in the river.*

Behind me the other racers were slowing, peeling off the track, being dragged to swearing halts and ridden back towards town. They created a melee that slowed my pursuers. There were no spectators beside the track now, only drifts of dead grass and beyond them, stretching down to the river, the hay and potato fields of the settlers. I wrestled the horse's head to the north. Trying to control him without reins was almost impossible now that he was no longer racing with the other horses along the straight track. I swung him over a low ridge, and along a gulley where a creek lay. Its ice shattered like clam shells as we crossed it and ran up the other side into a stand of poplar and willow. We dodged west for a few more minutes, then I wrestled the horse's head to the south and rode him down the long slope, through the tree shadows. Gunshot rang out twice, in the far distance, and the horse snorted and renewed his efforts.

Still heading south, we burst across the road, dodged some haystacks, rounded the corner of a cabin roofed in sod, and flew alongside a sod stable where chickens scattered underfoot. Ahead, sparkling in the sun, lay the river's bend, a loop as lazy as the letter 's'. We galloped towards the dark huddle of buildings on the point, thrashed for a quarter of a mile through a bank of tall reeds, and then ran along the far side of the cabin and barn. Inside a corral of peeled cedar poles, a dozen horses wheeled in excitement as we shot past. I caught a flash of grulla.

I leaned far forward, looped my arms beneath the horse's neck, and laced my fingers together. Then I swung down, my feet pounding on to the frozen ground with a shock that jarred my teeth. Gripping the halter rope, I hauled on it, finally bringing the horse to a skidding stop after twenty feet, my moccasins burning beneath my soles.

The wooden latch on the barn door lifted smoothly and I swung the door open on its leather hinges. The horse followed me into the dimness, where a cow turned her head and gazed at us in mild surprise, and chickens clucked on beams overhead. The door swung shut with a muffled thump, and the bedding of oat straw rustled as I led the horse inside. His sides heaved. I laid my face against his shoulder and waited for my heart to return to my body, for my spirit to come down from its flight with the angel *manitous* in the cold blue river of the sky.

I was shaking all over.

With my face pressed to a crack in the barn's chinking, I squinted out to the distant track, and waited until I had seen the buckskin and the bay horses jog past twice, once heading west and once heading back to the settlement. By then, they looked worn out, and the rider with the gun had returned his weapon to its holster and rode slumped in his saddle.

A grin trembled on my mouth, and then I turned my attention to the mud-brown horse with the black tail. I wondered whether I had made a foolish mistake.

I hummed a lullaby, *'wa wi wa way,'* and the horse lowered his head and pressed his face against my chest. I unfastened the hide and feather mask and slipped his face free of it, then of the halter beneath, and hung them both over a wooden stall partition. When I smoothed the hair on his forehead, I found a swirl like a current in a river. I lifted three of his feet and each one came up smoothly and easily to lie lightly in my hand. When I moved to the offside rear foot, the horse locked his leg joints together and refused to lift his foot until I sang to him some more; then he raised it grudgingly and pressed it heavy as a stone into my palm.

Setting the hoof down, I choked suddenly on tears and laughter.

I twisted stems of oat straw into a wisp and rubbed the sweating horse all over; my fingers remembered every inch of him; the length between fetlock and elbow, elbow and withers. I didn't know how his coat had been coloured muddy brown; perhaps with a dye made of birchbark, or plum roots or juniper berries; perhaps with minerals from rock and soil. At the stone fort, Cree women had shown me hides they coloured with substances brought in trade from far places. With a pang of sadness, I ran my hand over the cropped stubble of his mane, but it would grow back slowly, long and red as a bush fire again.

'Foxfire,' I murmured as I rubbed, and he turned his head to blow into my hair. I led him to a manger and filled it with hay from the rick outside the barn. Then I stood in the open doorway, watching the clouds roll in from the west. Shadow fell across the prairie like a blanket. When the stallion was cool, I found a tin pail which I carried down to the river and filled at a hole, kept open with an axe, at the edge of the ice. Being careful not to slosh cold water on to my leggings, I carried the pail back to the barn.

The first snowflakes began to fall as the stallion sucked water. When I stepped outside, the flakes touched my skin like the wings of white moths. I turned my face upwards, and closed my eyes, and stuck my tongue out. I could smell the winter rolling in from the west, and joy ran in bumps over my skin.

The snow thickened and a gusting wind sprang up, eddying around the corners of the barn while I sat in the oat straw and waited for Gabriel. I hoped that he hadn't been hurt in the fight, and that he had found Charlotte. Perhaps I dozed, for suddenly, or so it seemed, the light grew dim with evening. I moved to the barn door, and stared into the maelstrom of whirling flakes. At least the snow would cover the stallion's tracks, I thought. Perhaps no one would come here and find him now. But, surely, Gabriel would come soon? Peering towards the log cabin, I saw the rectangles of flickering light that marked the windows, and caught the hint of woodsmoke in the wind.

Suddenly, the shadowy horses in the corral began to wheel and nicker restlessly. Around the corner of the barn came a horse. Was some stranger coming, looking for a stolen stallion? I gripped my knife.

Then I heard Charlotte's voice and I jumped out of the barn doorway into the stifling whirl of snow. Gabriel pulled Hard Twist to a halt, and Charlotte slid from the gelding's back. I saw that he was pulling a travois of sticks and that my HBC chest was lashed on to it. A grin of delight split my face open, and I saw the shine of Gabriel's teeth. He led Hard Twist past me into the barn and pulled off his snowy saddle, his beautifully embroidered wool blanket, and his leather bridle studded with copper discs beaten from a kettle.

'Gabriel says we can stay here for Christmas!' Charlotte said, her eyes shining in the gloom, and I heard the catch of excitement in her voice. 'He says his sisters will play with me!'

'But your mother – she is not expecting us –'

'Our house is filled with visiting relatives. What's one or two more people?' Gabriel replied. 'Grab one handle of your chest.'

He unlashed the ropes holding it on the sticks of the travois, and then hefted it between us as we ploughed our way through the snow towards the lights of the cabin. What looked to be enough dogs for three teams were staked to logs nearby. Two carts and several wagons loomed near the back door and, when Gabriel opened it, the wail of a fiddle wafted out into the darkness and drifting snow. Lamplight and firelight dazzled my eyes. I stumbled in, pushing Charlotte ahead of me, and feeling suddenly shy as a roomful of eyes turned in my direction.

A tiny, quick woman, with brilliant earrings of glass beads and a vivid face, darted forward.

'Mother, this is Amelia who I told you about,' Gabriel said.

Her dark eyes sparked with merriment, and she hugged me. 'Welcome, daughter,' she said, and then stooped, her dark braids swinging, to unfasten Charlotte's snowy robe. Soon, we were seated by the open door of the wood stove with bowls of hot stew in our hands; the sweetness of berries and sunshine, the tang of the pine forests, the fertile soil of the valleys, were all united in that stew of berries and roots and moose meat. I ate so fast that my tongue burned.

A tall, wiry man was playing the fiddle, tapping his toes as he circled the room, and later I learned that he was Gabriel's father. A number of people were dancing, making the smooth plank flooring vibrate. At a table with a checked cloth, three small girls were cutting up old pieces of hide and making dolls. Gently I nudged Charlotte towards them, and in a moment her voice joined their chatter even though they spoke Michif and she spoke Swampy Cree.

'Will the stallion be safe in the barn?' I asked Gabriel. Seeing him in the lamplight, I noticed for the first time the knife gash that was swelling and turning purple on his left jaw.

'It is nothing, only a scratch,' he said, seeing my gaze resting on it. 'My uncles and I will take turns guarding the barn tonight.'

'Thank you, for helping with everything.'

'Come and dance,' he said in reply, holding out his hand. His mother had a set of spoons and beat a hard, fast rhythm while the fiddle notes leaped and soared, and a man blew into his harmonica. The lamplight shone along the stocks of guns hanging on the wall on wooden pegs, and babies slept in their cradle-boards, and little children lay on the sleeping benches along the walls, bundled in bearskins.

We danced late into the night while the snow fell and fell, blanketing the world in a whispering silence. In the barn, the stallion slept while a man sat at the door with a gun over his knees, and Charlotte snored softly beside me on a bench, her new doll and her old one both tucked under her arm.

All the following day, we feasted while relatives arrived and left again by horse-drawn sleigh and dog teams. The sun was brilliant on the new drifts when Gabriel and I took Hard Twist and Smoke Eyes out for a run. The mare had a saddle blanket decorated with yellow horses, like the ones I was stitching on Charlotte's robe and that one of Gabriel's sisters had admired that morning. She had given me some more yellow beads since my supply was running low. The drifted snow creamed around the horses' legs as we raced them over the swells of the land, so that it was as though they were running in river rapids. When we returned to the barn, it was filled with Métis relations all admiring the size and strength of the Norfolk stallion; they bombarded me with questions and ran their hands over his thick arched neck and the massive rounded strength of his hindquarters.

Inside the cabin again, Gabriel asked me to tell his family the story of the stallion's journey and of how he had learned to ride in a York boat. The Métis loved a story told well, and I hoped that I didn't disappoint them. Afterwards, there was more eating – baked sturgeon, mashed potatoes and turnips, fried white-fish with wild rice, roasted duck, huge cranberry tarts, cornmeal puddings with maple syrup – and then more games of cribbage and dice and change hands, and then more dancing. Gabriel unwrapped a fiddle and carried it over to me.

'Look, this is the fiddle that I told you about. It's the one I copied when I made my travelling fiddle. See here, on the back?'

He turned its smooth, shining body. I leaned forward, tracing the plaque of thin metal that was screwed to the wood. *'True heart is true riches,'* I read aloud. It sent a shock through me, to see those famil-iar words fastened to a fiddle, in this faraway place that I hadn't imagined when I stepped into a boat and began my journey westwards.

'Where did you get this?' I asked.

'From an old Assiniboine man who lives in St François Xavier.'

'Where did he get it from?'

'I don't know. Do you want to go and talk to him?'

'Yes.'

'A tune, Gabriel! A jig!' someone cried, and he lifted the fiddle to his chin and danced away from me, swinging over his bow while his mother played the spoons.

Again, we stayed up late and in the morning slept in while the horses whinnied and stamped in the corral, and the dog teams snarled and howled. At last, yawning, I followed Gabriel into the sharp snap of the cold to saddle the grulla mustangs and ride into the settlement. The old Assiniboine stepped outside when Gabriel knocked at the door of his low, sod-roofed cabin. His face was as creased as a mud flat when the tide runs out over it, and he pulled his striped blanket around his shoulders as wind lifted the ends of his long grey hair.

'Remember that fiddle I won from you at a race?' Gabriel asked. 'You wagered it, and I won. It was four winters ago.'

The old man inclined his head, his rheumy, sharp eyes gazing over Gabriel's shoulder at the mustangs that we had tied to a corral rail.

'I remember. There are too many winters in my fingers. I can't play a fiddle so well any more.'

'Did you get that fiddle from a man called Simon Mackenzie?' I asked. 'A white man. A Scot.'

The old man's gaze stilled as he considered my question. 'No, I've never heard of this man. Never heard that name.'

I let my held breath out in a sharp sigh. Until this moment, I hadn't realised how high my hope had climbed. Now it plummeted, an eagle falling from the clouds. I turned away from the men and stared across the white land, fighting back my tears.

'That's a nice mare,' the old man was saying to Gabriel when I turned back. His eyes were narrowed and assessing. 'How much would you take for that mare? I've got a new gun and some Congou tea you might like.'

Gabriel shook his head.

'How about I throw in some beads for your sisters, and a couple of good wolf pelts, and some fabric for your mother?'

Gabriel shook his head again and moved away to untie Hard Twist's reins from the corral's top rail.

The old Assiniboine followed, snow melting on his leggings. 'How about two guns, and some tobacco as well? And an axe? Sharp, new.'

Gabriel turned to the man with a grin.

'Dark Cloud,' he said, 'this mare is not for sale. And if she was, you would need to trade me a lot more than what you've offered. This is a fine mare. She's from Lightfoot's line.'

Lightfoot! I felt like a tall jack pine hit by a bolt of lightning.

'My father's horse –'

'Lightfoot,' said the old man. 'Hmnn. That was one fine stallion. People still tell stories about that buffalo runner. And funny thing . . . that man I got the fiddle from, he was called Lightfoot Stuart.'

'But where is he – where is this man?' I cried.

A dog trotted up to the old Assiniboine and nosed his hand, and Smoke Eyes breathed gustily against the back of my neck.

'Think he lives westwards,' the old man said, the sunlight lying in the ripples of his face. 'About three days' ride, little place on the Carlton Trail. But it was many winters ago. It was the winter when my wife died giving birth . . . maybe seven winters ago. I could get out my winter count and look for you.'

I was already fumbling with the reins, my fingers shaking. 'It's fine,' I said. 'Don't trouble about it.'

I was too impatient to wait while this old man searched in his cabin for the buffalo hide on which he painted his count of every winter, working in a spiral, remembering every year with one symbol: perhaps a buffalo, a horse, an axe, the stick figure of a person. I didn't want to wait while he traced his crooked fingers over the spirals, squinting at the symbols and trying to remember which year he'd got a fiddle.

'You sure you don't want to sell that mare?' Dark Cloud asked as I swung into the Métis woman's saddle with its decorations of brass tacks and blue beads.

'I could give you a few men's shirts too. And some gun flints. How about I add in a few knives?' he called as Gabriel mounted Hard Twist and we turned the horses westwards and gave them their heads. They sucked in the cold air and leaped away, racing with necks outstretched while the dog gave chase, yelping with excitement.

And all the way back as I galloped along, I thought about how, if I had never spoken to Angus, I would never have known the name of my father's horse.

'I will go and try to find this man for you,' Gabriel said when we reached his home.

'No! I will go myself!'

'Amelia, you have Charlotte here. And you need to get word to Mr Spencer that his stallion is in my father's barn. We don't want to be accused of stealing him ourselves.'

My face sobered. 'Then I will write a letter for you to take west,' I said. 'If Lightfoot Stuart is my father . . . if you find him . . . he can at least read my letter.'

'Write one then.'

In my chest, now shoved beneath a sleeping bench in the Gunner cabin, were a few sheets of paper that Orchid had given to me. I also had the stub of a pencil that I used for drawing patterns on hide before I embroidered them. By the light of the snow seeping through the thin fawn skin that covered the windows, I leaned over the paper and wondered what to write. My schooling, given to me by Mr Murdoch in the evenings, had been in the English tongue. I had learned all the letters of the alphabet, although I had little reason to use them. Would I remember now how to line them up on the page? And what should I write to this man, who might or might not be my father? And who, even if he was my father, might have long since forgotten about me, about my mother, about his promise. What could I say to such a man?

Gabriel's mother laid her small, slender hand upon my shoulder in passing. 'It is always best to speak from the heart,' she said, and then she moved on with her woollen gown swinging against her fringed leggings, and her very long braids trailing against her shoulders.

I sighed and pressed the tip of the pencil into the paper. Should I write the words *Dear Father*? How did the Scottish men write letters to their kin? Once, I had seen a letter that Ronald McTavish's mother had sent to him on the supply ship from Scotland. *My dearly beloved son*, she had written in blue ink with a smooth, gliding, looping hand. But my father was not dearly beloved; he was simply a stranger.

Dear Mr Litefoot Stuart, I finally wrote, while a baby began to cry in its wall hammock of woven thongs. Its mother went and stood beside it and nursed it without lifting it out.

I am looking for Mr Simon Mackenzie.

I am at the place called

I had to stop and ask Gabriel's mother for the spelling of the settlement's name, and even she was not too sure.

Sainte Fransis Exavier. Will you please tel me if you are mi father? Mi mother was Mary at York Factory. I have your broach.

Sighned Amelia Otterchild Mackenzie.

I looked up, surprised to find that the light was already growing dim as evening fell and brought more snow. Flakes whirled in as Gabriel, his father, and two of his uncles came inside on a gust of cold. They looked dishevelled and wild, their faces burning red in the cold. One of the uncles had a bleeding lip, and the other had a swollen eye.

'What's happened?' I asked.

Gabriel shrugged. 'Some men came wanting to look inside our barn. We sent them away again. Said we had nothing in there but a cow. Have you written your letter?'

I folded the paper and handed it to him.

'I have sent word to the stone fort with a man going north by dog team,' he said as he stowed the letter in a pouch. 'He will take the message to Mr Spencer that his horse is here waiting.'

Just for a moment, I thought that maybe Charlotte

and I should swing ourselves high up on that stallion's back, and turn his head towards the west, into the blowing snow of the Carlton Trail. No one might ever discover that we had taken him. And weren't he and I bound together by the times we had saved each other's lives? By my *pawakan*'s power? By my vision quest dreams? Then I thought of how that stallion's foals were going to make Orchid rich and build her a stone house with a veranda running around it, and maybe one day feed her babies. So I thanked Gabriel for sending the message to Mr Spencer, and went to wrap up some bannock, tea, and smoked tongue for his long ride.

He left early in the morning when the snow was still blue and unmarked by footprints, and with my letter in the pouch beneath his buffalo robe. I stood and watched until he was a speck in the distance, and the first rays of sun gleamed on the mustang's smoky flanks. Then I turned and went back into the cabin to help his mother sweep the plank flooring and stir porridge for breakfast.

I tried to hold my heart still, like a small bird captured in one hand and fluttering with the hope of flying.

Chapter 16

For three days I embroidered Charlotte's new buffalo robe with the help of Gabriel's sisters. And all the while, bent over my strings of beads, making the tiny legs and heads of the yellow horses amongst the roses, I thought about Gabriel riding west along the Carlton Trail. I imagined the mustang's hard black legs ploughing through the drifted snow, cresting the long swells of open land. I thought about the wind lifting the mustang's dark mane, and the long hair of his rider. I saw the clouds scudding through the boy's dark eyes. I saw the log cabins folded in some river valley, with smoke rising from their chimneys, and an oak door where Gabriel stood knocking. But when the door opened, I couldn't imagine the man who stood there, the man who might know where my father was, or what had happened to him. The man who might even be my father.

Today Gabriel will be starting to ride back, I told myself on the fourth morning, throwing fish to the sled dogs. I carried hay to the horses in the corral, and brushed the Norfolk stallion's muddy coat, and laid my face against his shoulder. With a strong *pawakan*, a person could survive anything, even this feeling of hope that was a longing as sharp as a pain in the belly.

On the fifth day of Gabriel's absence, a team of dogs trotted into the yard with their bells ringing. Their blankets, embroidered with red woollen fringes and flower patterns, were bright against their grey brindled coats. The standing irons on their necks stuck up jauntily, bright with yarn and fluttering ribbons. I stood against the corral rails, where I was brushing Smoke Eyes, and watched as a man in a buffalo coat climbed from the cariole sled that the dogs pulled; a second man swung along behind on snowshoes and carried a dog whip in one hand.

'Mr Spencer?' I asked uncertainly. He pushed his hat back from his sandy eyebrows while the dogs milled around, yipping a greeting to the dogs staked by the cabin door.

'Amelia, my dear young woman. You have the stallion here?' His blue eyes were sharp with agitation, and he didn't even seem to notice that his bright pink nose was running into his sandy moustache.

'He's here in the barn,' I agreed and felt Mr Spencer crowding against me in his haste as I turned to open the barn door. The cousin sitting with a gun across his knees rose to let us pass. When Foxfire nickered a welcome to me, I was seized by a pang of sorrow. *This is the last time he will speak to me,* I thought. *This is the last time that I will stand at his shoulder as he bends his head around, sheltering me in the curve of his neck, his breath running over my hands.* 'Heart of a bear,' I murmured to him.

This was the last time my face would hang reflected in his dark eye.

'Splendid! Simply splendid!' Mr Spencer was saying behind me. I ignored him as I slipped the stallion's halter from a nail in the wall and passed one hand beneath his neck. He lowered his head politely as he always did, and I slid his silky muzzle into the noseband, and fastened the buckle against his cheek.

'But what on earth has been done to him? This frightful colour! And how did you manage to recognise him?'

'I just did,' I said, running my hand over his cropped mane, over his flanks. Beneath my fingertips, I felt the flame of his coat, and the silver-like frost that would sprinkle it again as it grew back in and returned to a red roan color. With a smile, I recalled how I had first marvelled at this coat and how I'd wondered if the horse was turning white for winter like a hare or a ptarmigan changing colour. I had known nothing then about the nature of horses.

'Will you rest and have a drink?' the cousin was asking at the door, but Mr Spencer shook his head.

'No, I thank you. We are in haste to travel back to the Forks today.'

Like a dream walker, slow and gliding, my spirit not in my body, I led Foxfire outside into the sunshine; I ran my hand down his nearside foreleg to remove wisps of oat straw that clung there. His lips nuzzled the back of my neck as I bent down, as though he were kissing me goodbye. I remained there for a moment, after the straw had already been removed, and let the horse fumble at my hair.

'I have brought his bridle,' Mr Spencer was saying as I straightened slowly but I didn't look at him, only stretched out my hand for the bridle when he fetched it from the cariole. I pulled off my glove and warmed the cold shaft of the steel bit in my fist. The stallion bent his head again as I slid the headstall over his ears, and I smoothed his forelock over the brow band.

'I truly am most grateful. I am quite in your debt, Miss Amelia.'

I turned from the horse at last and stared at the white man who knew nothing about vision quests or the power of my *pawakan* spirit.

'You must care for this horse with your very life,' I said. 'His soul is precious. He is your future here in this land.'

A flicker of surprise crossed his ruddy face. 'Indeed, you are quite right. Have no fear; I shall indeed take the utmost good care of him. And if you ever wish to visit my wife, I am sure she would be most glad of your excellent company.'

'Thank you, Mr Spencer,' I said, although I knew that, beneath his gratitude, he still did not consider me to be company of the better sort for his wife to be keeping.

I held out the reins. For one last long moment, they lay across the palms of my gloves, and I stood in the warm shadow of that great creature who had swum to me in the fog of the Hayes River and saved me from drowning. Then Mr Spencer took the reins from me and the horse stepped forward. I laid my palm against his shoulder, then stepped back as Mr Spencer's companion gave him a leg-up, and he swung on to the stallion's high back. The other man climbed into the cariole and his whip cracked. The dogs leaned into the traces, whining with excitement, their toes scrabbling for purchase in the snow. The cariole began to slide forward. Foxfire gathered himself under Mr Spencer and began to move. I ran my hand along his sides, across his hindquarters; his tail flicked against my shoulder. Then he was four strides away, then five. Now he broke into a trot, tossing his head, neighing shrilly to the horses milling in the Gunner corral. The sleigh bells pealed on the dogs' harnesses.

I turned away, and went down to the river and bashed the water hole open with the axe, and then I led the mustangs down to drink. I watched their greedy lips and saw how their snorting breath made concentric rings of ripples in the dark cold water.

I felt gutted like a fish.

The next day, I did not embroider Charlotte's robe. *Today Gabriel will be riding towards home*, I reminded myself but no joy pricked on my numb skin. I cooked, I walked around outside, I lay bundled on a sleeping bench and turned my face to the peeled pine logs and the chinking of mud and grass. I thought about everything the red stallion had taught me about the nature of horses. With a strong *pawakan*, a person could survive anything. Even this gutted emptiness.

On the sixth day, I walked a long way westwards, chilled with the cold, straining my eyes for the sight of a grulla gelding trotting towards home. But as the afternoon waned and the light lay thin as one of Orchid's watercolour washes, the track to the west lay empty. Darkness fell as I trudged back to the Gunner cabin. All the next day as snow fell, coating the backs of the mustangs in the corral and lying along their dark necks, I waited and worried. Perhaps the knife wound had festered and Gabriel had fallen into the dark grip of a fever. Perhaps the gelding had placed a hoof in a gopher hole and broken his cannon bone, falling hard into the snow and thrashing there, helplessly. Perhaps Gabriel had lost his way and was drifting, roaming, fading away into the land like the *blanco diablo*, the white ghost horse of the Spanish nation.

'Fretting is like drinking poison slowly,' Gabriel's mother said, giving me a sharp look over the piles of babiche that we were using to net snowshoes. When she rose and put her arms around me from behind, I leaned my head back against her chest and, for a moment, I remembered my mother was dancing on the wolf road, in the brilliant light.

Today it has been a week since Gabriel left, I thought as I watered the mustangs early the next morning. *Surely, he will return today.* I gripped on to this hope as if it were a wild horse on the end of a rope. I held it all day, until my mind grew chafed and weary as I stitched mittens by the black wood stove where a pot of buffalo simmered in its dark, rich broth. Perhaps I dozed over my stitching, over the thousands of stitches I had made, for suddenly there were voices at the door, and a horse neighed, and men shouted, and sleigh bells rang on a dog team.

I started up from my plain wooden chair, laying the mitten on the checked tablecloth. Gabriel's mother, who had been lighting the lamp, moved towards the door carrying it in one hand. The draught almost blew the flame out as the door swung inwards and snow fell over the lintel and on to the planks. In the flickering light, Gabriel's hard dark face gleamed like polished wood, and I saw him grin, although his eyes were shadowed with fatigue. His mother gave a cry of delight and darted forward, catching him by the arm to pull him inside.

There was a man standing behind him.

Not an uncle, not a cousin. A tall white man in a buffalo robe and a marten hat. Gabriel turned and ushered the man inside; his eyes flickered around the room, taking in the children playing on the sleeping benches, the squat, dark wood stove, the herbs hanging from the open beams, the steam escaping from the buffalo stew, the fur and hide heaped on the table that we were making mittens from. His eyes flickered over me, and then returned to rest upon my face. His eyes, green in the wind-burned creases of his long, thin face.

I took a step towards him.

He tried to speak, cleared his throat. 'Amelia?'

I nodded.

'I am your father. I am Simon Mackenzie.'

We did not hug or shake hands or touch; we simply stared at one another while Gabriel went back outside to care for the horses, and his mother moved away to hang the lantern on the wall and stir the buffalo stew, and Charlotte crept up beside me and slipped her hand into mine.

'Where have you been, all these years?' I asked at last.

He pulled off his marten hat and I saw that his hair, once dark, was streaked with grey and worn long, pulled back into a single plait. Snow melted on the shoulders of his robe. The creases of his lean face shone with the scour of winter wind but his eyes, those eyes as green as my own, were clear and bright beneath his dark brows. I could see why my mother had waited so many years for him to return, a tall handsome man with a stern nose like a hawk's beak.

'I am sorry for your pain,' he said at last and I knew, in that moment, that he was a man who could read faces and hear thoughts. My letter to him had said nothing of pain.

'Take off your coat and come to the fire,' Gabriel's mother said, holding out her hands. My father shrugged out of his heavy layers of fur and moved to the wood stove with Charlotte and I beside him. He held his long lean hands, sinewy and callused, to the warmth. He was much thinner without his coat, dressed in buckskin leggings and a fringed buckskin jacket. A bracelet of blue beads and brass discs glinted on the bones of one wrist. For a moment, I thought that perhaps I was mistaken, that my father was a Métis and not a Scotsman, but then I remembered Betty's stories about my father coming off the Company supply ship at York Factory with the other Scottish men.

Gabriel's mother ladled out bowls of stew and pulled chairs to the stove. 'Please, eat,' she said. 'Empty stomachs do not make strong words.'

Then she returned to the table and began to stitch mittens with her daughters. When Gabriel and his father came inside from the dark, she shooed them to the end of the table and brought them their stew so that my father and Charlotte and I had the place beside the wood stove to ourselves.

My father ate thoughtfully, slowly, staring into his bowl as though it held answers to many questions. His dark beard was striped with grey. His lips were wide and thin and generous and once, when he caught Charlotte staring at him, his face lit up with a smile. All the creases ran the opposite direction so that I too stared at him; it was like looking at still water suddenly flowing, sparkling, running. The lantern light shone in his deep-set eyes.

When I pulled out the luckenbooth from my pouch, unwrapped it, and held it out to him, my father's gaze sharpened. A sound escaped his lips, part exclamation, part sigh – was it joy or regret that my father felt, reading that inscription, holding my mother's name in the palm of his hand after all these years?

'She is dead,' I said, my voice harsher than I had expected. 'She waited many years for you. She rejected a chief for you. Where were you?'

My father sighed again and this time, it was pure regret that I heard. 'I have loved your mother ever since I met her, a Swampy Cree woman bringing moccasins into the fort, smiling at me with those sparkling eyes. Mary.'

His mouth lingered on her name as though he had eaten a summer berry.

'When the Company sent me west to Pembina to

hunt buffalo, I wrote your mother a letter and asked her to bring you and to join me here. But she never replied and she never came.'

'She never received the letter!' I cried. From my chest I brought that letter, the one that a chief had persuaded his half-brother to hide behind a board in the York Factory post office, and that had never been given into my mother's hand. That chief, Eva's uncle, had not wanted my mother to get a letter from my father but instead to stay at York Factory and accept his gift of trade blankets and to marry him.

Now my father laid that ragged paper upon his knee, and smoothed it flat gently. He traced the water stains from when the paper had been damaged in the wreck of the York boat. I saw the black hair on the backs of his fingers. His lips moved as he silently read the puddled letters, those words that he himself had penned in blue ink and a flowing hand, on a summer evening by the bank of the Red River thirteen years ago: *This is a fair place . . . look forward to good prospects . . .*

I explained how Mr Murdoch had found the letter when they were preparing to tear down the old post office at York and build a new one, and how I had travelled west myself to try and find my father.

'But why didn't you write my mother another letter? Why didn't you come and find her for yourself? Find us?' I asked. I pressed my lips together to still their trembling.

My father sighed again and shook his head as though to clear them of the words in that letter but as he began to talk, his lean fingers kept smoothing the paper. The luckenbooth lay beside it, shining in the lantern light.

'After I wrote this letter to your mother, bad things befell me,' he began. In the corner of my eye, I saw the Gunner family lay down their spoons and their needles at the table, and listen to my father's story.

'I was hunting for the Company in Pembina, the fort to the south of the Red River colony on the war road to the Sioux nation. In those days, there were still two great trading companies, the Hudson's Bay Company and the North West Company. Men of both companies were trading with the Cree people and the Salteaux, with the Assiniboine and with the other tribes far to the west and the north. We were all trying to bring in the most pelts. Sometimes we helped each other out, but sometimes the men would fight. Lying and cheating and even murder have been committed in the competition between the men of the two rival companies.'

My father paused to sip the tea that Gabriel's mother handed to him in a tin mug.

We waited while he fumbled in his doeskin pouch for a pipe, and filled it with wild tobacco, and tamped it down with one thumb. He drew on the stem to make it burn.

'I had a horse, a buffalo runner called Lightfoot. That horse could outrun anything on the plains. It was descended from the Spanish stock brought over centuries ago, the stock that drifted north, traded by the tribes, running free. Lightfoot was a dappled grey, steel grey like a good gun barrel, like a stone. He had some of the *blanco diablo* blood in his veins.'

'Like the story,' Charlotte whispered in my ear and I nodded and hugged her closer.

'One day,' my father continued, 'Lightfoot was stolen, rustled away when I was buffalo hunting south towards the hills. I was pretty sure that a man from the North West Company had taken him. This man had been tampering with trap lines before this, making a nuisance of himself, stirring up the Cree people against the Company traders, offering them better prices for their furs.

'I set out on foot to find Lightfoot. I tracked him southwards and westwards for two days and then I came upon the body of the man, killed by the Sioux. I began to try burying him. The ground was soft, for it was early autumn and it had been raining. I thought if I could just scoop out a shallow grave, I would pile rocks upon the top of it. But while I was working, a band of North West Company men rode up to me; they had been tracking me while I was tracking their companion. They accused me of murder. They fought me to the ground and tied my hands behind my back, and led me north, walking behind a horse.

'They took me to Fort Gibraltar, and lodged a formal charge of murder. They knew it was a false charge, but they wanted me out of their way so they could trade with the Cree themselves. The charge was never proven, one way or another, but my name was tainted. The Hudson's Bay Company sent me back to England and terminated my contract. They shipped me out through Montreal. When I got back to Scotland, I found my old parents were dying, and I had two younger sisters who needed to be cared for. It took me several years to find them both good men to marry, and to see them settled. Then I took ship and came back, crossing at my own expense, coming up the St Lawrence River into Lower Canada, heading west to Rupert's Land by canoe and horse. I came back to the Red River colony and began my new life as a free trader. By now the two rival companies had merged, but I wanted to work only for myself amongst the tribes and with the Métis. They gave me a new name because the old one was tainted, and to keep alive the memory of that good buffalo running horse.'

'But what about my mother? Why didn't you come to find us?' I gulped tea, scalding my throat, choking and spluttering.

'I sent a message to her with a tripman heading back to York Factory, a verbal message this time. I asked her again to come and join me. But in the autumn, when the boats returned, the messenger told me that Mary Mackenzie had married another trader, the fort's baker, and had a second daughter.'

'That's me,' Charlotte piped up suddenly in her grave, sweet voice. My father inclined his head and smiled again; just for a moment, his face flowed upwards like river water in summer. Then it folded back into its long creases.

A log shifted in the wood stove. A baby wailed and was hushed. Children climbed beneath sleeping robes, giggling and talking in Michif.

My father's story soaked down into my understanding slowly, like rain soaking into ground after a long drought.

'What happened to Lightfoot?' I asked at last.

'Gone to be part of the Sioux nation, never seen again in these parts,' my father said, sucking on his pipe and gazing into the distance of the land. When the bowl was empty, he tamped the ashes out into the stove, and put the pipe bowl and stem away in his pouch. Gently, he refolded the letter and held it out to me along with the brooch.

'You must always keep these,' he said gently. 'They are a part of you.'

'Gabriel has a fiddle with these same words upon it,' I said. 'Is it a saying from the Scottish nation?'

'No, it is the motto of my family. A fiddle?'

Gabriel carried it over and laid it on my father's knees; his lean fingers smoothed the shining wood in loving recognition. 'Yes, this was mine once. I traded it for a horse, after I found out that Mary Mackenzie was never going to join me. I lost my music then.'

'But you can still play?' I asked.

My father tucked the fiddle beneath his chin and lifted the bow to the strings. A short ripple of notes tripped hesitantly over each other. A slow smile stretched my father's generous mouth. Faster, the bow slid over the strings and the fiddle sang out, pure and sweet. My father rose to his feet and began to play a sliding, swooping tune that sent prickles running up my spine and my neck, and up my arms. My toes twitched in their moccasins. Suddenly, my father let out a peal of laughter, and the bow flew over the fiddle, a blur like a branch in the wind, and his tall shadow leaped up the log walls as he danced by the wood stove, making the fiddle sing. Gabriel's mother began to play the spoons. Charlotte and the little girls danced, holding hands, giggling. But I just sat and watched, still soaking in the nearness of my father, Simon Mackenzie from the land far away across the ocean, with his long braided hair slapping on his back as he danced, and the creases in his face streaming upwards like river water.

He played jigs and reels and ballads. At last he stopped, laughing again, handing the fiddle back to Gabriel. 'No, no, you must keep it. It is yours now,' he said when Gabriel offered it to him.

Then he crossed to where I still sat, and pulled me to my feet, and pressed me against his buckskin jacket. I felt the fringing imprint itself on my cheek, and smelled the woodsmoke and horses and cold snowy distances in the hide. A single drop fell from his eyes and wetted my scalp, in the parting line.

'You look just like your mother, only with green eyes, Otterchild.' My father's hands smoothed my hair where it lay tight on the top of my head, pulled down into my braids.

'What do you want to do now?' he asked as we sat by the fire again. 'Do you want to come home with me?'

'Yes,' I whispered. I cleared my throat. 'I want somewhere for Charlotte to live with kin.'

'Amelia, there is one other thing. I did marry again. After I heard about your mother, I did marry a Plains Cree woman called Walking in the Wind, and we have children together. Two boys and a girl.'

'I didn't know,' I said stupidly. I wondered if my mother knew, up there on the ghost road, dancing in the light with the other spirits.

'Will she mind? Your wife?'

'No, she will make you welcome. She lost a girl once, before I met her. You would be about the age of the lost daughter. I have told her about you.'

'We will come,' I said.

'Good, we will set out tomorrow, early. I have brought a dog team with a cariole for you to ride in.'

Long after the lantern had been extinguished, and the heat had sunk low in the wood stove, I lay beneath the furs and thought about all my father's words until at last I fell into dreams. In my dreams, I was on a red horse, thundering westwards across the snowy land, rising up over slopes like a log riding the waves of a river under the wild, open sky scudding with bright clouds. With a strong *pawakan*, a person could travel great distances without tiring.

I awoke to dawn light seeping through the fawn skin window coverings, and the stamping of feet, and voices calling and shouting orders outside. I bundled into my furs and stepped out, blinking in the cold air and the thin light. My father was feeding his dogs and raised a hand to greet me. Beyond him, I could see the Gunner men harnessing horses to flat sleighs loaded with firewood, and heard Gabriel's voice calling in the corral. I went and leaned against the rails, watching the mustangs milling around inside. Gabriel's dark head emerged; the two grullas were following him on their halter ropes. I swung the gate open so that he could lead them out.

'We're leaving to hunt buffalo,' he explained. 'Their hides are worth the most now, in winter, because the hair is longest in the cold weather. The Company traders like the winter hides the best.'

'I am leaving soon too. My father is taking Charlotte and me home with him.'

'I am glad,' he said. 'In the spring, I am coming west along the Carlton Trail, heading for the new fort the Company men are building where the Qu'Appelle

River merges with the Assiniboine. I am going to be a horse herder there. The valley is very beautiful, filled with running water. The land is wide and open, and good for horses. One day, I will have a herd there of my own.'

'I am glad for you,' I said, but something inside me was whimpering like a puppy taken too soon from its litter-mates.

Gabriel reached for my hand, and our gloves fumbled together. 'I will see you in the spring. When I go west. Look for me in the moon when frogs sing. Don't forget about me.'

'I won't for –'

'Winter is very long,' he teased. 'You might have a short memory.'

I could feel his ribs heaving with laughter as he hugged me against them. When I stepped back, his eyes were filled with silence, sky and grass and long dusty trails.

'Gabriel!' shouted his father, and his glance broke from mine.

'Coming!' He strode away to the barn, the grulla mustangs following behind him, and I turned to run into the cabin and wake Charlotte up, and eat some porridge before packing my chest once more. I laid the luckenbooth and the water-stained letter on top of Charlotte's unfinished moose hide robe, and threw in a pair of mittens I had just begun to sew. Gabriel's mother gave me a pair of snowshoes, and kissed my cheek. 'Daughter, we will meet again,' she said, and slid a bundle of dried meat and tea into my hands.

When Charlotte and I dragged the chest outside, the yard was quiet, and the snow was trampled into a thousand ruts and ridges. The sleighs and horses and men were gone and only my father's dogs sat in their harnesses, ready to run. My father lifted Charlotte into the cariole's nest of buffalo furs, and wedged my chest in beside her as I bent to strap on my snowshoes.

'You won't need those, not with the horse to ride,' he said.

I squinted at him as the sunlight lifted over the horizon and gleamed on the Assiniboine's windswept ice. 'I don't have a horse.'

My father gestured towards the barn. 'Your mare? Gabriel said she was yours.'

She turned her head and whickered to me, tied to a ring in the barn wall, and saddled with a Métis woman's saddle decorated with blue beads and brass tacks. The first light gleamed over her thick winter coat, her coat that Kicimanitow had made from brown soil, wild honey and woodsmoke. Her dark eyes were banked embers.

'He said you had a bridle,' my father continued, strapping on his snowshoes at the same time that I was fumbling to undo the thongs on my own.

I shoved the snowshoes into the cariole beside Charlotte, and wrestled open the lid of my trunk.

Beneath the moose skin and the mittens lay the bridle that Gabriel had given me by the shore of Lake Winnipeg, the bridle that meant I would always have a horse to ride.

The mare slipped her head politely down into it and opened her mouth for the bit of twisted buffalo hair that lay softly between her teeth and around her lower jaw. 'Smoke Eyes,' I whispered, smoothing her forelock between her ears, feeling the energy bunched in her, ready to run. A horse, I remembered, was the very best gift that a person could give to anyone in this land.

'That's a nice mare,' my father said, swinging to my shoulder on his snowshoes.

'She's from Lightfoot's line.'

My father's face gleamed with pleasure and he ran a gloved hand over her back. 'A Spanish mare,' he said appreciatively. 'We will have to take good care of her. Did you know that she's in foal?'

I gave a start of surprise.

My father nodded. 'Gabriel says she's in foal to the red stallion from Norfolk, the horse you brought on your journey.'

My face broke open in amazement. 'But what – but when?'

'That young man said he put his mare with that stallion somewhere up on Lake Winnipeg when your York boat was beached by a storm. Said he couldn't resist – they're all the same, these men of the plains.

They cannot resist rustling a good horse. Even a stallion's seed!' My father guffawed. 'It will be a late foal, a very late foal due next September. But such a thing is not unheard of.'

Astonished joy prickled over me. I nudged my toe into the iron stirrup and swung on to the mare as my father untied her lead rope; before I had even settled my weight fully on her back she bounced sideways, snorting plumes of white air. My father strode to his dogs, the red stitching on his cap flaring in the light, and the sleigh bells ringing clear and sweet. I glimpsed Charlotte's heart-shaped face in the pile of buffalo robes as the dogs lunged forward yelping and the cariole runners glided over the snow.

I circled Smoke Eyes in the trampled yard so that I could wave to Gabriel's mother, standing in her cabin doorway. Then I turned the grulla's head and sent her running after my father's dogs, running westwards along the Carlton Trail towards my home, and the moon when frogs sing.

Horses in a
New World

Wild mustangs galloping over the plains! Cowboys and Indians! Stagecoaches pulling up in front of hotels on the muddy streets of pioneer towns. Explorers riding through mountains in search of the Pacific. Farmers heading west in wagons, hoping for the perfect new home. All these images conjure up tales of early white settlement in North America. But where did all the horses come from? And what kind of horses were they?

One million years ago, the ancestor of the modern horse was a small creature called *Equus caballus*. It spread from North America over the Bering land bridge into Asia, Europe and India. On the North American continent, however, *Equus* disappeared for unknown reasons. For centuries the grasslands and mountains of the great continent were empty of any horses. It was not until the Spanish conquistadores sailed westwards over the Atlantic that the thunder of hooves was once again heard in North America.

The Spanish horses were considered the best in Europe at the time; they were Barbs, Iberians and Andalusians with arched necks, convex heads and short coupling, to create strength and endurance. The Iberian Peninsula in Spain was the first place where horses were domesticated in Europe, and for centuries the purity of the Spanish bloodlines was maintained by Carthusian monks. Travelling west, these Spanish horses hung in slings in the bellies of caravels as they rolled across the sea to the New World. After the brutal subjugation of ancient cultures such as the Aztecs, which would ultimately lead to the decimation of these Native populations, the Spanish began to settle the continent, importing cattle to form the basis of vast ranches. Their horses were sometimes turned loose or abandoned, sometimes stolen, sometimes lost, or taken in warfare. Gradually at first, then faster, this wave of feral horses washed northwards over the deserts and plains, growing tougher, hardier and more numerous, with each year.

The indigenous peoples of the continent were quick to understand that the 'big dogs' of the Spanish could revolutionise their lives. Tribe after tribe – including Navajo, Nez Perce, Comanche, Blackfoot, Sioux, Shoshone, Cree and Métis – became people of the horse. The Native people learned to catch and tame the horses, using them to pull possessions on travois, to carry riders, to chase after buffalo. With horses, a raiding party could travel further and faster; a camp could be moved more easily. Tribes developed art forms based upon the pride they felt in their horses. They created beautifully woven saddle blankets, decorated saddles and bridles, as well as masks and carvings. The Native people became highly skilled at light cavalry and hunting on horseback.

By around 1900, there were an estimated one million horses roaming the American west. These mustangs (probably from the Spanish *mestengo* meaning stray or wild cattle) were of all colours: painted, spotted, grulla, roan, dun and other solid colours. Although their conformation was not as classically perfect as that of their Spanish ancestors, these mustangs were tough and wild and smart; they could survive predation from big cats, wolves and bears; they could find shelter in blizzards; they could survive drought, extremes of temperature and rocky footing.

As the number of mustangs increased, landowners became angry about the amount of range being grazed, and the mustangs were cruelly rounded up using planes and trucks. Thousands were slaughtered for dog food. Today, various mustang preserves have been created where the horses can run free in safety, and where they are protected by law. New breeding programmes aim to preserve the best characteristics of the Spanish horse and a breed standard has been established.

Horses did not only reach the New World from the south, however. The French sailed over the Atlantic and up the St Lawrence River of Canada, bringing with them black horses from the court of King Louis XIV. The settlers of Quebec (then known as Lower Canada) depended upon these sturdy, easy keepers for assistance in settling the land: they dragged logs from the forests, pulled ploughs through the virgin soil, hauled sleighs and wagons filled with farmers and their families, carried children on their backs to attend class in one-roomed schools. Today, the Canadian horse remains a solid, strong, docile creature with a black or dark brown coat.

As the Canadians moved westwards with settlers, and the mustangs moved northwards, it was inevitable that they would meet somewhere, someplace. It is believed that the crossing of these two breeds led to the development of the breed known as the Ojibwa pony or the Lac la Croix pony. The Ojibwa tribe did not need horses strong or large enough to pull ploughs or wagons, but did appreciate the ability to ride through the hills and forests on a smaller horse. Although almost extinct by 1970, this breed has been preserved. The modern ponies have comfortable riding paces, are very tolerant and tractable, have profusely haired ears and nostrils with flaps to keep out bad weather.

While the French were sailing up the St Lawrence, the English were reaching the continent along a more northerly route. At first, only the traders and other employees of the Hudson's Bay Company arrived. They sailed into Hudson Bay and from there travelled hundreds and even thousands of miles along the rivers, heading west, north and south over the land and bartering for furs (especially beaver) to ship back to England. Eventually, in the early 1800s, settlers began to arrive along this northerly route through the bay, and with them they brought domestic animals – chickens, sheep, dogs and oxen. They even brought a horse, a very special horse.

Fireaway was sixteen hands high, a red roan stallion from the English county of Norfolk. He was, in fact, a Norfolk Trotter, a strong and well-muscled breed with the ability to pull carriages or to carry a rider, moving at a swift and steady trot over long distances. Fireaway had been purchased by Lord Selkirk's experimental farm in the new colony of the Red River in southern Manitoba. The settlers needed to plough the prairie into fields for crops; they wanted big horses to haul wagons and move loads. The mustangs of the Native peoples seemed too small for these farming tasks. If a large stallion could be imported from England, and bred with the local mares of mustang stock, the large, strong foals would benefit the new settlement. So began Fireaway's journey.

Loaded into the belly of a three-masted ship in slings, he endured many weeks at sea, rolling across the Atlantic ocean, edging between ice floes, slipping into Hudson Bay in the few weeks of northern summer that it was free of ice. Then this great animal was persuaded to climb into a boat, an open, wooden boat, based upon Viking design and rowed by men sitting on benches. For six hundred miles, the Norfolk stallion stood or lay in the little boat, travelling west to help found a new line of horses in the Canadian west.

Norfolk Trotters were common in England at the time, and the breed's origins date to the 1300s when English royalty required the creation of a horse that was powerful and attractive, and could move at an excellent trot. Henry VII, Henry VIII and Elizabeth I all passed acts of Parliament concerning the breeding of trotting horses. The Yorkshire Roadster was a closely related breed to the Norfolk Trotter; both breeds were created by crossing native mares with Oriental stallions. Both breeds traced their line back to one especially influential stallion born in 1755 and named Original Shales, who in turn traced his line to the famous Darley Arabian. English riders liked to pit their trotters against one another in matches of speed and endurance; it was common for a horse to carry a heavy man at speeds of seventeen miles per hour over rough ground for many hours. By 1833, these trotters had formed the foundation stock for the modern Hackney, a handsome horse with high, elegant action.

The development of the railway led to the decline

of horses bred for travelling, and the Norfolk Trotter and Yorkshire Roadster both became extinct. However, their bloodlines live on in the showy Hackney, which remains a crowd favourite in the exhibition ring, and also in the Standardbred harness racing horse. This became an official breed in 1880. Still very popular on tracks in Canada and America, this breed retains its ancestor's ability to trot or pace at high speeds (often a mile in under two minutes) with a flowing, smooth action while pulling a light-weight sulky. It is propelled by powerful haunches and has hind legs placed behind the croup to give a piston-like action. The Standardbred's calm temperament makes it easy to train, handle, transport and race, and it is the horse of choice for pulling Amish buggies. When the racing career of a Standardbred ends, it adapts willingly to life as a pleasure mount.

And Fireaway? Although he arrived safely at the Red River colony, and was a subject of great admiration there, nothing seems to be known about his eventual fate. Somewhere, perhaps on a ranch in the Canadian prairie, there must still be fine horses that carry Fireaway's genetic material mingled with the ancient Andalusian strain beloved by European monarchs and generals, bullfighters and riders of *haute école*. And somewhere, perhaps on an oval track, there might be a Standardbred speeding along in a blur of legs, pulling its sulky and carrying the genes of the red roan Norfolk Trotter.

This novel, though fiction, was inspired by the remarkable true story of Fireaway, brave of heart, who came to help settle the New World in 1830.

Acknowledgements

With special thanks to dear Aimee and Leigh Adams, who so generously brought us a Standardbred gelding. It is inspirational to watch Malibu trotting through our fields!

My thanks to my friend, Barbara Mitchell, for giving my first draft an attentive, discerning read. It was a pleasure to compare notes about our research into fur-trade activities in Canada.

Also, my thanks to Mollie Cartmell and James Raffan at the Canadian Canoe Museum for taking time to answer questions about transporting animals along rivers. I am indebted also to staff at the Centre for Rupert's Land Society.

Once again, it has been a pleasure to work with my wonderful translator, Werner Löcker-Lawrence. Thanks also to Diana Hickman and Isabel Ford, my super editors in London, and to Caroline Abbey for so ably taking care of my novels in New York. Thank you all for your unflagging attention to the fine details of words!

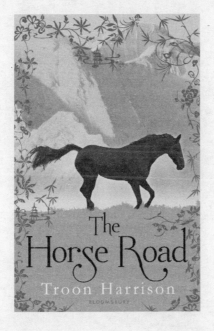

At last, we reached the ridgeline, and Batu edged along its sharpness, craning for a view of the eagle. I glanced downwards to where the horses grazed; they seemed contented in the grass and summer herbs, their backs gleaming. I straightened and looked to the south where the Pamir mountains rose in a vast wall, rumpled between us and the country called India. To the north, further away than I could see, lay the land from which my mother had come, a place of grass and tribes and the mighty Volga River. To the west lay deserts, and trading cities, and the bright Mediterranean Sea, and the land of Greece which my father had left when he was a young man filled with the spirit of adventure. And here I stood now, in the heart of all this world. I smiled to myself, and tipped my face towards the afternoon sun.

Then I inched forward to where the ridgeline fell away in a long drop into a deep valley. My head spun. I lay on my belly and peered over. For a moment, all I saw was miles of shimmering summer air, rocks, trees. Then movement caught my attention. I stared, knuckled my eyes, stared again.

No! It couldn't be!

I froze. Even my breathing became shallow with terror.

'Batu!' I whispered urgently. 'Batu, come here!'

Then I stared again, down into that valley where the track from the east trickled over the mountains towards Ferghana, my home and the heart of the world.

Batu dropped down beside me. 'Who is it?' he whispered harshly.

I scrutinised every detail: the foot soldiers marching doggedly along with light shining on the tips of their spears, the cavalry units on their small horses raising a pall of dust, the donkeys and black yaks and brown camels laden with boxes and bales of supplies, the loaded ox wagons lurching over stones. Above the army fluttered bright red banners made of the cloth called silk, the marvellous cloth that came from far away, in the east, and that my father longed to trade for. But to his frustration, our king in Ershi would not consent to trading agreements with the east; he was said to hate the emperor who ruled that foreign place.

'It's the Chinese,' I breathed. 'My father has described them to me. They are sending another army to attack Ershi.'

'For the horses?' Batu muttered.

'They want our Persian horses,' I agreed. 'Don't you remember? Years ago, they sent an ambassador over the roof of the world to ask the king of Ferghana for horses. But the king wouldn't give them any of our horses, and the ambassador and his men were attacked and beheaded.'

'Then what happened?' Batu asked, swivelling to look at me, his dark eyes serious.

'Then the Chinese emperor was very angry, and two years ago he sent an army over the mountains, a march of many starving months, but the army was defeated in the land of Osh, high above the valley of Ferghana. Now, he is sending another army to take our horses!'

Batu let out a long breath. 'The Middle Kingdom has long been the enemy of my people,' he muttered. 'The Hsiung-nu tribes have been driven westwards like sheep by its armies. Now the kingdom is building a great stone wall to hold back the nomads.'

'I have heard this too in the city,' I agreed.

Batu glared at the troops marching far below, massed like ants, pouring out of the mountains, filling the valley, steadily moving westwards towards the safety of Ershi, and my family's farm where our horse herd grazed the alfalfa in the shade of poplar trees.

'I must ride for my mother!' I cried, and I sprang up and began leaping and sliding down the mountain with Batu at my heels. Gryphon flung up his head, startled, grass trailing from his mouth. My mother would know what to do, I thought; my strong brave mother who had once been a warrior in her own Sarmatian tribe, far to the north. My mother, trainer of horses. She would know how to save us, our mares and foals, our pastures and stables. Gryphon. Me. And most important of all, my white mare, Swan. My most precious white mare.

'Hurry!' I screamed, fear clawing at my heart. 'Hurry, Batu! We must save the horses!'